OF SEA STORIES AND FAIRY TALES

The Time Before USS Hoquiam PF-5

Mark Douglas

Order this book online at www.trafford.com
or email orders@trafford.com

Most Trafford titles are also available at major online book retailers.

Printed in the United States of America.

ISBN: 978-1-4907-3547-4 (sc)
ISBN: 978-1-4907-3545-0 (e)

Library of Congress Control Number: 2014908321

Trafford rev. 05/02/2014

 www.trafford.com

North America & international
toll-free: 1 888 232 4444 (USA & Canada)
fax: 812 355 4082

Also by Mark Douglas

USS HOQUIAM PF-5 SERIES

Resurrected	2001
Road to Hungnam	2002
Hocky Maru	2012
Knock off Ship's Work	2012

MacArthur's Pacific Appeasement, December 8, 1941
   The Missing Ten Hours 2013

Editor

Nora-Gaye Hill Douglas, M.Ed

Disclaimer

This prequel answers several questions presented in the Hoquiam Series of four volumes. The story begins just before Lee Harrison Stewart joins the Navy. As you read, remember this all takes place in 1949-1950, about 65 years ago. In many cases, titles and processes have changed. For instance, I served as a Radioman throughout my twenty year career. In today's more modern age, radiomen are no more. Satellite communications caused more changes than can be written herein.

Most of the events in The Hoquiam Series and those events directly involving U.S.S. Hoquiam, are a matter of history. Commander Edward A. Lane's (C.O. of the USS Hoquiam) Hoquiam War Diaries, are public record. Some scenes are based around historical incidences off the East Coast of North Korea, involving other patrol frigates or destroyers for the purpose of this novel.

There may be persons alive who took part in events which were those described in these books.

Let me emphasize that all the characters herein and in the Hoquiam series are the complete creation of the author and entirely fictional.

There are exceptions, of course: those mentioned by name, such as MacArthur, Truman, Joy, Smith, and the rest of those historically public figures who were related to the Korean War.

The old sailor asked:
"You know the difference between
a fairy tale and a sea story?"
"No," responded the young boots.
"Well," he rasped, "a fairy tale begins:
"Yes, . . ."
"Once upon a time . . ."
"No shit?" they gasped.
"No shit!"

FEBRUARY 1949

February 14, 1949
179-F Magnuson Way
Eastpark, Manette
Bremerton, Washington

Lee was pissed. Eighteen-year-old Lee Harrison Stewart, slip sliding on the smooth red bark, climbed into his favorite madrone tree, settling into his regular tree fork that was worn smooth by uncounted hours of sitting and daydreaming. Scratches, a 4-year old multicolored cat, clawed her way up the trunk and settled down in Lee's lap to be petted, and purred in response.

He glowered as he looked down on two parts of Puget Sound near Bremerton, watching a sleek gray destroyer leave Bremerton Naval Shipyard until it was out of sight. His eyes were slits narrowed in anger.

Lee knew what he must do even though it meant giving up a cherished dream that two years of education at Olympic Junior College would have given him: a shot at attending the U.S. Navy Officer's Candidate School at Newport, Rhode

Island. Lee also knew his mother would be in a towering rage to find he was out of OJC.

I'll just have to bite the bullet and enlist.

Lee felt in his cord's front pocket and rubbed the Mercury Head dime.

I'm down to my last dime and no jobs in sight. Chief Halleran will help me out, I'm sure of that. Lord knows I've taken enough of those preliminary tests to qualify for Navy Electronics Technician School. Those advanced courses at OJC in Trig, Physics, and Radio Electricity helped out, too. I'll go see him bright and early tomorrow morning. I won't tell Mom until after I'm all signed up and ready to go.

Bremerton was still in the grips of widespread unemployment following the end of World War Two. The Bremerton Navy Shipyard had laid off most of its workers following the Japanese surrender in September 1945.

It was bad enough that jobs and money were scarce as hen's teeth. No full time jobs were available. Lee had been able to find a few very short-term jobs for a few dollars each: he held two small part-time jobs at twenty-five cents per hour.

His Bremerton Sun paper route in East Park had fallen apart as all the Yard workers left for home, many without paying their monthly bill for the paper. The money he made didn't even pay his bus fare back and forth to OJC. He walked the four miles just about the last week of every month. Lee had run up a bill at Olympic Junior College that family funds could not handle, and more to the point, neither could he.

This morning, OJC Admissions Office turned away his Winter schedule registration because he owed so much. His first semester grades would be held in abeyance until the debt was paid in full. Lee had no idea where he could raise

$138.17, plus additional money for the Winter Schedule registration, Student Body Card, books, and lab fees.

2:30 PM, February 15
Navy Recruiting Station (Metro)
214 Second Avenue
Seattle 4, Washington

The bus stopped to pick him up and he dropped his last dime into the slot, listening to it go ka-chunk ka-chunk. Lee sat down behind the driver and watched the war housing drift by.

At least, this bus turns around right in front of the Navy Recruiting Office.

He had to wait around until Chief Halleran appeared to open his office. The Chief looked at him with curiosity because he did not expect to see Stewart for some time.

"Come on in, Stewart. The coffee will be ready chop chop. What are you doing here this morning? the Chief asked.

"Wanted to sign up, Chief." Lee said, looking at the Chief.

Completing the final paper work and submitting to the Navy Doctors' physical examination processes weren't as bad as Lee expected. Now, the final event was at hand. The Recruiting Officer was going to swear them into the Navy.

Floor wax and stale cigar and cigarette smoke hit Lee square in the nose as he walked through the door following the other fellows. The teenaged civilians stood nervously while the Yeoman tried to arrange the recruits into three rows in front of the Recruiting Officer's door.

The door opened. The Yeoman instantly called, "Attention on deck."

Eighteen young men stiffened up as straight as they could, as a Navy Lieutenant walked across the polished floor, heel noise marking his steps, to stop directly in front of them.

The Lieutenant's navy blue uniform was sharply creased and spotless, lending a solemn, formal air to the ceremony that was about to take place. In a measured voice, he began speaking: "men, you all have passed your physical examinations and have signed your Shipping Articles of Enlistment. I shall now swear you in as sailors in the United States Navy with the rank of Recruit. Raise your right hands and repeat after me . . ."

Lee's heart was racing, his belly was thumping, water was pouring from his armpits, and his throat was so dry he couldn't swallow. His right hand quivered as he raised it. This was the single, most important thing he had ever done in his life. He hoped his voice would remain steady.

"I, say-your-full-name . . ."

"I, Lee Harrison Stewart."

Even as he repeated the words of the lieutenant, Lee began reviewing his reasons for being here.

Slender at 150 pounds and a quarter of an inch under six feet tall, his build didn't really make him stand out. He looked as young as he was with blond hair that had a slight wave to it, offset by a cowlick that stood straight up at the back of his head. His ears stuck out so far from his head that his mother had taped them to his head when he was a baby in an effort to pull them in. A straight nose, blue eyes, and a scattering of freckles made up a face that was slightly longer than wide—a family trait.

Life for an eighteen-year-old is miserable in a shipyard town where layoff after World War Two was still holding Bremerton in its terrible grip. Grown men, desperate for money to leave town with their families, hawked papers on corners and shined shoes. What chance did an eighteen-year-old kid have?

"do solemnly swear or affirm . . ."

Dad, a Navy Lieutenant with four mouths to feed, didn't have enough left over to offer much help with college tuition, lab fees, and books. Raised in a family where debt is a big time sin, Lee's debt to Olympic Junior College was just too much for them to carry, or for him to pay.

Thirty-five cents bought a ticket to the movies. Lee had only seven dates the whole two years he was at Bremerton High School. Sure, he was a little shy but that wasn't it. There was no money to spend. Two-and-a-half bucks was enough to take a girl to the movies at the State Theater and have a pair of hamburgers and shakes at the Owl Drug Store afterwards, including the nickel bus fares. Thirty-five cents might as well be a king's ransom.

Now Lee was so broke, Chief Halleran even had to buy his ferry ticket from Bremerton to Seattle. That last dime on the bus to get downtown to the Bremerton Recruiting Office emptied his pockets. During last night's sleepless hours, Lee had thought back to the time he had decided to join the Navy. It was ten years back when he was eight years old.

In the fall of 1939, he and his mother used to take the bus downtown, and walk way out on Rainbow Pier at the south end of the Pike in Long Beach, California. Although he enjoyed watching the waves crash against the big rocks below, he was too young to understand why his mom kept looking across the empty seas toward the mountain out there. She told him that was Santa Catalina Island.

Then one morning as he peered through the Rainbow Pier guardrail, he couldn't believe his eyes. All those big gray boats sitting out there! His mom told him those were Navy battleships, cruisers, aircraft carriers, and destroyers anchored out there. It was almost more than a boy could take. The Pacific Fleet had just returned from the Fall War Games. He understood that his dad was on one of those ships, but he couldn't figure out which one. His mother said his dad would be home that afternoon or the next day.

When he did come home, his dad, Ivan Stewart, (Interior Communications) Electrician's Mate Second Class, or EM2, (later IC2), announced that he judged Lee was finally old enough that dad could take the family out to his ship, U.S.S. Saratoga CV-3, for Thanksgiving dinner aboard.

Lee got to ride out to his dad's ship in one of the fifty-foot motor launches. He remembered standing at the Pico Street Landing over by all the oil wells and cargo ship piers in Long Beach. There were a lot of sailors and their families going out to other ships, not just the Saratoga. Boys and girls stood excitedly with their mothers and fathers, watching the motor launches arrive and depart with engine exhausts bubbling and bells clanging, waiting their turn.

When it was finally Lee's turn to ride in the big motor launch, he was furious as only an eight-year-old can be because the boat crew handed him into the boat instead of letting him climb in by himself.

Lots of people got sick on the way out but Lee loved it. His dad pointed out his ship, and for the first time, Lee identified his dad as a sailor on 'that' ship, the one with the big vertical black stripe on the funny square thing with smoke coming out of its top.

It didn't seem so big until the boat came alongside the ship and he had to look up, way, way up to the big, flat deck Dad called the Flight Deck. He was really impressed. All those steps Dad called ladders, going up and down were even more impressive and tiring.

They joined a lot of other people riding on the big airplane elevator up to the flight deck to look at the modern F2F-A Brewster Buffalo fighter planes all lined up on the flight deck. They weren't allowed to climb in those airplanes, but he did touch one of the wheels. The F2F was famous for having the very first retractable landing gear in America.

Watching that beautiful bi-winged seaplane, Dad called it a Grumman J2F Duck Scout Observation plane, being catapulted from the Saratoga's flight deck had been awesome. Then he got to go through one of the big twin eight-inch gun turrets. They were so big! His dad had handed him up through the bottom hatch to another sailor inside the turret. That sailor let him touch one of the big shells that lay in a trough, and he got to look up through the barrel of the other gun.

Dad had taken him by the hand down many ladders where Mom couldn't go, and showed him his bunk, then showed him where he had slept in a hammock when he reported aboard in 1934.

Lee saw his father and mother kidding with his shipmates and drinking coffee down in the IC—Interior Communications—repair shop where Dad worked. Their coffee smelled funny, though.

Finally, his dad led them up to his mess deck. The long mess tables were filled with places for everyone to sit. He remembered being overwhelmed with the table settings and the variety and amount of food. Each place had a plate and soup bowl. Behind those two were a package of cigarettes and a cigar. Within reach were bowls of hard candy and all kinds of different olives—the black ones were his favorites. He didn't like the green ones 'cause they made his eyes water; his mom would only let him have two black ones.

With a parent on each side of him, they made sure he had turkey and ham, turkey dressing, sweet potatoes and mashed potatoes, gravy, cranberry sauce, and vegetables. He got pretty full. Even so, he had just enough room left over for a piece of pumpkin pie with whipped cream on it.

Riding back to the Pico Street Landing later, he watched the Saratoga get smaller and smaller. Finally, he had been on a Navy ship, and he knew he would always be able to recognize his dad's ship. That day had sealed young Lee's fate. He knew then he was going to join the Navy when he grew up.

"do solemnly swear"

Because of his finances, his lifetime desire to join the Navy after a couple of years of junior college took on a practical view, join the Navy now and see what happens later.

The Bremerton Navy Recruiter, Chief Carpenter's Mate Vincent Halleran, lived just a couple of doors away from the Stewart's half of a duplex at the top of the hill on Magnuson Way in Eastpark. Lee and the Chief had worked out choices over several weeks. Lee had already completed the preliminary tests before actually signing the enlistment papers. All he had to do was make the jump.

"that I will bear true faith and allegiance"

Chief Halleran gave Lee the final series of pre-enlistment papers to complete. Lee's previous test results assured a seat in Electronics Technician training. Lee's major had been Radio Electricity at Olympic Junior College.

"that I will bear true faith and allegiance"

"When do you want to go to Boot Camp, Lee?" Chief Halleran had asked as he filled two coffee cups with fresh coffee and handed Lee one.

"I want to enlist for three years today, Chief."

The Chief took a sip of his coffee as he looked at Lee and slowly shook his head.

"Can't do it, Lee." Lee looked at him in shock and put down his coffee.

"Well, why not, Chief?" he asked.

"Because there is a twenty-one month waiting list now."

"You mean I'd have to wait almost two years to enlist for three years?" he blurted incredulously.

Chief Halleran nodded and sipped some more coffee.

"That's screwy. Do I have to wait for a four year hitch?"

The Chief nodded again. "No one wants to be drafted into the Army. So, they are reserving their enlistment into the Navy. Not only that, you can't jump ahead of them, either. You do have a draft card, don't you, Lee?"

"Yeah, Chief, got it last month, but what about four years?"

Chief Halleran shook his head slowly left to right.

"Sorry, that's full up for fifteen more months. In this Navy town, a lot of high school grads join the Navy."

"to the United States of America; . . ."

It was really tough around here. There just weren't any jobs for a young guy. Lee wanted to go now. He'd had it here in Bremerton. Olympic Junior College was asking for money he didn't have, so there was no signing up for the second semester.

Where am I going to go?

"to the United States of America;"

Lee had looked out the window and listened to the street noises as he thought over his options. It was only 9:45 A.M., and already Hoagy Carmichael was A-Huggin' and A-Chalkin' was booming from the Fred's Bar across the street.

"Well, Chief, you know I plan to stay in the Navy. What about the six year enlistment?"

"Sorry Lee, that's full for another eight months."

Crap!

"Chief, too late for a Minority Cruise, huh?"

Young men between their seventeenth and eighteenth birthdays could enlist, with their parents' written consent, to serve until the day before their twenty-first birthday.

"that I will serve them honestly and faithfully"

The Chief sipped on his coffee, frowning at Lee's frustration.

"Sorry again, Lee. You know you can't have reached your eighteenth birthday. You're twenty-nine days too late."

"that I will serve them honestly and faithfully"

Lee had felt like screaming. Here's all these posters calling to him to "Join the Navy and See the World," and he'd have to take a number.

I want to go now and can't because other guys have reserved spaces and are not going now. This doesn't make any kind of sense.

He started moving toward the door.

If angered, Lee was inclined to jut out his chin, draw his lips tight and thin against his teeth, and narrow his eyes. His normally high tenor voice would deepen and become strident. His face and voice showed that anger now as he neared the door.

"To hell with it. Tear up my papers. I'll go next door and join the Marines!"

"against all their enemies whosoever; . . ."

Chief Halleran jumped up and came around the desk, almost spilling his coffee, holding out his hand like a traffic cop.

"Hold on now! Let's don't be hasty, Lee. You don't ever want to do something like that. You really need to go right now?"

Lee nodded, swallowing hard and not daring to try to speak, as he watched the Chief. He was really disgusted with this turn of events and was afraid he was going to cry. The Chief's eyes narrowed.

"You're not in any trouble with a girl, are you?"

Lee held his arms wide, appealed to him with a choked up voice. "Chief, I don't have enough money to get that close to a girl!"

"Hmm. Well, there is another program that just came in yesterday, that lets you join right now. There is this E.V. program you qualify for."

"E V? What's E V?" Lee asked desperately. By this time, anything sounded good.

"against all their enemies whosoever;"

The Chief explained that the Enlisted Volunteer program allowed a man to enter immediately for one year on active duty, followed by four or six years as a reservist.

"You could leave today if you like. There is no quota system for this program."

> "and that I will obey the orders of the President of the United States . . ."

"Chief, we've always talked about the three, four, and six year enlistments. How come you never mentioned this one-year deal before? All these guys on the three-year waiting list would probably jump at it. Is there something you're hiding from me?"

Lee had known the Chief as a neighbor for over a year and had cut his lawn and washed his car for some money. Even so, he had heard tales about Recruiters and didn't want to sign for something that would not help him make a career of the Navy.

"and that I will obey the orders of the President of the United States"

"It's a brand new program, Lee. I haven't even signed anyone up for it yet. You would be the first to join in the EV program."

He moved over to his desk, pulled a pamphlet from his PENDING basket, and tossed it to Lee.

"This is all I have on it. Take a look at it while I finish my coffee."

"Chief?" asked Lee, swallowing after looking at the pamphlet, "are you sure I can reenlist in the REGULAR NAVY following this one-year E V reserve enlistment?"

Chief Halleran had finally convinced him it was his best option.

Lee signed all the papers and turned in his draft card for the Draft Board. Knowing he was flat broke, Chief Halleran handed him a Black Ball Bremerton-to-Seattle ferry one way ticket, also gave Lee a large envelope with his papers sealed inside, and had shaken his hand one last time. Lee left for Seattle on the 10:20AM ferry, the streamliner MV Kalakala.

> "and the orders of the officers appointed over me,"

In the Seattle Navy Recruiting Station, Lee learned the Chief had not been completely truthful. His initial enlistment was designated USN-EV, all right. He would serve one year on active duty. If he chose not to reenlist, he would serve four years in an Active Navy Reserve unit, attending regular meetings once per month in uniform with pay. Otherwise, he would serve six years in the Inactive Navy Reserve, attend no meetings, not be a member of any reserve unit, and receive no pay.

However, since Lee would be on active duty such a short time, he could not attend ANY school, much less the year long Electronics Technician's School at Great Lakes Naval Training Center. Also, he was not permitted to change to a longer enlistment today. Besides, it was too late to back out now.

> **"and the orders of the officers appointed over me,"**

I wonder what it would have been like in the Marines? he mused. *Those uniforms are sure swell. I can take long hikes and read maps. I don't get lost in the woods. I like camping and cooking over a campfire.*

> "according to regulations and the Uniform Code of Military Justice. . ."

But, what would Dad think? What on earth would he tell his fellow officers in the wardroom?

> **"according to regulations and the Uniform Code of Military Justice."**

The Stewart's had eaten dinner in the Wardroom a few times when his dad's ship was in the Bremerton Navy Shipyard, and he could just picture his father saying, "Hey guess what, gentlemen? It grieves me to say my son Lee—you know, the one who wants to join the Navy? Well, today he joined the Marines."

Oh shit! I'd never live it down. How could I face him if I did join the Marines? Nope, I made the right choice. It has to be the Navy.

> "And I do further swear or affirm that all statements made by me as now given in this record are correct."

Here we go!

> **"And I do further swear that all statements made by me as now given in this record are correct."**

The Lieutenant paused for a moment and spoke in a very solemn tone:

"Put your hands down," he said, glancing around. "Men, you are now members of the United States Navy and subject to all its orders and Rules and Regulations of the United States Navy. To miss a military movement, such as going to the Recruit Training Command in San Diego, is a very serious offense. Listen carefully as I read Article 87 of the Universal Code of Military Justice about missing a military movement." He raised a large sheet of paper and read Article 87 slowly.

> "Any person subject to UCMJ Article 87 who through neglect or design misses the movement of a ship, aircraft, or unit with which he is required in the course of duty to move shall be punished as a court-martial may direct."

As the Lieutenant read to the recruits, he looked at them, raising and lowering his eyebrows to emphasize each point, before directing his gaze back to the paper.

His Dad had said this many times, but now it was personal; this Article 87 was right up there with the Ten Commandments.

"In a few minutes," the Lieutenant concluded, "you will leave for the train station and take a Pullman train to San Diego, to begin your Naval Career. Good luck to you."

Then the Lieutenant turned, and with his heels marking time once again, walked back into his office and shut the door without looking back.

These young men, now Navy Recruits, most of them just out of high school, were from Alaska, Washington, Idaho, and Montana. That afternoon, the recruits, with one of them in charge of the detail, "sort of" marched from the Navy Recruiting Station down to the King Street Railroad Station. There they waited until called to board the afternoon Seattle, Portland, and Spokane Railway coach-sleeper to Portland.

Lee snapped his fingers and looked around for a pay telephone.

I gotta call Mom; she didn't know I was going to join up today.

He turned to one of the other recruits and borrowed a nickel for the phone.

"Number, please," said the operator.

"Yes, I'd like to call collect to Bremerton 3476-M, please."

"Who is calling, please?"

"Tell my mom it's Lee."

"One moment, please." Lee heard the phone ringing its one long and two short rings twice before the phone was picked up.

"Hello?"

"Will you accept a collect call from Lee, please?"

"Lee?"

"Yes, ma'am, Lee."

"Where is he that he has to call collect, operator?" his mother asked.

"He's at the railroad station in Seattle, ma'am. Will you accept his call, please?"

"Yes, yes. Let me talk to him."

"Go ahead with your call now."

"Thank you, operator. Hi Mom."

I don't think this is going to be easy.

"Lee, what are you doing in Seattle?" She paused, then shouted, "At the railroad station?"

"Yeah. Things happened really fast after I left this morning, and before you could say Jack Armstrong, I was in the Seattle Recruiting Station getting sworn into the Navy, and now here I am waiting to board a train for Boot Camp in San Diego."

"San Diego—you joined the Navy, Lee? Without asking my permission?"

I didn't need to ask your permission.

"Sorry Mom, everything is rotten for me in Bremerton. OJC won't let me continue until I pay off my Fall semester debt. Just had to go."

Besides, I didn't need to ask your permission. I'm eighteen now.

"Why didn't you get a job, Lee? There ought to be something you could do."

Wake up, Mom.

"Mom, you know I've looked. The little bits at the Roxy Theater doing the marquee and Bremerton Sun stuffing sections didn't even pay my bus fare to and from OJC."

She sighed. "Well, I'll write and tell your Dad what you did. I think he would like to hear from you also. How long are you in for, Lee?"

Easier than I thought.

"One year to start with and nineteen more to follow, Mom. I had expected . . . "

"Your three minutes are up, signal when done, please."

"Gotta go, Mom. Love you."

A catch in her voice, "God speed, Son. I love you, too."

Lee hung up and took the nickel back to the guy that loaned it to him. Then, he took time to look around the train station.

Lee was doubly excited. He had actually joined the Navy and was riding on a train for the first time. When they boarded the SP&S train, he found out he could go to the open platform on the last car. He stood there and watched the world go by, for the entire trip to Portland. It was wonderful watching the countryside, people, and highways as the train raced by.

Arriving in Portland after 9:00 P.M., they had a long wait in the Portland Train Station. The Portland Station Master advised all passengers on the Southern Pacific Coast Starlight that heavy snowfall and avalanches had blocked the rail in the Oregon and California Siskiyou mountains.

Around 2:00 A.M., passengers were allowed to board the Southern Pacific Coast Starlight train to Los Angeles. The Recruits had Pullman berths for that two day ride.

During the day, Lee spent most of his time on the rear open platform watching the scenery. When the train stopped at stations along the line, he would step off just to feel the ground and see what was going on.

His time was his own, except for Paolasso, the guy from Spokane that the Recruiting Officer had placed in charge of the recruits.

"Stewart!"

Lee turned at that and saw Paolasso glaring at him.

"Hi Paolasso. What's up?" Lee asked.

"Getcher ass back on this train, right now."

"Hey, I'm enjoying the train and watching what's going on. I have no intention of missing the train. Besides, I can see the Conductor and he isn't ready to signal the train Engineer.

"I don't care, Stewart. Get back on board this train right now."

Lee studied him for a moment and climbed back on the platform.

"Good, now you come on inside to our compartment." Paolasso angrily ordered.

That's carrying this shit too far.

Arms akimbo and fists on his hips, he slowly turned and said, "Fuck off, Paolasso. I am staying here and you can't order me around. I'll see you in time for chow, though."

Paolasso glared back. "If you don't show up for lunch or dinner, you'll go hungry 'cause I'll tear up your meal tickets." Then he turned and went back inside the club car.

As it turned out, most passengers including the Recruits got off the train to watch the Southern Pacific mechanics and crews service the engine with water and coal, and passenger cars, disconnect the helper engine, itself promptly serviced and turned to wait for the next upbound train over Black Bear Pass, and the re-coaling and watering of the Starlight at Dunsmuir, California. This would be repeated at Bakersfield, adding a helper engine to climb Tehachapi Pass.

The SP Coast Starlight struggled up the grade to Tehachapi. Finally, the SP passenger train re-watered and re-coaled on top of the pass. Most passengers got off the train to watch the engine service in the very cold weather.

The Engineer reached up and pulled the whistle twice: the train began to move. The Engineer was saying he was leaving to go down grade to Mojave.

Delayed by the heavy snow in the Cascade and Siskiyou Mountains, the Starlight pulled into Los Angeles Union Station at noon of the second day. The recruits moved again as a group across the platform to the Santa Fe silver streamliner—the San Diegan—for the ride to their final destination, the San Diego Broadway Train Station.

In San Diego, sailors with SP armbands guided the recruits, arriving on the SF train and Greyhound buses from all the western states, to gray Navy Bluebird school-type buses. As each bus was filled with the recruits, it left for the U.S. Navy Recruit Training Command, San Diego—commonly known as Boot Camp.

During the next eleven weeks, the recruits studied Naval Traditions, the Universal Code of Military Justice—UCMJ, Navy Regulations, and Naval Courtesies, such as saluting all officers, using the word 'sir', often appended to 'aye aye', 'yes', and 'no'. Additionally, they learned to march, do calisthenics with Springfield rifles to march music, and roll and fold their uniforms so that everything fit into their white, canvas seabag. They also received a variety of inoculations in both arms.

They were even granted liberty three times during the eleven weeks, between Noon and 2200 (10 P.M.).

Lee took advantage on one of the liberties to go up to Long Beach and visit his old girl friend, Elizabeth Thompson, whom he had not seen in over two years. Unfortunately, she was now spoken for.

Finally, after much practice, the recruits marched to the big field, did their exercises, passed in review, and were dismissed on Recruit Leave of eleven days. Lee, of course, now a Seaman Apprentice (SA), took Greyhound to Bremerton to see his folks and friends, after which he would return to the Naval Training Center for his first Fleet assignment.

MAY 1949

0915, May 10
Broadway Pier
San Diego, California

Lee Stewart (ex-SR), having completed recruit training and been promoted to Seaman Apprentice (SA), waited impatiently for his first sea duty assignment. A SA's monthly pay was $62.50.

Lee sat on the ground leaning against the barracks wall in his work clothes. That is, he wore black, shined, high top shoes, black socks, dark blue dungaree trousers with a dark blue web belt, a light blue long sleeved chambray shirt, carefully tucked into his trousers, and a round white hat. Everything he wore including his boxer shorts and tee shirt were stenciled in various combinations of his last name, first name and middle initial, and his service number.

Lee was still glum about Boot Leave back in Bremerton.

A zero, an absolute zero.

He had walked up to the house from the bus stop and noticed there were no curtains in the windows and looked inside.

It's empty!
Hey! Where'd everybody go?

It was a shock to find his old home empty. Neighbors said they left just two days before. Dad had been transferred to a baby flattop, the U.S.S. Siboney CVE-114 in Norfolk.

Well, hell. If I'da known that I wouldn't have taken Boot Leave. Guess my home is my Navy bunk from now on.

His buddy Larry lived two duplexes away, so he trudged over there sooner than he had intended. This time he didn't just walk in the door like always. He knocked on the door and stepped back.

Mrs. Wilson opened the door curiously and gasped. "Lee Stewart. Look at you," She hugged him, then held him at arm's length and inspected him from head to toe.

"Hi, Mrs. Wilson," he grinned, "can Larry come out to play?"

She laughed in remembrance of other times. "No, he can't, Lee. He's over at Fort Lewis in Basic Training. He's a soldier now. He got his draft notice a week after you went to Boot Camp."

Mrs. Wilson fed Lee her special spaghetti dinner and wrote down Larry's Army address for Lee while she caught him up on the neighborhood gossip. He slept in Larry's bed that night.

The next morning Mrs. Wilson let him use a phone book to call several other guys he knew in high school and OJC. They had reorganized themselves into new groups and he didn't fit anymore. Lee thanked Mrs. Wilson and went downtown.

He got a room at the YMCA where he could wash his scivvies and dry them in the room. He tried wearing his uniform to Bremerton High School but it was as if he were invisible. None of the girls he knew would be caught dead with a sailor, much less acknowledge the presence of a sailor.

Discouraged and ready to begin his life in the Navy, he checked out of the YMCA after three days—a week early— and caught a Greyhound bus back to San Diego. This time, he entered the Naval Training Center at the opposite end of the base and checked in to a nice barracks to wait for his first duty assignment.

A letter from his Mom explained she hoped he got this letter before Lee went on leave. They had to move in a hurry and hoped he would understand. It might be a long time before they got back together again.

So now he sat in the warmth of the sun reading one of Zane Grey's classic westerns while he waited to be called.

The speakers clicked and hissed. "Now hear this," the speaker crackled, and several young wet-behind-the-ears sailors cocked their heads. "The following named personnel report to the office with your seabag in five minutes. Uniform of the day will be Dress Blue Baker. Stewart, Lee H. . . ."

The speaker droned on with several names. But the important one was Stewart, as far as Lee was concerned.

"My orders are in!" Lee whispered with glee.

He stuffed the Zane Gray pocketbook he had been reading in his dungaree back pocket and raced into his barracks. First, he stripped his mattress cover off the mattress and folded the mattress back.

Unlocking his white seabag where it was secured to the bunk, he pulled out his Dress Blues, unrolled and smoothed them out on his bunk. Then he stripped off his dungarees and and rolled them just like he had been practicing for the past three months. He inserted his dungarees, work shoes, and folded mattress cover into his white seabag and pounded them down. They were followed by his two white blankets, which were first twisted, then coiled into the top of the sea bag.

Next to go in was his pillow with pillowcase still on it.

Now let's see. What did I forget?

He looked around and discovered he had forgotten his ditty bag, towel, and washcloth on the end of his bunk. He stuffed them in. Stewart bounced his white seabag several times to pack it down. He threaded the steel cable through the grommets and pulled the top so tight, a golf ball couldn't have slipped through the opening. As he slipped into his Dress Blues and tied his neckerchief, he took another quick look around to make sure he hadn't forgotten anything.

Placing his white hat squarely on his head, he grabbed his white seabag by the canvas side handle and the top.

Grunting, he heaved the eighty-six pound seabag up to his shoulder and hurried off to the Shipping Out window, dropping his white seabag next to him. His voice quivering with excitement, he asked, "Stewart, Lee H. reporting, Sir, where'm I going?"

At last, into the Navy for real, hopefully a fast destroyer.

The Yeoman Third Class (YN3) looked kindly at him. "Stewart, you're out of Boots now. Don't say sir to another white hat or chief. You got that now, or do I write it on the inside of your eyelids?" Stewart's cheeks reddened as he realized his error and he nodded his head in understanding.

"Here's your orders and records. Note they are sealed. Do NOT," he said firmly, "open your records." Stewart nodded again and took the bulging envelope.

"Your first ship is the U.S.S. Chilton APA-38 (Amphibious, Personnel, Attack, Hull Number 38), and you are in luck. She's over at the Broadway Pier, just back from Tsingtao, China. They brought some of the Marines home. She won't be going anywhere for a while. Just climb on that bus with the other sailors."

There is an entirely different class of ship that carries troops from port to port—do not participate in combat landings on foreign beaches. These are former passenger liners, pressed into the Army Transportation Corps or Navy. Their designation is "AP"—instead of APA—meaning Auxiliary Personnel.

Not going anywhere? When will I get to sea?

He sighed in disappointment, grabbed his seabag again and boarded the Navy bus. The gray Navy Bluebird school bus traveled only three miles from the U.S. Navy Recruit Training Command, San Diego, California. Caught by the red traffic signal, the bus stopped at the intersection of Pacific Coast Highway (US-101) and the foot of Broadway in downtown San Diego and waited for the signal to change.

Stewart edged forward in his seat trying to catch a glimpse of the ships tied up at the pier as the Seaman (SN) driver pulled the handle of the turn arrow up into the right turn position and latched it. As the light changed, he turned onto the Broadway Pier, reached out and flipped the lever to let the arrow drop back to the side of the bus as he brought it to a halt.

U.S.S. Chilton APA-38, and her sister ship, U.S.S. Bayfield APA-33, were tied up there. Ships just back from an overseas assignment were permitted to dock at the Broadway Pier as a special treat for the families of the crew and passengers. Stewart groaned. It would be a long walk to the gangway where the Chilton was tied up.

U.S.S. CHILTON (APA-38) was formerly a merchant cargo ship of the C3SA2 class. (I have no idea what that means.) It was launched as the SS Sea Needle, one of six of that class cargo ship purchased by the Navy. They were destined to be part of its fleet of amphibious transports and cargo ships at the beginning of World War Two. The Bayfield class APA, including Chilton, is one of the larger amphibious attack transports.

A Navy crew of 250 officers and men serve in these ships that can carry as many as 1600 combat troops and much of their initial combat supplies.

Merchant seamen are inclined to look at Navy crews contemptuously and laugh about how they could handle that ship with 50 Merchant Marine officers and men. True, and so could the Navy, as far as ship handling at sea and shore goes. The civilians tended to overlook the fact they only move freight or passengers between two points. And, they conveniently forget to mention the weapons of war that require the extra 200 or so Navy officers and men on a ship of this size required to protect their troops.

These Navy amphibious transport ships are named for state counties across the U.S. The Chilton was commissioned on December 24, 1942, and placed in regular service in the Pacific Fleet.

When Chilton is fully combat-loaded, she displaces 8,100 tons of seawater. Her overall length is 492 feet and she can make 27 knots top speed, about 30 miles per hour.

Chilton's nominal armament includes two single dual-purpose 5-inch, 38-caliber guns in open gun tubs, mounted on the forecastle (pronounced fok'sil) and on top of the after deckhouse at the stern. There are four twin 40mm dual-purpose anti-aircraft guns similarly mounted, two forward on the forecastle and two on the after deckhouse. Eight twin 20-mm machine guns are located around the superstructure on the exposed upper decks.

However, Chilton's main armament is not her guns: it is in the landing craft that move combat troops and cargo between the ship and the beachhead. There are eight Landing Craft, Mechanized (LCM), twenty-two Landing Craft, Vehicle/Personnel (LCVP), two Landing Craft, Personnel, Ramped (LCPR), and one Landing Craft, Personnel (LCP), not ramped, that also serves as the Captain's Gig.

Each ship in the amphibious fleet is assigned a one or two-letter ship-identifier that is painted on the outside of each landing craft's ramp, such as the designator "L" for Chilton.

The acronym APA originally meant Auxiliary, Personnel, Amphibious ship. During World War Two, the Naval Bureau of Ships, or BuShips, re-designated several classes of vessels. APA became Amphibious, Personnel, Attack ship.

An LCM (also called M-boat or Mike boat) can carry a battle-ready light tank and crew, a loaded six-by-six, with trailing 105mm howitzer and serving crews, a platoon of combat-loaded troops, or an equivalent weight in combat-ready supplies. LCM's are driven by twin diesel engines. These M-boats were very large, flat bottomed, metal boats. A pair of single 20mm machine guns could be mounted aft, to fire at the beach or attacking aircraft.

An LCVP (also called P-boat or Peter boat) was much smaller. The 26-foot plywood hull, metal-ramp boat, originally called a Higgins boat after its designer, was powered by a single diesel engine. It could carry thirty-six combat-loaded troops, a jeep and loaded trailer, or an equivalent amount of combat supplies. P-boats could mount a pair of single air-cooled .30 caliber machine guns. Anything heavier would rip away the wooden plywood decking.

Aboard Navy ships, looking down from above, the Main Deck is the first deck that runs continuously from bow to stern. As you descend below the Main Deck, each lower deck is numbered 2, 3, and 4, spoken as the second, third or fourth deck. As you ascend above the Main Deck, the higher decks are numbered 01, 02, possibly as high as 07, spoken as the oh one level or oh one deck. Larger ships have more decks below and platforms above the Main Deck.

The ten new sailors stood looking at Chilton and Bayfield a moment, muttering excited half-embarrassed words of chatter. Lee squinted along the Chilton's cluttered lines, seeing greasy cargo cables everywhere.

My first ship! Sure not a ship of the line, though. Time to get squared away for reporting aboard.

Stewart quickly dusted his uniform with the flat of his hands. He reached up and squared his hat two-finger widths above his right eyebrow. He straightened and pulled his neckerchief's square knot down to the vee of his Dress Blue jumper.

Stewart checked to make sure all fourteen buttons on his trousers were fastened, even though only thirteen show. He also made sure his wallet was safely tucked over the top of his trousers and pulled the bottom of the jumper down to hide his wallet. He looked at both wrist cuffs to make sure all six buttons showed. He sucked in his belly and gently shoved his Camels and matches into his trouser waistband. Only his ID card was in his jumper pocket.

Finally, he rubbed his shoes on the back of his trousers to get rid of the dust. They were sparkling black as only spit-shined shoes can be.

Lee stood with his hands on his hips and his head cocked to one side as he judged the distance to the brow.

Think I'm going to have to shift twice; I want my seabag on my left shoulder when I arrive at the Quarterdeck.

"Hey, guys, there's no time like the present to report aboard," Stewart called.

He hoisted the 86-pound white seabag to his right shoulder and started walking smartly, as straight upright as he could, along the side of the ship. He knew sailors on deck above were watching them.

By the time Stewart reached the Quarterdeck, his seabag was back on his left shoulder. Both shoulders ached. The sweat rolled down his chest and back and his uniform wasn't as neat as it had been a few minutes earlier. The other fellows were struggling just as much with their own gear. Stewart passed the manila envelope containing his orders and records to his left hand, praying he wouldn't drop his orders and records into the water below the gangway.

He turned aft to salute the National Ensign, flying at the stern. As Stewart did, the Officer of the Deck saluted with him. Then Stewart turned toward him, raised his arm in salute again, and held it. The Officer of the Deck returned and held his salute as Stewart announced as fiercely as only an eighteen-year-old sailor with eleven weeks in the Navy could while trying not to breathe hard, "Stewart, Lee Harrison, Seaman Apprentice, 3-9-2-5-1-4-4, reporting for duty, Sir! Request permission to come aboard, Sir!"

The Officer of the Deck dropped his salute and Stewart followed suit. "Permission granted, Stewart." He responded with a smile. "Welcome aboard. Just step over there with your seabag and the Quartermaster of the Watch will log you in."

Stewart walked a few steps to the Quartermaster's desk and eased his seabag to the deck with relief. Stewart felt a rush of elation.

I'm here!

The feeling was strong and welled up into his throat. He was grinning from ear to ear as he handed the orders to the Quartermaster striker (QMSN) (striker: similar to a civilian learning a trade, an apprentice.) Lee began to look around with overwhelming curiosity while the Quartermaster was busy logging information on Stewart's orders into the logbook.

Stewart was surprised at the amount of noise he could hear. There were blowers running all around him. Farther up the deck, he saw one sailor scraping paint from the deck, and another one painting a spot on the superstructure bulkhead. He looked back at the Quartermaster who seemed to be stalled. The QMSN read Stewart's orders again and looked at Stewart with an odd expression.

"USN EV. Stewart, are you a sailor in the Navy, or some kind of Midshipman or cadet?"

In the meantime, the other nine guys were reporting aboard, one at a time. The Officer of the Deck, hearing the Quartermaster, looked over his shoulder at the two sailors standing by the log.

He suddenly held up his hand like a traffic cop, and stopped accepting the men, leaving one man still saluting and holding his seabag on his left shoulder. The Lieutenant J.G. (Junior Grade) stepped swiftly to the log, looked at the entry, and held out his hand to the Quartermaster of the Watch for the orders. He looked down and read the orders thoroughly, then looked over the paper at Stewart.

"That's a very good question. Just exactly what are you?"

Uh oh!

So began Stewart's first tour of duty.

The ten USN EV sailors were a new breed, never seen before, a puzzle to all that beheld them. They were among the very first Enlisted Volunteers to reach the Atlantic or

Pacific fleets. All were automatically thought of as *Draft Avoiders*, not to be mistaken for real sailors. Division Officers and Chiefs didn't know what to make of them or what to do with them. So they asked the Personnel Officer about EV's.

The Personnel Officer explained that the Enlisted Volunteer program was an experiment. In theory, the Navy would get the cream of the crop coming out of high school before the draft could catch them. If these kids decided they liked the Navy after one year, they could ship over for 3, 4, or 6 years. If they decided not to ship over, they were still part of the Navy Reserves and not subject to the Draft. The Navy still got better personnel this way. Since the EV's could not go to any schools, they were sent to ships for Navy sea duty experience.

For the most part, EV's would become Air, Deck, and Engineering fodder. Advancement to the next step, Airman (AN), Constructionman (CN) of the SeeBees, Dental Technician (DTSN), Fireman (FN) of the Engineering gang, Hospitalman (HN), Steward's Mate (TN), or Seaman (SN), was hard enough to come by as it was. A ship certainly was not going to waste that reward on any EV who would leave shortly, after less than eight months aboard ship! Many Regular Navy sailors were already struggling to advance—sailors who had been around, and would be around, for a lot longer.

0945, May 10
Personnel Office
U.S.S. Chilton APA-38
Broadway Pier,
San Diego, California

The yeoman opened the top-half of the dutch door to the Personnel Office and looked out into the passageway. Ten nervous, young sailors stood there waiting. Their eyes swung to the door as it opened, tension showing on their faces.

"Come here, Boots," he said with a smile, looking at them.

They shuffled forward timidly until they stood close to him. He began calling out names and handing each named sailor a slip of paper along with their medical and dental records.

"All right sailors, listen up. My name is Quinn, Yeoman First Class, or YN1, Leading Petty Officer (LPO) of Personnel. I just gave you your own check-in chit, and medical and dental records. Before you move, make sure all the information on the check-in chit is correct; that is, spelling, proper last name, first name, and middle initial, and your Navy Service Number."

Quinn paused for a moment while he watched the kids check. He was glad to see this first draft of new sailors come to the ship. Nearly everyone on board was a World War Two veteran waiting for his enlistment to run out. Almost one-quarter of the crew left the ship for discharge when it arrived here a few days ago.

"Every one of those boxes on your check-in chit has to be initialed by someone in that department's office, and it is very important they copy your correct name and service number. You can leave your seabags where they are; no one will take them. Besides, you don't know yet where your bunk is located, and you sure don't want to be carrying your seabag as you waltz around looking for these offices— right?" A few sailors smiled back at him as their tension began to ease.

"Note the last line on the chit is this office, Personnel. Next to the office name—Personnel—is its deck and frame number, One dash seventy-four." The young sailors studied their check-in slips as Quinn waited quietly.

"We are located at frame seventy four on the Main, or First deck. Make sure you leave your Medical records in Sick Bay and Dental records at the Dental Office. Your department will assign you to a specific division and issue you a Watch, Quarter, and Station Bill card." A few wrinkled brows appeared at that.

"When you finish that, come back here and turn in your completely signed off chit. Got it?" He looked at their puzzled faces and grinned broadly.

"Good! Go do it and get back here soon." The yeoman leaned back in and shut the upper half of the door.

The sailors looked at each other for a moment, and almost in unison, looked at their chits. Slowly, they realized that for the first time, they were expected to follow an order without someone, three feet away, shouting orders. They had to think for themselves. Hesitantly, they began to move away from the office door, looking at door signs and frame numbers painted on the passageway bulkheads.

In the coming days, Stewart and the other boots would learn that everyone in the Navy—officers included—fit into a specific slot. Each person has an assigned task to keep the ship maintained in fighting trim, clean, and out of danger. Ship's personnel are assigned to Departments, such as Deck, Engineering, Supply, Operations—and Air, in the case of aircraft carriers. The size and nature of a given ship's function determines personnel specialties and how many personnel are assigned to carry out a department's responsibility.

The Commanding Officer—CO—not necessarily a Navy Captain wearing four gold stripes on his sleeve or eagles on his collar, is always addressed as Captain. Department Heads report to the Executive Officer—XO—who is second in command. Each Department has one or more Divisions, headed by an officer more senior than the other officers in that department.

The Deck Department maintains all gunnery and deck spaces from the bow to stern. The department head is responsible for Damage Control and all amphibious boat operations. There are several divisions for this purpose: First, Second, Third, Gunnery, and Damage Control Divisions.

The First Division is responsible for the forward section of the ship. The Second Division for the middle section, and the Third Division for the after section. These divisions normally have a Chief Boatswain's Mate (BMC) as their enlisted leader.

Gunnery maintains all guns, the Armory, ammunition storage, associated training loaders, and trains all assigned ship's personnel in gunnery safety and practice, by Gunner's Mates (GM).

Damage Control (DC) personnel are specially trained to respond to damage from battle or collisions and underway, are stationed throughout the ship.

Enlisted men work and live in their section of the ship. Chiefs, or CPO's, live and mess—eat—in a specific area set aside somewhere on the ship called the Chiefs' Quarters. Most non-rated men considered it pretty choice duty if they got selected to be Chiefs' Mess Cook or Compartment Cleaner. The Chiefs paid them extra money to keep their quarters squared away.

All officers live in Officers' Country, a godlike territory amidships where enlisted personnel may not enter on pain of punishment. However if ordered there, an enlisted man must quietly open the chained passageway, immediately remove their hat as they pass the sign "Officers' Country—Remove your hat—Maintain quiet", and nearly tiptoe to remain quiet. Officers have staterooms with beds, desks, private safes, and telephones. Steward's Mates, or SD's, always men of color, attend the officer's quarters—men maintained in the Navy for just that purpose. Their work duties include everything from shining shoes, and changing and making beds, to preparing and serving meals in the Wardroom.

In the Deck Department, for example, there are a few Chief Boatswain's Mates, or BMC. These Chiefs are thoroughly knowledgeable in seamanship, marlinspike seamanship, and boat handling. The most senior of those chiefs is the First Lieutenant's advisor, right hand man, and "Department" Chief. He is similar to the First Sergeant in the Marine Corps, Army, and Air Force. (At this particular time in the Navy, there was not a designated Chief Petty Officer who compared to Sergeants Major in the other services.)

It is this Chief's job to make sure each division carries out its functions properly. He only speaks to the officers and other chiefs or leading petty officers about duty matters. He seldom talks with lesser-rated white hats other than smiles of greeting, or frowns of something untoward. All Chiefs help the Department Head train his young officers to become learned in the lore of the department.

Some divisions don't have chiefs. There, the senior enlisted man, a white hat, so-called because enlisted personnel below chief petty officer wear the round turned up white hat, is called the Division Leading Petty Officer, or LPO.

Each division is further divided into watch or duty sections. All hands except the Captain and Executive Officer fall into the Port or Starboard watch. Those two watches are split into two other watches, a total of four watches or sections: Sections One and Three in the Port Watch, and Sections Two and Four in the Starboard Watch. To form just three duty sections while at sea, the men from Section Four are equally distributed among the other three Sections.

Men in each duty section have a specific function to fulfill. Enlisted personnel functions are published on a special list in two parts: first part is general personal information written in pencil by name, service number, rate, bunk and locker number, duty section, and liberty section. Each individual has a special location or duty as listed under several functions in the second part—written in ink or typed: Fair Weather Quarters, Foul Weather Quarters, Cleaning Station, duty or watch station in port and at sea, General Quarters, Fire, Collision, Fire and Rescue, Man Overboard, Abandon Ship, Repel Boarders, Boarding Party, and Prize Crew.

This list is known as the Watch, Quarter, and Station Bill. It can be so complex that some commands issue individual cards with specific information to each man, as it is terrifically hard for a new man to remember. Other people may need to know where to find a sailor under any given condition. A very large, lined, cardboard form with this information is kept behind a locked glass front. The first part on each line is written in pencil because of frequent changes as men come and go. Only the Division Officer, Chief or Leading Petty Officer, can change the Watch, Quarter, and Station Bill.

A group of Chief Petty Officers and Leading Petty Officers were standing on Number Three Hatch cover next to the Mess Deck scullery on the Second Deck, talking with the Chief Master-At-Arms, or CMAA. The Chief had just handed them slips of paper with names: ten kids just out of Boots on their first duty assignment. Each Petty Officer in the group was receiving one of these Boots into their division.

"What kind of unadulterated bullshit is this?" growled one Petty Officer.

"What the fuck am I going to do with this kid?" said another in puzzlement.

Another Petty Officer asked, "What kind of work we gonna get out of these kids? They'll be gone in eight months."

The Chief Master-At-Arms, Chief of Police, or Sheriff so to speak, had a different idea.

"They are running around checking in right now. Make them Mess Cooks for three months and Compartment Cleaners for another three. Then, put them on a division cleaning station. That'll do for the eight months, anyway."

Certainly, this would be a superior method of convincing the EV's this was the life for them.

"Make sure you get them listed on the Watch, Quarter, and Station Bill right away. Then, check each of these young sailors to make sure they know where to go for each of the drills. I don't want the Captain down on me like that last fuck up at Administrative Inspection." The divisions' P.O.s nodded and strode off in different directions, coffee cups refilled and in hand.

Stewart stopped at an open door with benches welded to the passageway deck beside the door. He compared the name and frame number to the title SICK BAY, stenciled on the door to the information his check-in slip. The odor of alcohol and other things drifted out from the door.

Must be it.

A sailor sitting at a desk inside glanced up at Stewart. His face was neither friendly nor hostile. Without a word, he placed the blue covered book he was reading face down on his desk and held out his hand.

In a second, Stewart thrust the check-in slip and his Medical Record toward the Corpsman's hand. Since the sailor was dressed in dungarees, Stewart had no idea what rate or rank the sailor was. (Years later, iron-on Petty Officer badges were available to press onto a dungaree shirt sleeve.)

"Hey, Chief?" the sailor called over his shoulder. "Here's another Boot to process. Think he needs Yellow Fever."

There was the sound of a chair creaking and rolling. A head and shoulders leaning way back around a bulkhead, looked at Stewart, then at the sailor sitting near the door.

"Give him back his record and send him in to me, Saint." Said the Chief.

Saint handed Stewart his check-in slip and Medical Records, and jerked his thumb toward the Chief. As Stewart walked by him, he saw the book was Hospital Corpsman, Third Class Training Manual.

Guess he's a Hospitalman Seaman—or is that just Hospitalman—an HN?

Passing the separation bulkhead, he stopped behind the Chief and waited. The Chief looked up at him, extended his hand, and smiled. "Morning. How you doing today—umm,

Stewart?" he greeted him as he caught Stewart's name on the slip.

"Just fine, Chief," answered Stewart nervously.

What was that Saint said?   I thought I had all my shots in Boot Camp.

The Chief chuckled and glanced back up at Stewart as he went down the list of inoculations.

"Here's the deal, Stewart. In Boot Camp, they give you a standard issue of shots good in the United States. You're in the 'Gator Navy' now and we go to some strange ports-of-call where all kinds of bad beasties live. Yellow Fever and Malaria are the two most prevalent. You definitely want a Yellow Fever shot. Take off your jumper, Stewart, and push up your skivvy shirt sleeve."

Stewart shuddered and removed his jumper reluctantly. He hated to feel a needle, and some of the serum could be really ugly. While he was undressing for the Chief, the Chief was making preparations, getting alcohol and swab to clean the spot where the needle would be inserted, then drawing the Yellow Fever serum into a syringe through its needle.

The Chief turned to Stewart who was standing rigidly, staring straight ahead, almost not breathing.

"Hey Stewart. Relax, this is not going to kill you."

So you say.

"Really. Flop your arm around and stand loose. You don't want tight muscles. Let it slide in, don't fight it." The Chief continued to talk, trying to make Stewart relax. "Here, let me massage your shoulder for you."

I just wish he'd get it over with!

"Come on, Stewart. Relax a little and breathe while you put your jumper back on." The Chief said, grinning at Stewart.

Stewart looked at the Chief in surprise. "Aren't you going to give me that shot, Chief?"

"You done got the shaft, Stewart. On your way," he grinned.

Stewart's head snapped around at the Chief, then looked down at his shoulder. The shine of alcohol was still there, along with a tiny red spot.

Son of a gun, that wasn't so bad!

The Dentist didn't have anything scheduled this morning, so he was checking the new arrivals' teeth. Stewart's teeth checked out fine.

When he arrived at the Disbursing office, a sailor at the dutch door got his jollies off by announcing that since payday had just been conducted, his first pay aboard ship would be on June First. The good news was he will see two pay raises on his first payday: first for being promoted to Seaman Apprentice; and second, for Sea Pay.

Oh crap! I've got four bucks and jingle to last me two weeks.

As much as Stewart thought he knew about the Navy, he didn't know that each ship had its own police force until he checked in at the Master-At-Arms shack. There, a petty officer wearing a policeman-type badge advised him to always pay close attention and obey orders of a Master-At-Arms.

"Oh yeah, Stewart," he concluded, "after you unpack and load your locker, bring your seabag to me. We'll put it in the seabag locker until you leave."

"Why not just stuff it in the bottom of my locker?"

"Two reasons. You won't have enough room for it and all your personal effects in that locker. Okay?"

"You said two reasons."

"You won't pass locker inspection which is every six months." Stewart's face took on a disgusted expression.

"How does this differ from a seabag inspection? I just had one last week at Boot Camp when I came off Boot Leave."

"You still got your Blue Jacket's Manual, don't you?" Stewart nodded. "Okay then. It's all in there."

Deacon Jones, Boatswain's Mate Second Class (BM2), was tall and very thin with a slightly flattened nose on his weathered face. His faded dungaree patch-pocket bell-bottom trousers were clean and pressed, as was his light blue chambray shirt, no mean feat in the Amphibs, or 'Gator Navy. His black shoes sparkled.

He smiled most of the time. His happiness was accentuated by what seemed to be a too small white hat perched on top of his head of closely cropped hair. Nothing seemed to bother him much. He picked up his nickname— Deacon—by his practice of saying grace before every meal, in spite of the stares and some ribbing of his shipmates. Deacon Jones was a former Steward's Mate, a rate restricted to men of color—Oriental, Filipino and Negro. Until four years ago that was the only rating he could ever hold in the Navy. Jones was a Negro. Nowadays, he was a Boatswain's Mate Second Class, P.O. in charge of a very special group of non-rated men drawn from all the three deck divisions.

Jones got the word that a draft of new men just out of Boot Camp had reported aboard this morning. He found the Chief Master-At-Arms in his office on the Second deck.

"Sheriff, I could use some new Side Cleaners. The ones I got are due to go back to their divisions soon."

The Chief's perennial frown disappeared and his eyes lit up.

"Now, that sounds like a winner, Deak. I'll see that you get one or two." The Chief beamed as he thought about it.

That handles the troublesome EV's neatly. Each can perform a necessary task, without getting in the way of real sailors.

Yeah! Compartment cleaners, mess cooks and at least one Side Cleaner.

He picked up his phone and called the First Lieutenant's Office while throwing a friendly wave as Deak left the Master-At-Arms office.

Assigned to the Deck Department, Stewart had trouble associating the First Lieutenant's Office with the Deck Department. He hadn't known that the Deck Department head's title was First Lieutenant. He had already seen some Marines in their Dress Blues while he was wandering around finding the various offices. The title First Lieutenant made him think of a Marine officer. It was a little confusing to learn that the First Lieutenant was really a Lieutenant Commander.

The sign over the open dutch door said First Lieutenant, and a Seaman was sitting at a desk typing. He looked up as Stewart appeared, picked up his notepad and joined Stewart at the door. "Reporting aboard from Boot Camp, I betcha?" he asked. Stewart nodded without a word.

The First Lieutenant's Yeoman jotted down some information and signed the check-in slip. "Okay, Stewart. You're going to be in the First Division. Chief Abernathy is your division chief. One of his P.O.'s will pick you up at Personnel and give you a tour of the division spaces. After the chief puts you in one of the duty sections, I'll type up a Watch, Quarter and Station billet card for you," said the yeoman.

The phone rang as he was explaining this. The yeoman grabbed the phone before it rang a second time.

"First Lieutenant's Office. Young, Yeoman Seaman (YNSN), speaking, sir."

He listened for a minute and looked up at Stewart as he listened.

Whoops. What's this?

"Just a sec, Chief. I have one in front of me now." He looked at Stewart and held up a finger. "Stewart, change of plans. Hang loose for a minute," Young said, and then spoke back into the phone.

"Okay Chief, I'm going to assign Stewart—yeah, Stewart spelled with an e w—to the Side Cleaners, from the First Division allowance. Should he report to Chief Abernathy or directly to Deak?" The yeoman nodded in response to something the Chief said. "Right, Chief," responded Young as he hung up the phone.

Stewart had been watching and listening as this was going on.

Whatever it was was about him. What the hell did he say— side cleaners?

The yeoman erased what he had written next to Stewart's name and jotted new information in its place. Stewart leaned in the dutch door trying to see what he had written.

"You've been assigned to the Side Cleaners . . ."

"What the fuck is that?"

Young ignored Stewart's outburst. "You take this chit and get Jones BM2 to sign it. You report to him from now on, at least for three months." The yeoman handed the chit back to Stewart. Stewart automatically took it but still didn't have an answer to his basic question. "But what's a Side Cleaner, Young?"

"You take this chit and get Jones to sign it. He'll tell you all about it."

1045, May 10
U.S.S. Chilton APA-38
Broadway Pier
San Diego, California

Stewart didn't go far. Jones, who had already gotten the word, was leaning against the bulkhead behind Stewart while he was getting directions. Stewart turned around and Jones held up his hand like a traffic cop.

"I'm Jones, Stewart. Give me your chit."

Stewart handed the slip of paper to him, trying to cover his surprise at seeing a colored man in charge. He studied Jones as Jones initialed the chit. Jones shot a look at Stewart. "Surprised at seeing a negro in charge, Stewart?" he asked with a rumbly voice.

"Yeah, 'cause I thought men of color could only be Steward's Mates. That's all."

"Okay, you have any problem with me?"

"Uh, no. I grew up in California alongside every kind of people," Stewart answered with a tentative smile.

If first impressions count, Jones is an all right kind of guy.

Jones looked at him thoughtfully for a second. "Okay, now come along with me, Stewart, and we'll get rid of this chit."

Jones led the way back to Personnel to turn in his check-in chit.

"Okay, Stewart, you got a bunk and locker yet?"

"No. Been walking around getting signatures about 0945, Jones." It was nearly 1100. Not time for the noon meal yet and Stewart was all checked in. Right now, he had three goals. He had to find out where to eat, live and work—whatever 'Side Cleaners' was.

"Let's get you settled in right now," Jones said. "Grab your seabag and come with me."

And so saying, he turned away. Stewart selected his seabag from among the others and slung it over his shoulder. They stepped through the latched open watertight door onto the weather deck. As they walked aft, Stewart had to stop when Jones occasionally stopped and looked over the side, inspecting something. He followed Jones all the way back to the fantail, where he quickly disappeared down a ladder. As Steward approached the deck hatch, he found Jones looking back up at him.

"You want to carry the seabag or toss it down to me?"

Stewart looked down the ladder, shook his head, and started down with his seabag still balanced on his shoulder, turning slightly sideways so more of each foot would land on the steel treads. He still remembered following his Dad up and down ladders on the Saratoga ten years before.

"Don't slip on the treads and fall," Jones called.

Indignant at the thought he might slip, Stewart went down the ladder, loosely holding onto the chain rail as he had seen Jones do. Jones smiled and flashed his teeth at Stewart. He spread out his arms as he spoke.

"Home Sweet Home, Stewart. This is our compartment. We share it with a couple of other Divisions. You're assigned to be a Side Cleaner—that's your cleaning station—from the First Division of the Deck Department for about three months. You understand?"

"Yeah, everything but what a Side Cleaner is," Stewart answered.

Jones chuckled and sat down on a bench, tossing his white hat on the table. He pulled out his Luckies and offered one to Stewart. Lee smiled and reached for the offered cigarette. Jones flicked his Zippo lid and thumbed the flint wheel twice before it flamed, and lit both of their cigarettes. He then leaned back against the table, pointing to another bench for Stewart.

"It's easy. We clean the sides of the ship from stem to stern, from bulwark down to the water. We normally don't worry about anything that rises above the Main Deck, excepting the King Posts once-in-a-while." Lee's brow wrinkled in question.

King Post? What's a King Post?

Deak took another drag on his cigarette and let the smoke trickle from his nose, as he watched Stewart closely, looking for his reaction.

"The nastiest job is when the snipes spill oil over the side. Can't paint over it. Gotta wash it with diesel, then soap and water. Ain't no fun in that. Otherwise, we see a rust spot, we chip the paint back to clean, clear metal, wire brush the metal clean and smooth, and paint it a couple of times.

"What's a snipe?" asked Stewart, mortified he didn't recognize that rate. Jones chuckled quietly. "Any engineer, a member of the black gang, is a snipe. Okay?"

Stewart nodded his understanding but shrugged.

No big deal. Sounds like a lot of simple hard work. Sure as shit isn't going to be like working in the Electronic Technician's shop.

He was resigned to whatever fate held, so long as he wouldn't be stuck there at the end of his EV year.

"There's a catch to it, though." Jones paused and Stewart looked up, waiting for the other shoe. "You have to go over the side to do this work."

Now Stewart understood why Jones was watching him so closely. Stewart shrugged. That didn't seem to bother him either, so Jones tried again, speaking carefully.

"Sometimes, when we are coming into port, the Captain wants the sides all pretty. So we get to paint while underway. He does slow down though."

That got Stewart's attention. He started grinning at the prospect of being close to the water as the ship moved.

This should be pretty interesting, being down close to the water while underway, banging, brushing, and painting. It sure won't be dull around here!

"Okay, Jones, what happens now? Do I get a bunk and locker before chow so I can put away my gear and change into dungarees?" Stewart looked down at himself, still in his Dress Blues from reporting aboard.

"Just a minute, Stewart, let me take a look around," he said.

As Jones looked for a bunk with a locker close by, Stewart looked around. The first thing he had noticed was how noisy the blowers were, and there were a lot of them to provide compartment ventilation.

Man, an awful lot of people could live and sleep in here.

He got his first close look at a bunk aboard ship. This compartment had many tiers of bunks. Each tier held six bunks, three on a side, separated by two vertical 3-inch poles. The bunks were stacked so that the lowest one was about six inches above the deck. The middle one was waist high, and the highest one was about armpit high if you were six feet tall. More than sixty sailors called this compartment home.

A bunk was similar to an old wooden-framed camping cot: a very narrow, single bed with a tubular, metal frame you could call a pipe-frame bunk. Chains hanging from the overhead suspended three or four frames levelly above the deck. A piece of heavy canvas about three feet wide and six feet long was suspended within each frame, equally from all four sides, and stretched very tight. The canvas bottom had holes every four inches along the edge.

Each hole was protected with a brass grommet. Quarter-inch manila line was fed through a hole, around the bunk frame, through the next hole, and on around the frame. Then the whole thing was pulled drum tight, like drawing up shoelaces. When properly woven, the canvas was suspended equally between all four sides of the frame.

A two-inch thick, six-foot long, cotton-filled mattress was slipped into a mattress cover called a fart sack. Two blankets, properly folded with stenciled last name showing on the top blanket, were stacked just so, at one end of the bunk under an adjustable web belt.

At the other end of the bunk, a pillow, with stenciled last name on the pillowcase showing next to the aisle, also under an adjustable web belt with hooks on the ends, was hooked to the bunk frame. The towel, stenciled name showing, and washcloth, stenciled initials showing, hung from a special rack built inside the locker door. Each bunk was alternated so those two sailors' heads were never next to each other. "Toes to nose, and nose to toes," as the saying went. That way a man didn't breathe the other guy's germs, just his toe perfume.

The tiers against the side of ship were favored. Sailors like to listen to the slap and rush of seas outside the hull. There was a better reason. The side curved outward here. This set of bunks only had bunks on one side of the stanchions, away from the hull. Each bunk had considerable space between the stanchions and hull to illegally hang or store personal things.

The tiers ran from the forward bulkhead toward the after bulkhead, but stopped about ten feet short. There, Stewart sat at a portable mess table with two portable benches. On the Starboard side, a small dogged (secured) deck hatch led down somewhere. Two rather large deck lockers were fastened against the after bulkhead. One was open. He could see peacoats inside. The other locker was taller and contained raincoats hanging inside. Over on the Port side was an open doorway into the head, where trough urinals, trough stools, wash basins, and showers were located.

"Uh, Stewart, come over here, will you?"

He's asking me!

Stewart hurried to him. Jones was halfway forward and just starboard of the ship's centerline, standing in front of an empty bunk frame. Stewart looked at it with a sickening feeling and then back up at Jones with dismay written all over his face.

"Okay, Stewart, here's your bunk and there's your locker. Since you just came out of Boots, I know you have no idea how to do this right. The first thing you want to do is clean your locker so clean clothes won't get dirty. Then, load your locker.

"Next, change into the Working Uniform of the Day—dungarees, just like I'm dressed—and wear your boondockers instead of your dress shoes, and keep those boondockers shined.

Boondockers? Oh, he means my high-topped work shoes.

Then, I'm sorry to say . . ."

He's sorry?

". . . you need to put your bunk together. Got all that?" Jones was watching Stewart closely.

"Right Jones, I got it. Put things away, change, and make my bunk. Aren't there any real bunks in here?" he asked, as he looked around for other open bunks.

"No, this is where the Side Cleaners live. Other Divisions have the rest of the compartment. You can't change bunk or locker without permission. I'm turning this," he waved a slip of paper in his hand, "over to the First Lieutenant's Office to add to the Watch, Quarter, and Station Bill. I'll get you a card tomorrow."

That's the second time I've heard that name. What card is Jones talking about?

"Another thing, Stewart, call me Boats or Deacon. You're in the Navy now, not in a Boot Company! Also, . . ."

Stewart opened his mouth to respond. "Wait just a minute," Jones said as he held up his hand, "also, the Compartment Cleaners will be down here in a few minutes. They will explain how to make your bunk, and some other things about living down here."

That changed Stewart's train of thoughts.

"A compartment cleaner?" he asked.

Jones looked at the new man tolerantly and sighed. "Stewart, just how do you think the compartment stays this clean? A compartment cleaner is a non-rated man just like you who has been assigned the compartment as his cleaning station. You will also spend three months in here— probably on the Mess Deck as a Mess Cook, too. See those huge bags over there?"

Stewart twisted around and saw two tall bags: one was white and the other a pale blue. He nodded yes.

"That's where you put your dirty clothes: white things in the white bag and dungarees and black sox in the blue bag. The Compartment Cleaners have to take those big bags to the laundry every week and bring them back after the laundrymen have washed and dried everything."

"One of the ways you'll learn where everyone sleeps is by helping to sort all the clean laundry. You need to know where everyone sleeps without turning on the compartment lights when it's your turn to wake the next watch.

"Now, get with the program. When they pipe Chow Down, go with the Compartment Cleaners and eat lunch. I'll pick you up down here at 1300."

"Okay, Boats, I'll be ready."

As Jones clattered up the ladder, rattling the chains, Stewart opened his locker.

Hey! How about that! It's already clean.

He opened the seabag and rummaged around the top for his Bluejackets' Manual. Checking the index, he found the section with a picture illustrating how to keep this style of locker properly stowed away.

In short order, the locker was shipshape according to the Manual.

Okay. What do I do with my Ditty Bag?

Stewart looked around to see what the other sailors did. He saw that everyone had his tied on his chain.

Have to wait a bit for that 'til I get my bunk put together.

He was still considering his next move when both compartment cleaners came down the ladder, laughing and talking as they did. They fell silent when they spotted Stewart.

As they looked each other over, Stewart could see how green he really was. Their dungaree work uniforms—dark blue pants and light blue chambry shirts—were faded from long use and their white hats were blocked and squared. By comparison, his hat was a round, limp noodle, no shape to it, and his dungaree work uniform were blue from almost no use.

The shorter of the two walked over to Stewart, looked at the way he had stowed his locker and announced, "Well, well, you know how to set up your locker, at least. Mr. Mason will be pleased to see that."

Stewart felt relief wash over him. Smiling, he held up the Blue Jacket's Manual still in his hand.

"Who's Mr. Mason, umm—Bertram?" He asked. Bertram's last name was neatly stenciled on his shirt pocket.

"Mr. Mason is First Division Officer and he's real hardnosed about locker inspection, Stewart. You oughta do real good on that since locker inspection is in four days. I'll give you a hint. The Captain don't like pinup girls taped inside your locker. Family pictures are okay."

Holy Crap! I don't even have any pictures of Mom and Dad.

"You're going to be a Side Cleaner, right?" Bertram asked.

Stewart nodded yes.

"Did Deacon bring you down here?"

"Yeah, he said you'd cut me in on some things I need to know." Stewart looked at both of them a little tentatively.

"Where do I find the line and canvas to make up this bunk? I haven't the foggiest idea how this is done," he confessed.

Bertram grinned and walked over to the after bulkhead where a metal rack was mounted. Various forms were stuffed in slots.

"This is where you start. All of these colored forms are chits for different purposes," he explained as he waved his arm at them.

He reached out and pulled a few out to look at. He then thrust one at Stewart.

"This is the most important chit. This is a Request Chit. You fill this out when you want to Request Special Captain's Mast."

"Why would I ever want to see the Captain if I weren't in trouble?"

"If you want to swap duty because you have a hot date, need special payday, or any number of things. But this blue chit right here is to draw paint and other such things. You fill it out showing what you want, and have it signed off by Deacon and the Chief.

"Then you take it to the right place and get what you need. But most of these places are only open until 0900 in the morning. After that, it's tough titty."

The other compartment cleaner laughed, saying as he walked away. "No sweat, that coon'll take care of you after chow."

Stewart was shocked at what he called Deacon. "Won't you get in trouble calling him that?"

"Not if you don't say anything, I won't. I don't like niggers, and I'd go over the hill before I'd ever work for a nigger. I'm in Third Division, not the Side Cleaners."

Hmmm. It appeared that life was not going to be as rosy aboard ship as he thought.

"Here, Stew. "Is it okay to call you Stew? Bertram's eyebrows were raised in question.

"Yeah, sure, Stew's okay."

"Okay, look, you need to get your peacoat and raincoat hung in those lockers. Check your bunk number and find the same number in the lockers. That's where you store them. There are enough hangers to go around."

Stewart nodded, pulling those items from the bottom of his seabag, he shook them out and hung them in their respective numbered slots, and stood back to admire the nearly full lockers.

"There's still a few minutes to go before chow, so why don't you set up a clean mattress—here's one—with a fart sack. You can lay that on my bunk temporarily. The MAA's won't take them this time. They know you're trying to settle in. Oh, yeah, pillow and blankets."

Stewart nodded and tossed his pillow on his mattress. Then he began pulling out his two blankets. He heard Bertram whistle.

"Wow, hey those are nice blankets. Is that what they issue in Boots now?"

"I guess so, Bertram. That's what I got the first day, along with everyone else."

"Yeah, well you make sure those are properly stenciled or you gonna wake up cold one morning. Look at our thin khaki ones." Stewart nodded and folded both blankets according to regulations.

He looked down in his bag. Only thing left were his clodhoppers—the hightop black workshoes—leggings (sometimes called puttees), and galoshes. He changed into his clodhoppers and put away his good shoes. Peering into the bottom section of his locker, he thought he had enough room for his galoshes.

"Stew. You still got leggings? You can toss those. Not used anymore and Mr. Mason doesn't look for them."

A Bos'un's Pipe began to warble a long call over the compartment speakers.

"Okay, Stew, there goes chow call. I'll help you to lace up your bunk after chow. I know someone who will let you have the line for your bunk, and we have canvas down here."

Stewart felt a wave of relief slide over him. Bertram was really helping out.

Stewart stood in line behind Bertram as everyone shuffled toward the stack of trays.

"Hey, Stew, you ever eat aboard ship before?" Stewart had an immediate flash of Dad's ships: the Saratoga Engineering Mess Deck—and later when he was commissioned, to the Union and Lexington II wardrooms—and grinned.

"No, Bert—okay to call you Bert?" Bertram nodded. "But I am looking forward to it. I'll just follow your lead, is that all right?"

"Sure, just pick out what you want. Sometimes you can even get seconds."

Stewart watched Bertram stuff a knife, fork, and spoon in his shirt pocket, and followed suit. Ditto for a very hot tray and white mug without a handle. Bertram took soup. Stewart wasn't much for soup and passed.

Bertram leaned back and whispered, "Cookee is gonna be upset with you. He spends an awful lot of time making sure his soup is just right. It is, too."

"Nah, I'll pass this time," Stewart turned and nudged Bertram to get moving. He took mashed potatoes and brown gravy, Lima beans, a pork chop just a little too wet with oil, a biscuit, and milk. Stewart followed Bertram to a table and sat down beside him.

"I'm curious, Bert. Why don't the cooks use both steam lines and both sides of the mess deck?"

Bertram nodded as he chewed and swallowed. He forked some mashed potatoes and explained. "Well, you see, next week we'll be using the starboard side steam line and tables. He alternates every week to make sure everything is always in top shape. Never do to have a fuckup when the troops come aboard." He took a bite of pork chop. "This is where we see movies except when it is godawful hot, then we go up on deck to Number Three hatchcover," he said while pointing straight up.

Bertram nudged him and pointed with his nose. "Stew, Deak is motioning for you." Stewart looked up to see Deak beckoning to him. Stewart left his bench seat and tray, and hurried over to Jones.

"Stewart, this is Davis, my leading seaman. He is going to take you around and show you what we really do this afternoon. Have you got your bunk and locker all squared away?"

"No, Boats. Bertram is going to help me lace my bunk if it's okay with you."

"All right. Finish that so you have a place to sack out tonight. You're in the duty section today but no watches to stand cause you're not checked out yet."

"Okay." Stewart went back to Bertram and finished his lunch.

Of course, Stewart had no means of comparison but he felt that duty in the Side Cleaners was going to be interesting, possibly exciting when he was dropped over the side to work, maybe even fun. However, before he would be allowed to work over the side, he had to be thoroughly grounded in the topside tender tasks.

Davis took him patiently through all the steps in Side cleaning, literally teaching him the ropes. Nautical terms that Stewart had thought went out with Richard Dana's "Two Years Before the Mast" were still commonly in use.

Boatswain's Mates didn't yell across the ship at their men. They pulled out their Bosun's Pipe and shrilled out an order in special pipe tunes, or sometimes they blew the pipes just to attract attention, then make hand motions. As with any musical instrument, some Boatswain's Mates were more proficient with a pipe than others. Each pipe even had its own tone. It wouldn't be many days before Stewart could pick out Deak's pipe from the others, not that his was particularly pleasing, it was the way he played it.

Stewart had to learn to be a line tender to handle a Side Cleaner's lines before he could ride the chair, though. Davis taught Stewart how to lower and raise someone in the chair and secure lines with clove hitches, sheet bends, bowlines, or square knots, so the man wouldn't drop in the water.

Tools had to be tied with marlin, a kind of rough, tarred, thin line, and lowered to the Side Cleaner when he called for something. Two lines, called tender lines, were attached to the chair and led away about twenty feet forward and aft of the chair's vertical position. When a Side Cleaner spotted something to correct that was out of reach, his Tender would loosen both Tender Lines and pull in the direction the side cleaner wanted, then refasten both lines.

Sometimes, dragging the chair off to the side was enough to complete the work. More often than not, the Side Cleaner had to be pulled topside and the Bosun's Chair moved to a new place.

The Tender drew the tools for his Side Cleaner: a chipping hammer to chip paint from the metal surfaces; a sharp paint scraper to scrape paint from metal surfaces—one never knew which of those two would work the best—a wire brush to smooth the surface and buff out rust and a gallon or two of Haze gray paint, a gallon of yellow chromate and two brushes.

When the day's work was finished, the Tender returned these items, including any left over paint, and cleaned the brushes for use by the next sailor.

Side Cleaners wore a lifejacket and gray battle helmet liner without chinstrap whenever they were over the side, just in case a line broke or something dropped, both of which can happen very easily.

Stewart impatiently waited through his learning period until he could go over the side in a Bosun's Chair. He was eager to go down there and swing above the water to do his work, be part of the team. Stewart hovered over the Bosun's chair and the Side Cleaner nervously, his eyes darting around the deck, wondering if a Petty Officer was going to chew him out because he looked idle. He spotted Deacon walking along the bulwark checking the progress of his other four crews over the side. Like most of the other Boatswain's Mates, he carried a steaming cup of coffee in the crook of his right index finger, while jamming his left hand flatly into his back patch pocket. The pose was like a badge of honor.

Deacon stopped and smiled at him, sipping his coffee.

"How's it going, Stewart? Having any problems handling the lines?"

"Nah. That's pretty easy." Deacon's eyebrows rose in amusement.

"It's the standing around waiting for some Boats to come jump me for not doing anything that bothers me."

"No sweat, Stewart. They all know what your job is. Just keep doing it like you have been."

After another week, Deacon decided Stewart was ready go over the side. Oh yes indeedy, Deacon Jones had studied Tom Sawyer's white-washed fence very well.

It was as exciting as Stewart thought it would be, and just as hard. First time he climbed in the chair and was lowered, he tingled with apprehension. That morning was a particularly cool morning and his hands were stiff with cold as he started to chip and scrape rust spots. However, he soon settled down, critically looking for rust to eliminate.

Now when you are dangling over the side about fifteen feet down from the Main Deck in a Bosun's Chair, you have nothing to push against. You need force to push a wirebrush or paint scraper back and forth. When you start to push, the Chair moves away from the hull, reacting to your force. The first few days were miserable as he learned the tricks.

0830, May 23
Buoy 17, San Diego Channel
U.S.S. Chilton APA-38

The day the San Diego Harbor Master remembered to move the Chilton and Bayfield from the Broadway Pier was the day Deacon decided Stewart was ready to go down through the Bull Nose. The Bull Nose is a small, closed chock—that is, a large hole where mooring lines, cables, or chain can be passed through, even the Bosun's Chair would fit—when mooring or tying up the ship.

This chock is high up and at the very front of the bow, at the peak of the stem. After being pushed through the Bull Nose, the Bosun's Chair is pulled to one side where the Side Cleaner can mount the chair. Back in position on the stem under the Bull Nose, it looks like the Side Cleaner came through that itty bitty hole.

The anchor chain rubs against the stem of the bow as wind, tide, and currents move a ship around at anchor. The rubbing action removes paint, causes rust, and is very unsightly: ergo, Side Cleaners to the rescue.

Davis, Leading Seaman of the Side Cleaners, was breaking in a new sailor, Easton of the Third Division, just as Stewart had been educated a couple of weeks earlier. Stewart carefully eased his way into the chair. Davis was giving instructions to Easton as Stewart got tied in and settled, ready to take his toolbag and gallon cans of paint.

The Yellow Chromate paint pot hung on the left side of his chair. The other, with Haze Gray in it, hung on his right side. Stewart had discovered earlier there were quite a few distinctive shades of gray paint used by the Navy: light machinery gray, dark machinery gray, light gray deck, dark gray deck, battleship gray, and haze gray.

He still remembered with embarrassment the scornful look and caustic comments Davis offered about his intelligence and future when Stewart had drawn light gray deck instead of haze gray. Stewart never did figure out why the undercoating paint—chromate—came in yellow and pale green. He knew Davis had him return the green chromate paint when he had drawn that by mistake.

"Hey Easton, let me down about six feet so I can see the sides better."

Easton's face appeared over the peak to check Stewart out before lowering him. Again, Stewart heard Davis talking to Easton. Then, with a rattling creaky squeal from the block and sheave just above his head, Stewart slid down the ship's stem.

The Captain had used the port anchor when the Chilton anchored off the Silver Strand for amphibious exercises the previous day, so Stewart just glanced at the Starboard side. Sure enough, no scrapes there; still nice and clean. A look at the Port side under the anchor showed scrapes where the anchor flukes had touched, and of course, the stem where he was.

"Okay, let me down another couple of feet, then pull me under the Port anchor. I'll be there about five minutes, I think."

There was a hollar from topside. The chair dropped jerkily a couple of feet and stopped. Easton looked down at Stewart.

"How's that?"

"Okay fine, now pull me over by the anchor."

"Okay."

"Yaaaaa!"

Stewart let out a screech of sheer terror as suddenly he was in free fall. The sheaves screamed as the line paid out. He hit the water with a big splash, scattering the contents of both paint cans around him.

That son of a bitch dropped me in the water.

He struggled out of the Bos'un's Chair and frantically splashed the floating yellow and gray paint away from him.

This fucking water is cold.

Then realizing what happened, he looked up for Easton.

"Easton, you bastard! You better know how to swim 'cause you're going over the side."

Stewart's screams of rage attracted both the Boatswain's Mate of the Watch and Deacon who had been checking another crew.

"You okay, Stewart?" Deacon Jones asked with genuine concern. His laughter was scarcely concealed. The Officer of the Deck joined the Boatswain's Mate of the Watch and they both joined Deacon in a good laugh at Stewart's expense, who meanwhile was muttering dire, vile things he was going to do to Easton when he caught him.

"Fuck yeah, I'm okay. I always like a bath in this shitty water," he answered with an enraged voice. Stewart swam over to the camel and clambered onto it and then up to the pier. A few stiff, angry strides, dripping water as he went, and he was on his way up the gangway.

Stewart looked aft and saluted the colors and turned to salute the Officer of the Deck. The Officer of the Deck was looking at Stewart, dripping from head to foot, with a frown.

"Stewart, I didn't give you permission to leave the ship." Said he, looking Stewart up and down.

Stewart looked at the OOD with his mouth open, surprised. He saw Deacon, the Messenger of the Watch, and the Boatswain's Mate of the Watch all grinning from ear to ear.

Funny, ha ha.

Stewart replied through teeth chattering with cold. "Sir, I was occupied with a rapidly changing scene and forgot to ask. Request permission to come aboard, sir."

Amidst the laughter, the OOD granted permission and Stewart stepped on board.

When Deak finally got Stewart calmed down, Stewart found out Easton had held Stewart's line with his foot instead of stopping it around a cleat. The dumb shit let him drop when he moved his foot to fasten the tender lines.

The Side Cleaners often worked in pairs along the waterline in little boats called punts. Force would tend to push the boat away from the hull. One Side Cleaner would try to hold the punt against the hull by paddling while the other worked on the hull. Side Cleaners, absorbed as they were, tended to lean over further as they worked. Green Side Cleaners, like Stewart, tended to take cold, saltwater baths when they weren't careful.

Sometimes Deacon would get permission to use a P-boat to gently push and hold a punt against the hull. Work got done much faster. Several days later, Deacon gave Stewart a chance, after appropriate begging, to move the P-boat during Side cleaning work along the waterline.

1330, May 27
Buoy 17, San Diego Channel
U.S.S. Chilton APA-38

Chief Abernathy, First Division Chief, had noticed Stewart handling a P-boat and talked to Deacon about it. For the first time, Stewart's Sea Scout background came in handy.

Stewart, faking down a half-inch line, looked up as Chief Abernathy and Deacon approached him.

What's the Chief looking at me like that for?

He stood from where he'd been kneeling.

He's smiling.

Stewart got an uneasy feeling in his belly. "Morning, Chief," he murmured, acknowledging the man's presence.

"Stewart," the Chief nodded. "Take five, Stewart. Got a few questions for you."

Stewart nodded assent, waiting.

"I've seen you fumbling around in the P-boats. You act like you know something about boat handling, Stewart. You wanna tell me about that?"

Stewart thought a second.

He's here to see me about something. Is he going to laugh about the Sea Scouts, too?

"Uh, well, Chief, my family moved around a lot and only thing I really found every place was scouting. So, I was in the Cub Scouts and later the Boy Scouts. After World War Two, I joined the Sea Scouts in SSS Malolo in Long Beach and later transferred to a Sea Scout Ship in Bremerton in SSS Sinclair." He grinned as he thought of something. "If you count the time I was in Sea Scouts, I've been wearing Blues for over three years."

The Chief and Deacon laughed, appreciatively. Deacon clowned a little.

"Forgive me, Stew. And here I thought you were just another Boot."

The Chief glanced sharply at Deacon and smiled thinly.

"I wouldn't try to take that to the Paymaster, Stewart." He paused, then, ""Sounds like you're a Navy Brat, Stewart. Is that right?" Stewart nodded in return.

"Your father retired?"

"Nah, Chief, Dad's a Mustang Lieutenant. Was an IC Electrician."

Chief Abernathy grunted. "He stationed around here?" He asked, waving his arm in a circle.

"No, Chief, he was on the Lexington-II CV-16 in Bremerton. My Mom wrote a letter a few weeks ago to say Dad was transferred to the Siboney CVE-114 in Norfolk, as Engineering Assistant. And they've already moved from Bremerton. I figure I don't have a home ashore anymore. This is home."

The Chief seemed to reach a decision. He reached in his back pocket, pulled out his wallet, and began rummaging through cards and scraps of papers.

"Okay then, Stewart. Tell me more about your Sea Scouting experience."

On familiar ground, Stewart relaxed some—which was what Chief Abernathy was trying to accomplish.

"I don't carry my papers with me anymore, Chief, but I was a qualified coxswain on the Sinclair and a qualified predicted log race observer for the yacht clubs around Puget Sound. We had a decked-over 50-foot motor launch with an old Chevy engine in it. I was a qualified Puget Sound Navigator and passed the Coast Guard's Pilot examination for Inland Rules of the Road."

Deacon looked at him strangely, as he learned new things about his Side Cleaner.

"Okay Stewart, I'm not familiar with those predicted log races. We don't have anything like that around here."

What does he mean — around here?

"The yacht clubs up there have what they call predicted log races. If a yachtsman wants to enter, he pays his fee and picks up the program. Ahh—they start from their own yacht club. They must estimate the time they will pass several checkpoints, and the time they're supposed to cross the finish line. The yatchsmen check the tide charts, expected winds and currents, and lay out their predicted course and times in ink, in a logbook.

"The observer logs the actual time. I was an observer." Stewart had begun hesitantly but grew more confident as he continued.

Chief Abernathy was smiling as he handed a familiar looking card to Stewart.

"I wouldn't want this to get around, Stewart, but as you can see, I am the Sea Scout Master of SSS Malolo here in San Diego. Yeah, I know your qualifications very well. I've been looking for some qualified Mates."

He broke off abruptly. "That's not what this is all about. I'm pretty particular who gets behind the wheel of any of my boats. You understand that?"

Stewart, watchful now, nodded. "Yes, Chief."

"And I've seen you handling the P-boats. Pretty bad, so far, but better than a lot. He looked at Deacon thoughtfully, nodded as if making a decision, and turned back to Stewart. Sticking out his hand, he said, "Break out your Watch, Quarter, and Station card, Stewart. I'm going to have a new one issued to you."

Stewart's eyes darted from the Chief to Deak and back to the Chief again.

"Why's that, Chief?" he asked as he reached for his own wallet.

"You're going to stay in First Division, Section Two, Side cleaning for regular cleaning duties, but I'm moving you around some. Instead of standing Fire Watch at sea and Messenger of the Watch on the Quarterdeck in Port, I'm putting you in Carter's crew for liberty boat runs in a P-boat, as a bowhook or sternhook. At sea, you'll join the lifeboat crew and alternate between there and Port Lookout when you're on watch. What do you say to that?"

"When do I start, Chief?" answered Stewart with a big grin on his face.

Chief Abernathy smiled approvingly.

"Just as soon as I run it by the First Lieutenant and he signs it off. Deak will let you know because he has to change your schedule. Each day at 1300, you report to Carter so he can run you through P-boat orientation, and teach you how to be a boathook—okay?"

"Okay with me, Chief. Thanks."

Chief Abernathy laughed, "Don't thank me yet. If you work out, we'll start training you as an Assault Boat Coxswain. Just wait 'til you learn to crank the bow ramp while retracting from the beach." Then he nodded at Deak and walked away.

Boat crewmen, designated as Bowhook and Sternhook, derive their title from the boathooks they hold sometimes as they approach a dock or ship. A boathook is an eight-foot long wooden pole with a brass hook—shaped something like a wall coathook. The hook is used to push away or grasp lines (rope)—or to reach out to someone in the water.

The Chilton moved out into the Pacific off the Silver Strand South of NAS North Island and anchored for three days each week. Officers and men of the Amphibious Operations Section practiced unloading and loading LCVP's and LCM's with simulated cargo in the various holds. The boat crews practiced the assault landing and retracting in lively surf.

Stewart began training as a member of an Assault Boat Crew.

A designated Boatswain's Mate striker, Jones BMSN, sat down beside Stewart on the Mess Deck one Tuesday morning after securing from Special Sea and Anchor Detail.

"Stewart, I'm the Assault Boat Coxswain on P-boat 18, and you've been assigned to me as Bowhook. Deak knows I'm talking to you, so after you eat, meet me up on the 02 deck by Whalen Davit Number One. I want to see what you know. This ain't going to be like those liberty boat runs, you see." The crew of LCVP's is the Coxswain, an Engineer and two 'Hooks.

Stewart was surprised even though he had been expecting something like this. He took in the sailor sitting along side him and liked what he saw.

A Coxswain is always the boss of his boat and I'm about to be part of his crew.

"Okay," Stewart responded between bites, "be ready in about ten minutes. Mind telling me how long you've been in the boats, Jones?"

"Yeah. I went directly from Boots to the Chilton in Tsingtao, China, in January 1948. The ship had to keep the Chinese away from the ship because they could be serious trouble. Some of them wanted our Galley garbage, some had girls in the bumboats, and some had things to sell. Those were understandable, if exasperating, by their constant crowding around the fantail, bow, and gangways.

"Mostly, ships of all navies used fire hoses to keep them away. But it was sabotage they worried about. That's why several P-boats circled the ship day and night, keeping the bumboats at a distance."

"Sometimes, those bumboats wouldn't take no for an answer. Then, I'd push them away with the bow ramp. They got damaged but not hurt or sunk or anything like that."

Stewart was fascinated by this and other stories he heard. They got up with their trays and took them to the scullery. White hats on and squared after clearing the Mess Deck, Jones led the way to the 02 deck where his boat was resting. Stewart was beginning to feel comfortable on board. Just barely a month ago, he had joined the Chilton.

They stood there a moment studying the side and bottom of LCVP 38-18. Jones took a couple of steps closer, squatted down, pulled Stewart closer, and pointed to something on the bottom of the boat.

"Can you see that small drain hole next to the keel?"

It took a second before Stewart could focus on it.

"Yeah, now I see it."

"The Bowhook's number one job, Stewart, is to make damn well sure that hole is plugged before we hit the water. Its plug is always left next to the drain hole ready to screw in. It's got a big enough tee handle on it to make sure it's screwed in tight."

"Okay, what next?"

"Right. Let's walk around my boat . . .

Hmm, my boat, he sez . . .

. . . to check some things out."

Jones got up and led the way again, his hand trailing against the side of his boat. Peter-18 was sitting in a cradle on deck next to the edge. It didn't take a smart guy to figure out that the Eighteen boat was the second boat in the water after the one already connected to this davit. Jones stopped before they got to the ramp and pointed up to a winch on the P-boat's gunwhale, pronounced "gunnel".

"See that locking lever on the ratchet?"

Stewart squinted against the sun and nodded.

"When we hit the beach, I'll yell one word at both of you 'Hooks. On that word, you," tapping Stewart's chest a couple of times, "release this Ratchet lock," he said patting the side of the boat, "and Hendersen, the Stern Hook, releases the locking lever on the other side. The ramp drops to the beach and the troops charge out."

Stewart nodded, beginning to visualize what that task would be when they actually hit the beach for the first time.

"What's that word, Jones?"

Jones smiled at him. "Wondered if you were paying attention—the word I scream at you two is, '*now*'. You can't see it from here but inside the boat, a crank is stored in retaining clips on both sides. As soon as the troops are out of the boat, you 'Hooks push your crank onto the winches from the inside and start cranking."

He wasn't smiling now. "It's a tough job. You and Hendersen have to work together to bring the ramp up and seal the bow. And you have to do that while the boat is bouncing around in the surf and while I'm trying to retract from the beach. When you guys finally crank the ramp up all the way and latch the winch, you're ready to collapse."

Stewart chuckled, shaking his head.

"Stewart, when we finish here, I'll take you up to Hatch Three. Right now, Peter Ten has its ramp down for maintenance and you can—you will see what this is all about."

Jones continued, walking around the boat and pointing to different features, discussing their meaning as far as Stewart's duties were concerned. Then, climbing into Peter Eighteen, Jones had Stewart remove one section of deck plate and pull out the heavy lifting ring attached to its cables, to begin to get the feel of his job. Two rings are attached to the whalen davits cargo pelican hooks under its boom. It is the 'Hook's job to release the pelican hook on Jones's command so the ring drops into the boat. When arriving under the davit for retraction, the 'Hooks struggle with their ring to snap it into the pelican hook.

And there, right next to the keel is the drain hole and its plug in a clip, just like Jones said.

Stewart grabbed the drain plug by the tee and showed it to Jones. "The drain plug, right?"

"Yeah. You put that in on the way down to the water. Incidentally, we never know which cradle Eighteen boat is going to be in. Just depends on which boat is ready to be lifted first."

"Okay, Jones, when do I get to hit the beach as part of the crew?"

"This afternoon, guy."

This afternoon? Hoo boy!

"Oh yeah, wanted to show you something." He reached back for his wallet and pulled a card out. "Look familiar?" he asked and handed it to Stewart.

Well, I'll be damned. Chief Abernathy's Sea Scout First Mate.

"Isn't this kinda like carrying coals to Newcastle?"

"Nah. It's fun working with the kids. And besides, the Chief invites me over for a home-cooked meal once in a while. Even met a couple of girls at his house. But, now you know why you're on my crew."

"Does that mean I'm going to become a Sea Scout Mate, or will he invite me?"

"Just be a squared away sailor and let things develop, Stewart. Meanwhile, go back to work. When you hear the call for General Quarters One Able, you report here fast. Okay?"

"Got it," and with a final glance at Jones, he smiled and walked forward to see if he could find Deak.

By default, unless he left the ship at the end of his year as an EV, he was going to become a Boatswain's Mate. And Chief Abernathy had picked up the thought that Stewart was going to make a career of the Navy, following in his dad's footsteps.

JUNE

1600, June 3
Liberty Call
U.S.S. Chilton APA-38

Over on the Silver Strand, Stewart participated in fifteen practice landings and retractions in the surf, including five as part of waves of landing craft. Cranking that ramp was a bitch, but he could do it. During every practice, he alternated with Henderson to run the boat to feel the wave action. Jones had them practice trying to stay on the heel of a wave because that's where they wanted to be when the boat was pushing up on the beach. He saw what happened to LCVP's and LCM's that broached in the surf. They watch a broached P-boat get hit by a big wave and turn over, injuring the engineer.

At noon chow Friday, Bailey, Peter Eighteen's Engineer, sat down with Stewart. After nodding to each other and kidding around about the boat, Bailey got down to what was on his mind—monkey business.

"You going on liberty tonight?"

"Yeah, thought I'd hit the beach and see if I could get a USO ticket to watch the Padres play the Seals. Pass the salt and pepper, wouldja?"

"You a baseball freak or something, Stewart?" Bailey asked, grabbing the salt and pepper shakers and handing them to Stewart.

"Nah, it's something to do. Thanks," Stewart replied as he began to shake salt on his mashed potatoes. Putting that down, he picked up the pepper shaker and liberally coated his mashed potatoes with pepper.

"How about picking up some girls and seeing what develops?"

"You know some?" Stewart mumbled between mouthfuls of food.

"No, but if I try to find a single jane, my chances are slim to none. However, if we try to pick a pair, got a fair to middling chance of scoring. What say?"

Why not? Sure haven't had any dates so far in this town.

"Okay," Stewart grinned at Bailey. "Before or after chow?"

"Eat first. Save your money. Meet you here for dinner, Stew?" Chewing on a bite of chicken breast, Stewart nodded as Bailey got up and headed for the scullery.

Stewart and Bailey walked up Broadway from the Broadway Landing, window shopping at some of the Navy clothing stores and Locker Clubs, eventually making it to the Broadway Fountain Square where they hung around. Clip joints of all kinds, gyp joints, penny arcades where the cheapest shot was five cents, and high priced burlesque houses sat on three sides of the square—Broadway being the fourth side.

Bailey looked around. "Let's go over to those chains and set a spell. I bet some girls will come out of the buses that are just aching for some ass." Sitting in front of the bus stop on Broadway, they saw everyone getting on and off the buses.

"See, what did I tell you, there are all kinds of pussy coming into town for action." Bailey grinned at Stewart.

As they watched a bus pull up to stop, Stewart remembered his Dad saying that before he met his mother, he used to hang out with other Saratoga sailors in The Anchor Inn on Pacific Ocean Avenue. This was when sailors still wore their flat hats with ribbons emblazoned with the ship's name in gold lettering. A sailor in a new port, usually sailed his hat through the doorway. If it came sailing back out, he'd better not go in there. If it stayed there, the sailors inside were inviting him in—to drink or fight. Stewart wondered if this night would bring a girl or a fight.

A group of girls got off and separated. Two girls spotted Bailey and Stewart sitting on the chain fence, hesitated, then nonchalantly plopped down hard on the chain on the other side of the post from them. There was a wild scramble as Bailey and Stewart tried to keep their balance. In the end, they pulled each other down into the grass next to the sidewalk.

The girls giggled, the burst into a loud haw haw. They were dressed in matching cutoff blue jeans and men's white shirts with the sleeves rolled up and shirttails hanging out. Both of them had matching short curly hair that was in that indescribable shade of color, somewhere between light brown and not blonde. Bright red lipstick and clutch purses completed their ensembles. Both girls had nice figures with everything in the right places. They looked like your average Southern California working girls out for a good time.

It was apparent to girl-wise Bailey they had done this on purpose. Scrambling to his feet while brushing himself off, he laughed and said, "Hey, you got us good. I'm glad the pigeons and seagulls aren't around today." Bailey was obvious as he looked them up and down approvingly. "Very nice," he nodded smiling some more.

"You from National City?" he asked.

"East San Diego," replied the light brown haired girl. The lighter brown haired girl nodded agreement without saying a word.

"Oh yeah? Whatcha doing way up here on Broadway, then?" asked Bailey.

The darker-haired girl spoke up. "We thought we'd go to the zoo or go to the movies, maybe out to the beach. Why?"

"Well, me and my buddy here were thinking along the same lines, weren't we, Stew?" Lee nodded agreement.

"I'm George and this here is Lee. What's your names?"

The darker haired girl thumbed her chest. "I'm June and she's Alice."

By this time, Stewart had brushed himself off and was checking out Alice. She was about 5'5" with hazel eyes; a longish face and a crooked nose bent to the left. Her thin lips opened wide to whiney her laughs. Yet she spoke in a soft low voice. A nice set of boobs and a cute round bottom completed her makeup.

June, on the other hand, snickered through full lips and knowing eyes full of laughter. Her blue eyes, snub nose and freckles were set in a round face. Her bottom was under slung and he thought she was wearing falsies.

The four of them sat on the chains and kidded around, sizing each other up for about fifteen minutes. Lee had just about gotten up nerve to ask if they'd like to do something with them. George had other things in mind.

Bailey stood up, looked at the girls, and stretched. Stewart had no idea of what he was up to. Bailey smiled and looked at the girls.

"Well girls, you've had a chance to look us over, size us up, and make up your minds. Wanna fuck?"

Stewart was so shocked, his mind went blank momentarily as his body turned hot, then cold. He didn't know whether to run like hell, take a poke at Bailey, or out of curiosity, wait and see what the girls did.

I guess I'll wait to see what the girls do.

Bailey had already figured out June was the leader of the two and whatever she decided, Alice would go along. That's why he, therefore, had addressed his gross question to her.

Alice's mouth was open in surprise. June looked at Bailey with a crooked smile and winked at Stewart.

"Depends on where you plan to do it. I don't want grass or sand shoved up inside me. Right, Alice?" Alice nodded dumbly.

Stewart still couldn't believe this conversation. Bailey turned to him and in a low voice said, "We got pussy tonight. You got enough geetus to get a motel with twin beds?"

"I think so."

"Good. The girls and I will arrange for drinking material." Bailey pointed away from Broadway and spoke in a low voice. "Go over two blocks and turn right. There's a low life motel, green with yellow trim. Probably cost fifteen bucks for the night. You get it and meet us on the street."

Stewart was embarrassed. "Twin beds? You mean we'll see each other making love?"

"Kee-rist, Stew. We don't have to leave the lights on if that bothers you. Most likely these girls want to watch each other get it. Put your head in a sack for all I care. But this is sure stuff. Go on, shag ass," pushing Lee, "get the hell outta here and find the motel room."

Stewart gave one last look at the girls waiting for him to move, and he moved.

Stewart found the motel, quaintly named the Do Drop Inn. Inside, he filled out the card while a suspicious older woman looked him over.

"You ain't gonna have no wild parties are ya, sailor boy?"

"Uh, no Ma'am. My buddy and I want to get a restful night of sleep. Oh, we need twin beds."

The old woman began snickering, watching Stewart with knowing eyes. He felt himself turn red.

"Two double beds is all I got. That's sixteen fifty a night, take it or leave it."

Stewart pulled out his billfold and extracted the only twenty-dollar bill he had.

So much for cigarettes, soap, and razor blades.

Taking his change and a key to room twelve, he found the room and inspected it. It had an overhead hanging bare light bulb and one bedside lamp. A folding stand for a suitcase was in the open closet, and there was one straight back chair.

At least there is a door to the toilet.

He opened the door and studied the beat up fixtures.

Damn, I sure don't want to sit on that cracked lid.

He left the room and walked out to the street to wait for Bailey, June, and Alice. Nervously smoking his third cigarette, he watched and listened for the threesome to appear.

Damn it. I know I'm stuck with a room I have no desire to use. Wonder if I can stand here and raffle it off to the next guy and gal that come along? I'll wait ten more minutes. If they aren't here by then, fuck it, I'm going back to the ship.

He had just lit his fourth cigarette when he heard a girl shriek with laughter and a boy and girl haw-hawing raucously. He relaxed, took a deep drag, and leaned back against the telephone pole.

The three appeared around the corner, Bailey between the two girls. Bailey spotted Stewart and held up a paper sack for him to see. Stewart held up the motel key and shook it for them to see. June, followed a second later by Alice, clasped her hands over her head in a sign of victory.

"Hey, Stew, what's your first name? I never knew it—mine is George."

He already said that.

"Lee," he replied, while looking at how cozy the three stood together.

"Okay, Lee."

They all huddled together, Bailey with a hand playing with June's bottom. Mentally shrugging, Stewart patted Alice's behind and left his hand there. She looked up at him with a sly smile and knowing eyes as she wiggled a little bit under his hand.

Whoa, Junior!

A conspicuous bulge rapidly appeared on the front of Lee's pants.

"Here's the plan, Lee. June says variety is the spice of life, but they have to catch the 10:30PM bus back home. In about two hours then, we're gonna swap partners for twice the pleasure."

Alice was playing with his thigh now letting her hand slide closer to his erection, which was beginning to throb. He found it hard to concentrate on what Bailey was saying.

"Do we have to check in?"

"No, but we do need to sneak by her window and be quiet, George. She also said we can't have any wild parties."

George laughed. "She's kidding you, Lee. This is a hot sheet pleasure palace. Ten minutes after we leave; the maid will have fresh sheets in there. Come on, lead us back to the room—didja check for glasses?"

"Ah, no, didn't even think of that."

Alice held his hand as they quietly walked back and went into room twelve and closed the door. June moved over to the window and pulled the blind all the way down.

"No peep shows allowed," she whispered and sat down on the bed closest to the door.

"Okay guys, you got rubbers? No rubbers, no pussy!"

Lee looked at George in embarrassment.

I don't even know how to put one on.

George, pouring Four Roses into four glasses, looked up at June in dismay.

"No, I didn't even think of them."

Alice picked up her purse and rummaged through it. She pulled out a handful triumphantly. "Ta Daaaaa!" she trilled.

George made a sound of disgust. "Rubbers are like galoshes in the shower." He grumbled as he grabbed one. He flipped the light switch and now just a bare glow from outside lights illuminated the room.

"Hey, why no lights, George?"

"Cause Lee likes it dark—he's shy."

"Lee, don't you like to watch? That's part of the fun." June asked, with a pout in her voice.

She got up and flipped the lights back on. Lee was trying to figure out what to do next when his bed bounced and Alice slid up next to him, grabbing Junior.

"Oh, what a nice boner," she chuckled, squeezing it.

Oh wow, she's already got all her clothes off.

"Lee, you stuck in neutral or something? Get your uniform off. Here, let me play with the buttons and you take off your jumper."

There was a quiet rustle as Stewart tore off his jumper and threw it aside. Alice had his thirteen-button flap open playing with Junior as Lee struggled to remove his pants, skivvies, and shoes and socks. Alice continued to stroke and pull Junior. "You got a nice dick, Lee." She leaned over and sucked it deeply and laid down. Then he flopped down beside her on his side and she cuddled close. Lee took a deep breath and reached over with his lips for a breast.

I can't believe I'm going to have a piece of ass for the first time—and with two girls. Holy Shit!

Much later, with the lights back off, Lee lay along side June, stroking her soft belly as she spoke.

"Alice, who was best, do you think?" asked June languidly.

"No question, George is. Hey, Lee, you were a virgin, weren't you?"

I didn't know it was so obvious.

"Yeah. How did you know, Alice?" he asked sleepily.

"Cause you wanted to hop right on and go for it without playing around. Didja like it?"

"Oh yeah."

"And you said you're eighteen, right?"

"Yeah. What's that got to do with anything?"

"How about that, June? Copped the cherry of a guy three years older than me."

"Scooz me. What did you say?" Stewart stared into the darkness in shock. There was a thud as feet hit the floor, then the light turned on. George was standing by the door. He stared at Alice, and looked back at June.

"How old are you, June?"

"I'm sixteen—so what? Did you like my pussy or not?"

Oh, Fuck!

Bailey and Stewart looked at each other and then at both of the girls. As one, they grabbed their uniforms and began dressing as fast as they could.

"Hey, where you guys going? It's only 9:30. We got another whole hour to do it."

"We're getting the fuck away from you as fast as we can, that's where," panted Lee as he jammed his legs into his trousers as rapidly as possible.

"But why, Lee?" asked a puzzled June.

"Cause fifteen will get you twenty every time, June."

Minutes later, Bailey and Stewart, fully dressed, left room twelve and hurried away.

"You can sure pick 'em, Bailey. Truly, you can."

"Okay, okay, they sure looked old enough and they damn well fucked old enough. They may have busted your cherry, Lee, but I can tell you, those broads have been passing it out for quite a while."

0630, June 6
Broadway Pier
San Diego, California

Stewart watched from his side cleaner station on the Main Deck as bus after bus of Marines from Camp Pendleton drew up to the gangway and unloaded Marines in their combat fatigues, packs, and weapons, mostly Garand

M1 rifles slung on their right shoulders. Jeeps and trucks with trailers were loaded into Cargo Holds Three and Four.

Wonder if this is in memory of D-Day, five years ago?

In company with the Bayfield and Noble, two other APA's, they sailed up to Camp Pendleton and conducted a live landing.

Peter Eighteen made three waves before the engine began running rough, and they had to tie up for repairs on the after port boom. Chief Abernathy met them at the top of the starboard quarter boat boom Jacob's Ladder.

"How'd it go, Jones?"

"Not too shabby. Everything was going great guns until the engine began to stall, so we had to come in. Don't know what's wrong yet." He and the Chief strolled off for a private conversation as they watched the rest of Jones's crew. Chief Abernathy motioned with his head and they strolled back to confront the crew.

"Bailey, Hendersen, Stewart. How you feeling? Everything okay?"

I sure don't know what's wrong with my engine, Chief. Wasn't anything I did back there, but it ain't safe for any more landings," Bailey growled in exasperation.

"Okay, Bailey. Go find your Chief and see about repairs. How about you, Hendersen? Any complaints?"

Hendersen smiled tightly. "Glad to be back aboard, Chief," as he stretched his sore muscles.

"Stewart?"

He broke into a grin. "Other than wanting a cup of coffee, everything is great. Really different with troops aboard, isn't it? Any idea if we get to go back out today?" He asked with a wider grin.

The Chief and Jones exchanged a glance that was not lost on Stewart.

Uh ohhhh. Now what?

"Jones, I'm going to borrow Stewart for another little task, if you don't mind."

Jones laughed and shook his head. "Have fun, Stewart."

The Chief walked off, beckoning Stewart to follow. Back inside the ship, he pulled Stewart to the side.

"We're going up to see the First Lieutenant, Stewart."

"Hey, Chief, I haven't done anything wrong." There was a worried sound in his voice.

"I want to tell you something, Stewart. Ordinarily, you would not get the task I'm assigning because you're not that experienced yet. However, you looked very good on Silver Strand and here again today. You get it because I said so and because the First Lieutenant, knowing about your Sea Scouting and previous experience in Puget Sound, believes me. He just wants to look at you to check the size of your balls and reassure him I'm making the right move."

What the hell is he talking about?

"Most of the coxswains are tired as all get out right now, or busy landing troops. I have to have someone take the LCPR with Marine Public Information people out to take movies of the landing. Do you feel you could do that?"

Stewart kinda swallowed and nodded to the Chief. He felt a little tingly all of a sudden. "Yeah, I think I can, Chief." His eyes glowed in anticipation.

"Okay. You got it then. Remember, as coxswain, you are in charge of your craft, right?"

"True, that's right, Chief."

"Okay then. Let's go see the Man."

Chief Abernathy led the way up to the 03 deck and the Amphibious Operations Office. Stepping inside, Stewart was surprised to see so many Marines sitting at desks, talking on radios. The Chief nudged him, pointing to the First Lieutenant. He was beckoning to him.

Stewart pointed to himself with raised eyebrows. At the nod, he walked over to this Lieutenant Commander he had only seen in passing three times since Stewart had reported aboard.

"Good morning, Mr. Ambrose. You wanted to see me, sir?"

"Stewart, you ever handled the LCPR?"

"Uh, yes sir. On the Strand, I 'Hooked for Sawyer and he let me run it around a little bit. It's a lot faster and more maneuverable than a P-boat. Only holds a squad, though."

Mr. Ambrose nodded. "Well, we're up against it this morning, trying to make landing schedules and no extra coxswains to go around. Chief Abernathy says you can handle this detail." He paused and, after glancing at Chief Abernathy, looked into Stewart's eyes with serious but friendly eyes.

"Do you feel you could run a few people around the landing area without getting into trouble?"

"Yes, sir. I'd sure like to give it a try, Mr. Ambrose," he responded in a more relaxed stance.

"All right then. There is a Marine Corps Public Information Office contingent on board that wants to run around taking movies and pictures of their landing on the beach."

That doesn't sound bad at all.

"Chief, take him off and tell him things I don't want to go into."

"Aye aye, sir."

"Thank you, Mr. Ambrose. I'll take care of the R-boat," Stewart said with pride in his voice.

"You do that, sailor." His voice came sternly but there was a smile on his face.

The Chief tugged on Stewart's shirt and they stepped outside. "That PIO Marine Major might want you to do some stupid things for his cameras. You feel it's dangerous, tell him so and don't do it. Got it?"

Marine Major?

Stewart swallowed with a frown wrinkling his brow. "Tell a major no?"

"That's right, and he understands your position."

"What happens if he insists and I still say no?" Lee still had a worried look on his face.

Me, a Seaman Apprentice, telling a Major, USMC, where to go or not to go was very not good.

"You're driving, Stewart!" He smiled broadly, then turned serious again.

"Here's generally what the major wants to do. He has movie cameras and still cameras. He will ask you to get close to an LCVP filled with troops, or maybe one with jeep and trailer, and run parallel while they use their cameras. They will want you closer than you know is safe. Don't go closer than you know is safe."

Stewart nodded. "Okay, Chief."

"I know from past experience they will also want you to run across the front of a wave. If you decide it is too dangerous for that wave of landing craft, pick a later wave."

Stewart nodded.

"Now then, when running across a wave of boats, make sure your far point is way seaward of where the combers start to break. Otherwise, sure as shit, you'll broach and I'll be pissed off, the major will be mad enough to shoot you for dumping his expensive equipment, and the Captain will have something to say to the First Lieutenant, which means me, which means you. Got it?"

"Got it, Chief. If I run across the front of a wave, I'll need battle speed. Can I use that?"

"Yes. Mostly, you'll be dashing from one point to another."

"What if he wants me to make a landing and retract?"

The Chief looked at him with stone cold eyes and didn't answer him.

I think that means don't fuck up.

"Do I have time to make a head run and maybe grab a sandwich, Chief?"

"Yeah, Stewart. Meet me at the forward Quarterdeck in thirty minutes."

"Aye aye, Chief," looking down at his wristwatch. Lee disappeared below. Chief Abernathy looked after him with a thoughtful look on his face.

I hope Stewart is a good choice. Otherwise, we're fucked!

He'd only been out of the Chief's sight for twenty minutes but as Stewart looked at his wrist watch and approached the Quarterdeck, he saw Chief Abernathy looking for him.

"Right here, Chief."

Chief Abernathy stood next to a Marine Major, two Marine Staff Sergeants, and a Marine Corporal, guarding three olive drab wooden cases; they were in khakis with fore-and-aft caps, not in combat fatigues, which surprised Stewart.

"Stewart, this is Major Hathaway," Stewart rendered a snappy salute, which was returned with a friendly smile, "Staff Sergeants Smith and Williams," who both nodded, "and Corporal Dowd," who smiled. "Major Hathaway will explain what he wants for each shot. Just don't bend the boat, Stewart." Stewart grinned and nodded to the Chief.

"Aye aye, Chief, I won't." Stewart turned to the Marines. "Major Hathaway, are you ready to leave, sir?"

"That's right, Stewart. The sooner the better."

Oh shit, I haven't even checked on my crew yet.

He looked down the gangway at the LCPR. Three sailors sat looking up at him. Stewart held up a thumb in question. Three thumbs popped up, in answer. He waved to them and turned back to the major.

"We're ready, major." He turned to help the Marines with their boxes, but they waved him away.

"Don't sweat it, Stewart. We handle our own gear," said Staff Sergeant Smith. As they gathered up their boxes, the major turned to the Officer of the Deck and saluted.

"Request permission to leave the ship on assignment, sir."

Returning his salute, the Officer of the Deck responded, "Permission granted, sir."

Major Hathaway stepped on the landing, saluted aft and descended to the rolling LCPR. His crew followed him in turn.

Stewart stepped forward, saluting. "Request permission to leave the ship on assigned duties, sir?"

"Do you know when you'll return?" asked the Officer of the Deck.

"No, sir. No idea at all. I'm under orders of the major, sir."

"Very well, Coxswain. Carry out your orders." Stewart swelled with pride.

He called me coxswain!

"Aye aye, sir," saluting the Officer of the Deck, which was returned.

Stewart stepped on the landing, saluted aft, and clattered down the gangway and into the boat. With eight people in the LCPR, the boat settled down nicely, rising and falling with the swells. There were no seats—standing room only.

He looked at his crew. He didn't know any of them. The 'Hooks were from the Second Division, and he'd never seen the Fireman before.

At least, I can read their stenciled names.

Stewart turned to the Engineer and read his stenciled name.

"Roberts, all set?" Roberts flicked a switch and Stewart heard the exhaust fan start.

"All set, Stewart."

The Stern Hook was standing right behind Stewart, using his boat hook to hold the LCPR to the lower landing. Stewart looked at him with a grin and raised his eyebrows in question. Getz responded with a smile and nodded. The Bow Hook, Baker, waved affirmative to Stewart's raised eyebrows.

Stewart reached down, moved the throttle-shifter arm experimentally to make sure it was in neutral, checked the movement of the wheel, and pushed the primer three times. Stewart gave a look to Roberts: "Okay to start now?" Roberts nodded.

Stewart moved the combined throttle-shifter to neutral , twisted the throttle to start position and pressed the starter button. The engine roared to life, echoing off the metal hull of the Chilton.

He eased the throttle to a nice idle and looked to the upper landing. The Officer of the Deck was standing there with a megaphone.

"Shove off, Coxswain. Carry out your orders."

"Aye aye, sir." Stewart grinned and saluted. He waved at his 'Hooks.

"Push off." They pushed against the lower landing, raised their boat hooks away to show they were clear, and lowered them into their respective retaining clips.

Pushing the lever forward to engine forward gear, Stewart stayed at idle until he knew which way the rudder was pointed. Turning the wheel a quarter turn, he increased the engine's RPMs to get away from the ship, then cranked the throttle-shifter up to 1500 RPMs heading outward in a sweeping curve toward the beach.

Straightening and seeing no boat traffic, he called his crew to him. The Marines were getting set up to shoot. Stewart and the rest of the crew had to get their signals straight rapidly.

"Roberts, you know I'm authorized battle RPMs, don't you?"

"Yeah, just remember, you keep it up there too long and you'll burn the diesel jets."

Stewart acknowledged that with a nod and smile.

"Getz and Baker, you got a free ride until we return to the ship. Making a landing is not part of this trip—leastways, Chief Abernathy didn't say yes, when I asked. So, find a place out of their way."

"Roberts, when the major tells me exactly what he wants, I expect to go to 2250 RPM to get there. So, we play it by ear. Okay?"

"No sweat, Stew."

The three ships were about six thousand yards off the beach. The LCPR wouldn't arrive at the Beach Control Vessel for about twenty minutes. Stewart studied the sea and set a course to quarter across the swells. Then, he played with the throttle until the boat's pitching and rolling was soft and smooth; it kept down the spray over the square bow ramp. Stewart was delighted with the way the LCPR handled.

"Hey, Stewart!" He looked up into the eyes of three cameras.

What the fuck?

Then, he laughed.

Major Hathaway called out directions to him.

"Look back at your ship—okay, now glance forward and then study your compass for a moment. That's right, now look forward again. Good, okay, that's very good."

The cameras all came down. Major Hathaway came back to him.

"Stewart, we're going to take a series of shots as we approach the jump off point, such as that wave of Peter boats or those Mike boats heading to the Control Vessel. When I want you to do something, I'll let you know."

"Aye aye, sir."

"Is there any way you can speed up?"

"Yes, sir." He looked at Roberts and caught his attention. "Time to go to battle."

He dropped his hand to the throttle and waited as Roberts ducked out of sight. Then a hand came up. Stewart dropped to idle and a moment later the hand rotated. Stewart opened the throttle all the way and the LCPR began to move much faster than before.

"How's that, major?"

"Fine," he beamed until sea spray caught him full in the face. Wiping his face off, he looked at Stewart in appeal. Stewart tried not to grin but wiped off his own face and pointed at the throttle as if to say blame it on the throttle.

Staff Sergeant Williams tapped the major on the shoulder and pointed to a wave set up in column formation. The major looked where he was pointing.

"Yes, that's a good start, Williams." the major said, nodding approval.

He turned to Stewart. Pointing at the wave, he shouted, "Cross their front and go up the far side about fifty yards away."

"Aye aye, sir. Full speed or slow it down?" he asked as he spun the wheel and aimed for the oncoming wave.

The major looked back and forth between trying to judge the speed.

"Slow down after you cross the leading Peter boat's bow. When you pass the last one, make a loop back and overtake at high speed."

"Aye aye, sir."

The LCPR was fairly bouncing now with a great deal of spray splashing into the boat. All three cameramen were facing away from the bow, hunched over protecting their camera lenses. As Stewart curved back the other way and throttled back, the cameramen began shooting the line of LCVPs loaded with the Marines.

"Stewart, come in a little closer."

Stewart eased in closer as they ran by the second boat.

"Closer, Stewart, pull in closer."

He gave the rudder a little more pressure. They were now running less than twenty-five yards apart on this pass.

"Stewart, I can't see their faces this far off, I need to get closer."

Stewart leaned over the horizontal wheel, looked at the major, swallowed, and shook his head. "Sir, I can't get any closer on this head to head run."

Major Hathaway chewed on a fingernail, then nodded acceptance, and turned back to the shooting scene.

Passing the last LCVP, Stewart turned away, looping back. Major Hathaway came back to him.

"Got a question for you, Stewart. And only do it if it's safe. Use high speed to get just beyond the fourth boat in line, then pace them." He began to use hand motions to show his intentions.

"What I want to do, is cut a slow pan from the last boat up to the fourth boat which should be right about there," he said pointing to a spot in the water abeam of the R boat. Also, I want you to match that boat's speed and ease in real close so I can shoot those Marines in a close up view."

"No problem in that, Major, but I'll stop before it gets too hairy. The other coxswain hasn't the foggiest idea of what you're doing. The Wave Officer might get a little nervous, too, sir."

The Major nodded and moved off. Stewart eased the throttle up to full power and moved along the boats until he was even with the fourth boat. Easing back off the throttle until he matched speed, they were in position. Major Hathaway was nodding enthusiastically, and Corporal Dowd signaled a 4-O at Stewart. Stewart sidled a little left, drifting closer to that boat.

Suddenly, the Wave Officer who was riding in that boat, stood up and began to violently wave him away until the major made sure the lieutenant (junior grade) Wave Officer could see his gold leaf. Then he sat down again.

"Major Hathaway, he's going to circle in a moment. We're at the Beach Control Vessel."

"All right. Back off about seventy-five yards and we'll shoot that, too."

Stewart eased the rudder to the right, staying abreast of the boat, cutting to idle as the Wave Officer stood up on the motor housing and signaled his wave to slow down and circle.

In a few minutes, all the Marines came back to stand by him, happy with their shots so far. They dropped their cameras into the cases and flopped the lids shut.

"Stewart, is the smoking lamp lit?" asked Staff Sergeant Williams. Stewart nodded and pulled his soggy cigarettes.

Better than nothing, I guess.

The two 'Hooks had settled down in the after compartment with Roberts, both reading pocket books.

He listened to the Marines discussing the next action. Their worry was the sun. Even the sunshades couldn't hide all the sun when the LCPR was bouncing around.

"What if we were in the Beach Control Vessel's shadow, would that help any?" asked Stewart.

The Marines looked at each other and slowly nodded. Stewart moved the throttle to full ahead after Roberts released the latch again. He aimed at the Beach Control Vessel's Quarterdeck, and slowed down on the approach. Backing down with a strong squirt of throttle, he stopped within hailing distance.

"You want to tell him, Major, or should I?"

Major Hathaway stuck a thumb in his chest and moved clear of everyone. In a really loud voice, he called to the Officer of the Deck.

"Ahoy there." The Officer of the Deck reversed his megaphone to hear better.

"We are shooting movies and would like to camp in your shadow for about five minutes. Is that all right with you?" The Officer of the Deck turned his megaphone the right way and pointed it to the R-boat.

"Affirmative. Carry out your orders," he said and saluted the major.

Stewart moved the LCPR at an idle into the shadow of the bridge. Then to neutral except for a slow movement into ahead or reverse now and then to maintain their position. The Marines were delighted with their huge sunshade. So was Stewart.

The Major pointed at a wave just beginning to move into a line abreast. "We want to get a shot of that wave breaking out of the circle. As soon as that's over, let's move to the Line of Departure and look things over. Make our decision there as to which wave to shoot. Our next thing is to shoot across the front of a wave as they move from column into flank position."

"Yeah," he said thoughtfully. "I mean yes sir, Major." Stewart looked back and forth at several groups that were candidates for the cameras.

"It will be easy, Stewart. Don't worry about it."

"Okay, Major." Major Hathaway glanced at him for his informality but said nothing.

Oops, I think I'd better mind my P's and Q's.

"Stewart, let's move to the Line of Departure now."

"Aye aye, sir." He cranked the wheel and advanced the throttle to full, momentarily, to clear the ship. A lot of LCVP's were moving independently in this vicinity.

Like the Chief said—don't bend his boat.

After they arrived at the Line of Departure, Stewart dropped to neutral and waited for their choice of waves that were running about twelve minutes apart. The Marines looked at the choices of mixed LCVP and LCM waves, all LCVP or all LCM. As one, they turned to Stewart again.

"Can we shoot more than one wave, Stewart, or is one all we are allowed?" Asked Sergeant Williams, politely.

"It's your program, Sergeant. Tell me what you want and let's see if I can do it."

They turned to consider again, each cocking their eyes on the sun and holding their hands out to check the available sunlight.

"Okay, we'd like to shoot a wave of all LCM's . . .

Shit, that's going to be hairy!

" . . .and a wave of all LCVP's. If we have the time, it would be great to shoot a mixed wave too."

"We can get that one from the beach, Sergeant Williams." The Staff Sergeant looked at his major and nodded.

Wait a minute! Did he just say—from the beach? What the fuck am I going to do about that?

"Stewart, let's take this LCM wave just coming up on the line now. Get way off and come shooting back at an angle across the front. When you get across, swing behind them and return here. Okay?"

Sounds easy enough.

"Aye aye, sir." Stewart turned to the R-boat engineer.

"Roberts, here we go again. Give me battle speed." Roberts leaned forward and flipped the latch and Stewart twisted the throttle up to 2250 RPM. Twisting the wheel, he turned away from the oncoming LCMs.

"Keep going—farther—more—yeah, okay, come on back at full speed. Try to hold a steady line for us, " Major Hathaway instructed.

"It'll probably be a curved line, sir, but I'll do the best I can."

The major nodded and got down to business. Stewart's crew now stood up to watch this exercise.

I think those Mike boats are up to full speed now. Man oh man, look how low they are in the water.

He drew a virtual line with his eye and settled down to the run. He watched the far boat even as he watched the closest boat out of the corner of his eye.

Those Mikes sure push a big bow wave.

And suddenly, they were through. Stewart set an easy arc to come back along the line from the rear.

The second run with LCVPs and one LCM in the center, was a snap.

"Are you all done now, Major?"

Can we go home, please?

The major turned to him with a big smile.

"That's just about it, Stewart. For our finale, we want to shoot a wave landing on the beach."

Holy shit!

"Then, we'll just get off and continue shooting from the beach. You've done a fine job for us, Stewart."

"Thank you, Major Hathaway. The pleasure has been all mine. On this run in, if we cross in front of the wave and join it just ahead on the far side, you should get fine action of the beaching and ramps dropping, sir."

The major looked at him in surprise.

Shit, now I've got the major pissed at me.

"That's a hell of a good scene. Do you think you can pull it off?"

"Yes sir, so long as a broached boat isn't in the way, and we don't run into any mines or barriers."

Major Hathaway and his merry crew of combat photographers in training laughed their asses off. Meanwhile, Stewart was going through a case of nerves.

"Hey Stewart," called Roberts in a low voice, "can you land and retract the LCPR?"

"I'll let you know after this is over. I'm going to need battle speed again. How are your sand filters, Roberts?"

"They're in good shape." Stewart turned to the major who had overheard this conversation and was looking at him steadily.

"No bullshit, sailor. Can you beach this craft safely or not?"

"Yes sir, I can."

Retracting is what I'm worried about, but then you won't be on board.

"Let's get the show on the road then, Stewart."

"Roberts, gimme battle." Roberts smiled apprehensively and flipped the latch. Stewart brought the throttle smoothly up to 2250RPM and took a line across the oncoming mixed wave. Just as he passed the last LCVP and came forward of them, he throttled back a little to match the speed of the landing craft, and turned to face the beach.

Suddenly he turned and called to Getz and Baker.

"Better ease forward to handle that ramp, guys. I don't want them fumbling around."

They nodded and moved behind the cameras to crouch down by the narrow ramp.

Well, that's one break. There is no riptide right now.

Stewart kept making minor adjustments steering and leaving the throttle set—for the moment.

Beach is coming up pretty fast.

Twisting his head to the side and then back, he saw he was still just ahead of the wave, bearing down on the breaking combers.

His belly was pounding with excitement and his armpits were dripping water down his sides.

Now!

He entered the surf line, tightening his hold on the wheel and keeping his position perpendicular to the beach, twisting his head right and left. The two combers ahead of him were flattening out.

Won't be long now. Easy, baby!

"Stand by to beach," he yelled out. For the first time he glanced at the Marines.

What the hell?

Two of them were shooting him. The boat bumped, slid, and bumped some more. He hit the throttle to goose his way in farther. Then the boat ground to a stop.

"**NOW!**" he yelled, and the ramp dropped.

"See you, Coxswain; nice trip in."

"My pleasure, Major Hathaway."

Major Hathaway was already off and running up the beach. The Corporal, lugging two boxes, followed as best he could in the churned up sand and foam. The LCPR bumped forward as each Marine left. The 'Hooks reached over and pulled the light ramp up and latched it.

Stewart began retracting; goosing the engine just as a wave would reach the fantail and splash water over everyone. The engine bubbled and roared as the boat stern alternately grounded in the sand and lifted high on the next ocean wave. Light as this boat was, he noticed immediately how much easier it was to pull off the beach than one of the

LCVPs. True to his training, he kept steady medium throttle until a wave would lift the stern.

In a shorter time than Stewart thought possible, he was floating free and backing through the surf. He looked forward to make sure he was moving straight out and tried to figure out what he was seeing through his salt-stung eyes. Then it dawned on him.

Those guys were shooting us retracting from the beach.

No time to wave.

He checked behind to make sure he was clear before he turned. Then, as the next wave of landing craft came slashing by on his starboard side, Lee shifted to Forward gear, hit standard throttle, and twisted the wheel. Straightening out, he headed out to sea looking for the Chilton.

"Any of you guys recognize which one of those APA's out there is our ship?"

All of them stood and peered into the distance, right into the sun, beginning to set in the late afternoon. They couldn't make out the Chilton, either.

Fuck it, I'll steer for the middle and wait until I can recognize our hull number 38.

Stewart corrected his course, made sure he was at top throttle without battle speed, and leaned on the gunwhale to relax.

He idled down as they approached the forward gangway, and waited for the Officer of the Deck to get off the phone. The megaphone came up.

"LCPR, tie up to starboard after boom. Coxswain, report to Chief Abernathy."

"Aye aye, sir," saluting the Officer of the Deck as he departed.

I wonder what the Chief knows?

They leaned against the after deckhouse, sore and trembling after a couple of hours riding in ocean swells, afternoon chop, and surf in the LCPR. The Fireman had already gone to see about refueling his boat. The two 'Hooks waited for Chief Abernathy with him.

The Chief came up behind him. "Did you bend my boat, Stewart?"

"Nary a scratch, Chief."

"Have any problems out there, Stewart?"

"Not a one, Chief."

"Anything unusual happen?"

"Nooo, I can't think of anything, Chief."

"Did you have to override the major anytime?"

"No Chief, everything was hunky dory. I even got to make a couple of suggestions to help them out."

"I see. All right then. Usual stuff. Go shower, shave, and change into clean dungarees and white hat. Eat dinner, then come find me in the Chief's Quarters."

Oh yeah?

"Right, Chief, about forty-five minutes?"

"Sounds good to me, Stewart."

He turned and walked forward. Stewart dropped below to his compartment, eager for a nice hot shower and clean clothes. He'd rather have hit the sack and forget dinner, but the Chief had something on his mind.

Stewart arrived at the Chiefs' Quarters and asked for Chief Abernathy. The Mess Cook pointed across to Chief Abernathy who waved him in.

"Okay, Stewart, let's go see the boss." He got up and led the way out and up to the Amphibious Office on the 03 deck.

Stewart trailed Chief Abernathy into the Amphibious Operations room. Mr. Ambrose smiled at them but was busy on a radio circuit, and they waited. Finally, he waved them over.

"Well, Stewart. Pretty interesting day, would you say?" His voice drawled slowly and softly. His eyes were amused but friendly.

"Yes sir. It sure was interesting watching those Combat Photographers do their stuff."

"Would you like to know what they thought?"

"Er — sir?"

Shit, they've been talking on the radio.

"Major Hathaway said he doesn't believe they will have to reshoot anything."

"Oh that's nice, sir." He answered weakly.

"Yes. He was particularly pleased by your suggestion to sweep across the incoming wave and land just ahead of them so they could shoot from that perspective."

"Sir." Stewart felt a little weak. He hadn't been actually authorized to make that landing.

Oh shit, now I'm going to get it.

Chief Abernathy with a big smile, spoke up. "You know, Stewart, one of my friends here is the Chief Signalman. One of his good buddies is a Chief Signalman on the Beach Control Vessel. I asked that he keep an eye on you in case you got into a jam."

Uh oh.

"Stewart," asked the First Lieutenant, "how exactly did that trip to the beach come up?" who didn't see angry at all.

"Well, sir, Major Hathaway just did it natural like, as though the whole world but me knew about it. He said they were all done out there and I could go ahead and take them into the beach now."

Mr. Ambrose nodded, encouraging him to continue.

"It just came to me that a little flair in taking them to the beach wouldn't hurt, so I made the suggestion, sir."

"And you didn't object, is that it?" asked Chief Abernathy.

"That's right, Chief. How much trouble am I in for the landing?" He looked back and forth between the Chief and First Lieutenant, waiting for what he knew not.

"Stewart, Major Hathaway told me to tell you, 'Well Done,' I didn't tell him you had no previous experience landing and retracting a LCPR. But you certainly knew you should have refused on the grounds of safety. Whatever action will be taken is by Chief Abernathy. There will be nothing official about the 'Well Done' or any reprimand. One sort of cancels the other." He looked at the Chief whose red face looked like he was about to cough.

"That about cover it, Chief?"

"Yes, sir." Chief Abernathy tugged on Stewart's sleeve and they left. Out on the 03 deck, the Chief offered Stewart a cigarette and leaned back against the rails.

Stewart eyed Chief Abernathy, nervously. "Chief, when I specifically asked whether I was to honor the major if he asked to run ashore, you wouldn't answer. I took that to mean use my best judgment."

"Mr. Ambrose was surprised by that action. He did not suspect the Marine PIO's were going to go directly ashore. So, while I tested you today, Mr. Ambrose wanted to see if you were completely stupid, or just had a good pair of balls."

"So?"

"You passed, Stewart, four oh. The problem is, Coxswains are not supposed to be Seaman Apprentice. You, an EV, can't take the test for Seaman. Therefore, nothing goes in your record about this. Tough, but them's the true facts of life. This was a special day. I don't know when you'll have duty as a Coxswain again. Now, time for my coffee and tonight's movie on Cargo Hatch Three."

Lee was crestfallen about lack of recognition for a job well done. Chief Abernathy was looking at him fairly closely. "Stewart, if it's any consolation to you, remember that Mr. Ambrose and I know you did a 4.0 job this afternoon and got that 'Well Done' from Major Hathaway. You'll just have to accept that."

"Yeah, Chief, thanks. Is that all?"

Chief Abernathy nodded, smiled, and waved him off. "Get outa here."

0745, June 13
Buoy #21, San Diego Channel
U.S.S. Chilton APA-38

Seaman Apprentice Lee H. Stewart was excited. It was a great time of year up and down the Pacific Coast. Summer was the season after chill and before heat—just right, and the ship was going on an amphibious landing training exercise, named Operation Miki. The Chilton would sail to San Francisco and tie up at Treasure Island for three days of liberty.

Following that, they'd be underway again to his old hometown Bremerton, Washington at the Navy Shipyard, waiting for their turn to load near Fort Lewis. The Chilton's crew would have liberty in Bremerton before time to sail to Fort Lewis, take on Army troops and sail to Hawaii in a large convoy.

The Navy was conducting annual War Games. This joint Army/Navy amphibious operation was named Miki with opposing Fleets. Its purpose? The amphibious convoy would sneak over to one of the islands and land the Army troops before the enemy's carrier strike force found the amphibious convoy.

The chow line moved slowly forward until Stewart finally reached the trays. A Mess Cook had just reloaded the tray receptacle and his metal tray was hot. He grabbed a cup for milk and put that hot cup down in its designated depression. Grabbing the hot 'silver', he stuffed those utensils in his dungaree shirt pocket and immediately leaned forward so the hot knife, fork, and spoon wouldn't continue to burn his nipple. He pushed the hot tray along the steam line. S.O.S.

was his fare this morning. Whoever thought white gravy and little bitty granules of hamburger on toast was a great way to start the day, then call it *Shit On a Shingle*, had a weird sense of humor. Stewart took his breakfast over to the table with the other Side Cleaners, nodding to them as he threw his legs over the bench one at a time and sat down.

The tables were portable. A pair of three-inch vertical pipes (stanchions), between deck and overhead, passed through a table to hold it in position against the ship's motion. These pipes had three locking positions. The purpose of the upper locking position was for table and bench overhead stowage. The lowest position allowed the crew to sit on benches and eat, read, or watch movies. The middle position made the crew and troop passengers eat while standing up. People ate faster that way.

An APA's Mess Deck is designed to feed large numbers of combat troops on their way to or from a battleground. People just naturally tend to dawdle with their coffee and cigarettes after eating a meal. If you have to feed 250 men of the Ship's Company and 1600 troops, dawdling over coffee and cigarettes is just not going to work. When troops are aboard, mess table benches remain stored in the overhead. Mess tables are lowered half way so everyone eats standing up.

After all the chow hounds depart, Mess Cooks scour the table surfaces clean. Two Mess Cooks lift a table up the pipe stanchions clear to the overhead and latch it there, same as the table's benches, similarly placed and held against the overhead. When all the mess tables were stored in the overhead, the Mess Cooks scrubbed and swabbed the deck then used severely wrung out swabs to clamp the deck nice and dry.

Stewart hurried back to his compartment to change into undress blues for morning quarters. Today's Plan of the Day had been posted last night as usual. He knew he would be at quarters, standing at Parade Rest, while they left port. That took forty-five minutes to get the ship past the seaplane landing area and the Point Loma Coast Guard Station. Stewart was glad he wasn't a line handler or on the mooring detail. Those poor guys' blues were filthy in the short time because of handling the mooring gear. It cost 95¢ just to have one set of undress blues dry-cleaned.

The 1MC Public Address system opened and a good sounding pipe shrilled All Hands.

"Quarters—quarters for muster. The uniform of the day for enlisted men is undress blues with white hat and without neckerchief. Quarters for muster."

Before the ship got underway, it was vitally important to find out if anyone is missing unexpectedly. Division Officers also passed along pertinent information. Another pipe shrilled to the in-port boat crews for the Captain's Gig and an LCM bringing the ship's jeep, 4-door sedan, and van back from the pier. Large vessels carried their own vehicles in the cargo holds between ports. Finally, the two LCVP's used for liberty launches and work boats—all had to be lifted aboard.

"Boat crews, man your boats."

People were beginning to move a little faster. The Chilton was moored to Buoy 21 in the San Diego Harbor Channel. The standard plan was to slip the moorings, fore and aft. Two tugs would help the ship turn about facing down channel. Then, she would escape to the sea.

After muster, Stewart stood around with some of the other Side Cleaners waiting to get underway.

No side cleaning today. Let's see. I'm in Section Two. I wonder which section will take the watch when the Captain secures from Special Sea and Anchor Detail. The Boatswain's Mate of the Watch will let me know whether I stand Lifeboat crew or port lookout first.

The Side Cleaners smoked and watched the harbor water taxis and ships boats comings and goings. They had little to say. Harbor taxis were making their last morning rounds before 0800. They knew that Officers of the Deck didn't want them approaching while Morning Colors were being raised.

A gleaming, dark blue Martin Mariner PBM patrol bomber was being backed down the seaplane ramp from North Island by a wheeled tractor with a long boom. A sailor slipped into the water, unfastened the boom, and hurried out of the water. As the PBM hull rocked gently on its wing pontoons, first one engine, then the other coughed, sputtered, and roared into life echoing across the still morning water, settling down to a high idle.

The 1MC hissed again, no pipe this time.

"All hands not actually on watch or work detail, quarters for getting underway. Uniform of the Day is undress blues, white hat, and without neckerchief."

The Side Cleaners didn't move. They knew Deak would be here in a minute to form them in ranks. They smoked a last cigarette because the next smoke would be about an hour away. Deacon walked up lazily with a wide smile on his face.

"Put 'em out and fall in, sailors."

They grumbled good-naturedly, pinched out their cigarette tips and put the dead cigarettes in their pockets.

"Side Cleaners—A tenn SHUN!"

His crew snapped to and waited. Stewart watched Deak out of the corner of his eye but most of his attention was on the PBM, which would pass fairly close by as it taxied out to its watery airstrip.

"Close interval Dress right—DRESS."

Stewart's elbow came up automatically. Stewart looked down the line of noses right at Deacon who was checking the two ranks.

"Ready—FRONT."

Elbows snapped down, heads clicked forward. They waited.

"Side Cleaners—at ease."

They stood loosely, one foot in place, until their Division Officer showed up. Stewart's ears perked up. He could hear cadence and slapping as the Marines on the deck above them drilled at the manual of arms with their Garand M-1 rifles.

"Shift Colors—shift colors!"

That magic moment when the ship breaks its connection with the ground had arrived and passed. The next time shift colorswould be called is when the ship reaches out and grabs the ground—hopefully with anchor, mooring cable, or line to a pier—but not running aground! Lee felt the cold, foggy breeze begin to wet his cheeks and eyebrows. A barely perceptible trembling came up through his feet as the ship started to move slowly by ships still moored in the line of buoys.

The 1MC crackled. "Attention to Starboard." They were passing one of the AKAs.

"Division, Attention." Ordered Deak, as he faced outward,

"Hand Salute." Rendering honors—who know who was senior. Deak saluted for the division.

"To." Honors are over.

"Carry on."

"Division," spoke Deak. "At ease."

The Chilton did this three more times before passing the last moored ship, a Submarine Tender with four submarines tied up alongside the Tender.

A squadron of Chance-Vought F4U Corsairs took off ahead of the ship from North Island, roaring out to sea. A deep roar came to them from the Point Loma hillside. Stewart watched as the PBM came into sight lurching into the air, dripping water from its wing pontoons and hull.

The Chilton slowly turned to port heading out the channel. No more ships were moored here, but they couldn't pick up speed until after the ship passed the Coast Guard Station. A flight of Grumman F6F Hellcats took off and the Side Cleaners watched them roar over their heads as the fighters headed out to sea after the Corsairs.

San Diego was behind the ship now. The Pink Prison—U.S. Naval Hospital Balboa—showed starkly against the background of trees, houses, and hotels. The Captain, who had not felt the need for a Harbor Pilot to take the Chilton out, called for Standard Speed as they passed the end of the breakwater. Sea swells transmitted their message to their knees as brisk cold wind cut through their blues. They welcomed the sound of a pipe coming over the 1MC.

"Secure from quarters, secure from special sea and anchor detail. On deck, section one relieve the watch."

Okay, I stand the afternoon watch to start off.

"Stewart!"

"Yeah, Deak?"

"You got Lifeboat duty, then lookout on the afternoon Watch. Got it?"

"Got it."

0800, June 13
Quarters for Muster
U.S.S. Chilton APA-38

Their division officer, reading from a memo, advised them that word had come down from high: conserve your money. All the Armed Forces and Coast Guard were concerned that Congress might not pass the pay bill in time for July 1st payday.

1200, June 13
U.S.S. Chilton APA-38
Underway to San Francisco, California

Lee looked at the other members of the Lifeboat crew without recognition. Besides the regular LCVP crew, a

Hospital Corpsman with a large, heavy bag, was there to render aid to people taken from the water. After the Coxswain took muster and left to report to the Boatswain's Mate of the Watch, the crew straggled into the small ten by ten compartment on the 02 deck.

There were two doors and two narrow, metal benches. The quick release, watertight door opened out to the deck next to the Lifeboat. An LCVP hung over the side in its Whalen Davit with a belly cradle strap keeping the P-boat from swaying back and forth. The Lifeboat crew could be in the boat, ready to drop, within a minute of the emergency call, "Man Overboard".

A regular door on the opposite side of the Lifeboat crew compartment opened to the well where a ladder descended clear down to the Second Deck and ascended to the Flag Bridge (Sky One), at the 04 deck. The Main Bridge was down one deck at the 03 deck.

Duty in the Lifeboat compartment consisted of being ready to dash to the boat. Every hour, the Lifeboat crew swapped places with the bridge crew to specific jobs. During storms, they changed every half-hour. The Hooks were lookouts on the port and starboard bridge wings. The Coxswain became the Helmsman and the Engineer became the Lee Helmsman, manning engine enunciators, bell, RPM indicator, and sound powered phones with the Main Engine room.

During the daylight, they could read or study navy courses leading to promotion. At night, they were required to stay in the compartment wearing night goggles in the red-lighted compartment to maintain their night vision.

Stewart was fascinated to spot Radiomen and Electronic Technicians going through the door on the other side of the well opposite their compartment. Stewart learned he could spend time in the ET and Radio Shacks during the day so long as their door was open and the Coxswain could call him.

June 17
U.S. Naval Station Treasure Island
Pier 12
San Francisco, California

Stewart was a loner. He usually chose to go alone on liberty because his experience with group liberties had not gone well.

Jeez, going on liberty with Bailey in San Diego . . . What a rotten thing to say to those girls. Of course, he had been absolutely right on the money.
Funny thing was, those girls didn't care to see them again. As Alice said, all she wanted was a great piece of ass. He and Bailey had done as much as they could to fill her need. But Lordy, Lordy, San Quentin Quail!
Holy Toledo, the next time Bailey pulled that, though. Aye, yi yi! The one girl socked me hard enough to give me a bloody nose; the other one tried to kick Bailey's balls and then she screamed for a cop!

They had had to run hard for two blocks just to get away.

Stewart didn't like the idea of other sailors deciding what he would or wouldn't do. Group things were okay, like for ship's parties and baseball or football games, though.

Not yet nineteen, he didn't fit in with the older guys who went to their favorite bars and stayed there. Worse, this was the first time he was going on liberty in San Francisco.

I'm not about to try Bailey's shit again. Let's see, what have I heard about this port? Market Street is interesting to walk and has all kinds of movie houses.
Fleishhacker's Zoo is supposed to be great. I'd like to ride one of those five cent Cable Cars and I can do that to get off in China Town to look around. Then, spend another five cents to go see Fishermen's Wharf. It is expensive but lots of people go there.

Tomorrow, I could go to the Southern Pacific engine shops over by the Cow Palace. Maybe they will let me in to check out their engines. Might be able to pick up a' show ticket or two at the USO.

Stewart and others were disgusted because the Disbursing Officer didn't hold payday until after the Chilton was inside the 3-mile limit this morning, so they weren't able to buy a couple of cartons of Sea Store cigarettes at Seventy Cents per carton, instead of two dollars per carton.

Section Three was going to have the duty today, which meant he had duty on the last day before they sailed. It worked out just right because he wanted to save some money for liberty in Bremerton, when they arrived at the shipyard.

Wonder if Larry will be home on leave—no, Army calls it furlough—then. Better write a letter to him at Fort Lewis and find out.

Next, he decided to buy a picture post card today and send it to Larry, asking about a pass or furlough to meet him in Bremerton.

"Liberty Call—Liberty Call. Liberty Party muster on Hatch Three Cover for inspection. Liberty uniform for enlisted is Dress Blue Baker, peacoat optional. Liberty expires on board tomorrow morning at 0730. Liberty Call."

Stewart was in the fourth rank waiting to be inspected when he was tapped on his shoulder. Bailey was in the next rank, grinning at him, ready to go.

"Hey Stew. Whadaya say we go check out the snatch together?"

My ass, we will!

"Can't, Bailey. my Aunt Mathilda is expecting me for dinner."

"Yeah, well, if you change your mind, let me know. I'm going over to the beach by Golden Gate Park. There's pussy all over that place."

Sure—there's cops all around, too.

Stewart motioned Bailey to hush and came to attention as the Officer of the Deck approached. He examined Stewart carefully and checked his ID and Liberty Card. As he finished inspecting the fourth rank, he turned and announced,

"Okay fourth rank. Keep out of trouble and have a good time. Relieve your quarters." It was a strange way to handle liberty call instead of releasing the whole party, but it worked and nobody complained. They all saluted the O.O.D. and left the ship by the after gangway, saluting the Colors as they did.

Lee Stewart, liberty hound, pushed through the glass door of the streetcar station, not sure of the way to Market Street, paused as he looked around. A fellow behind him bumped into him and backed off apologetically. Lee smiled, waving it off, and asked, "Which way to Market Street, buddy?"

The guy's eyes jumped back and forth between Lee's crotch and his face.

Crap, a fucking fairy! Getting propositioned and I'm not even here, yet.

He swayed and pointed to a street. "That way about four blocks. I'll be glad to be your guide. What would you like to do?" he asked in a soft, sensuous voice.

"No thanks, I'll find Market, all right."

Lee strode off without looking back, hoping the fairy wouldn't follow him. The streets were dirty; the buildings were dirty, and the wind blew dirt and pieces of paper through the air. He kept squinting to keep the grit out of his eyes. Market was a lot more than four blocks away.

Finally, he ducked into a drug store at Market Street. Moving to the post card rack, Lee searched for and selected a funny postcard of a sailor and a girl.

"How much for this and a stamp, ma'am?"

"Fifteen cents." Lee reached into his pants change pocket, pulled out a nickel and dime, and handed them to her.

"Can I borrow a pencil a minute, please?"

She handed him a pencil silently and watched him write a brief note on the counter. He looked up at her and smiled as he pulled his wallet out.

"Gotta get my buddy's address." She smiled thinly and kept her eyes on the pencil as he wrote Larry's address on the card. Lee straightened up and gave her back the pencil.

"Thanks a lot, ma'am, appreciate it." She nodded.

"You can drop your post card in that slot, sailor," she said pointing to a wooden box. "We mail a lot of picture postcards every day."

Lee nodded, dropped the card into the wooden box, and stepped out onto Market. Looking left and right, he decided to go up toward a tunnel he could see in the distance.

By the time Lee had walked all the way to Van Ness Avenue at Market Street, he had arrived at several conclusions. First of all, it had been a dumb move. He could have ridden the streetcar and seen as much. It was cold out here on the sidewalk. Temperature dropped fast in the late afternoon. Second, he had no idea there were that many queers in San Francisco. He lost count after fifteen silent and vocal propositions on Market Street.

If he turned and walked back the same way, Stewart was sure some of those fairies would think he had changed his mind.

I'll ride the streetcar to Powell where the cable car turns around.

He spent another dime to ride the streetcar. At Powell, he and two other sailors helped the brakeman turn the cable car around on the "armstrong" turntable.

Paying his nickel, he sat on an outside bench and enjoyed the ride up the steep hill, through Chinatown and down the other side to the Fisherman's Wharf area. The cable car got very crowded, with people hanging onto the vertical grab bars, feet on the step.

At one point, a lady stood in front of him so close, he could have leaned forward just a bit and get a face full of breast cleavage. But he didn't dare.

I wonder if Bailey would have?

Two days in San Francisco had been expensive and not very fruitful. China Town restaurants were way too expensive for him, as was Fishermen's Wharf. The next day he had journeyed way out to the SP yards on city buses, only to be turned back at the gate. Both days, he ate hamburgers.

Maybe next time, I'll see if I can't get a date with a WAVE. She may know some interesting places to go.

June 23
U.S. Naval Shipyard
Bremerton, Washington

"Now hear this. Muster on Stations, muster on stations."

Stewart climbed up to the 02 deck, port side, to his cleaning station and began sweep down before swabbing the deck. As he swept, he looked across the bay to Port Orchard and remembered the girl he had met there.

What was her name? Allison? That had not worked out. As soon as he joined the Navy, she dropped him. Even so, Allison had been very nice for a while.

Typical of Bremerton, it was a dreary overcast morning. Hopefully, it would clear up by Noon. He bent to his cleaning duties and thought about the past.

What a difference it was from the last visit to the Shipyard. Two years ago, his Dad had been Chief Engineer on the U.S.S. Lexington II CV-16, just before it was decommissioned and put into mothballs there.

The family had dinner in the Wardroom several times. Now, Stewart was returning on his own ship, but certainly not eating in the Wardroom. Not only that, his family was in Norfolk, Virginia.

Stewart was disappointed in Bremerton. First thing, he called Larry's house and talked to Larry's Mother. Larry had lost Stewart's address but called his Mom to say he was being transferred as a Basic Infantryman replacement to the First Cavalry in northern Japan.

Lee tried to look up a few of his school friends without success. Now that he had a little money, he wanted to date some of those girls he remembered from high school and college. Those still here were engaged or wouldn't be caught dead with a guy in uniform, particularly a sailor in a Navy town, even a homegrown sailor.

Chiefs and white hats like Stewart were not allowed to have civilian clothes aboard ship. He even tried to find his recruiter, but Chief Halleran had already been transferred. Stewart painfully realized that since his folks had moved away, his home was under his white hat.

Back downtown from his old drive-in hangout, Lee decided to go by the Roxy Theater where he had been employed as the marquee sign changer. He only worked twice a week at twenty-five cents per hour for a small amount of money and got to see all the movies free. He had even taken his folks to the movies one night!

His old boss, Mr. Bauer, had moved on, but the cashier and ticket taker remembered him and let him in free. Lee rolled his hat rim down and slid it up under the front of his jumper. Lee found a seat high in the back where he could see the movie and watch the local action.

Lee noticed a girl come in and wave off the usherette. She looked around and slowly came up his aisle until she got even with his row. Casually looking around, she slipped past him and sat down three seats away.

She looks familiar.

He waited until a light portion of the movie and studied her features.

Son of a bitch—that's Edith Zimmerman. I'm sure of it. She graduated from Bremerton High School with me.

He waited again for another light portion of the movie and whispered to her. "Edith, is that you?"

The girl glanced at him, then looked again, and leaned over in his direction. In the dark all Lee could tell was that she had shoulder length hair, a plaid, pleated skirt, and a light colored blouse topped with a button sweater. The sweater and blouse did not hide her nice looking breasts.

"Do I know you, sailor? You look kinda familiar."

I hope to shit in your flat hat, you do!

He was sure now.

"You ought to, Edith Zimmerman, you were one of the very few girls I dated before we graduated."

Edith moved over one seat closer so there was still space between them, and peered closely at him.

"Oh my God, Lee." She scrambled up and over the armrest into the seat next to him and squeezed his arm. "Whatever are you doing here and in the Navy, of all things?", accenting the first words of each sentence. Her voice had risen to regular conversation levels, irritating some customers.

"Knock it off, lady. I'm trying to watch the movie!" She glanced over her shoulder and whispered, "Sorry, fella," and turned her attention back to Lee. Edith moved as close as she could and put her head next to his ear.

"Will this be better?" she giggled. Lee chuckled a yes and looked up behind them.

Yep, that dark section of seats is empty and no one around.

"Let's go up there, Edith. We can whisper a little louder without disturbing anyone." She nodded and they went up to the rear row and close to the projection booth—very dark here.

If it hasn't been fixed, the armrest will be missing between the last two seats in the corner next to the projection booth.

He sidestepped across to the last seat, grinning as he felt for the armrest and couldn't find it.

Bingo!

"Hey, where's the armrest?"

"I thought everyone at BHS knew, Edith. Been missing as long as I've been around the Roxy. Is something wrong?" He put his arm along her seat back. She shook her head and slid over tight against his side and pulled his hand down over her shoulder onto her left breast.

"We never did get a chance to do anything on our date that night, did we, Lee?"

Wham! Up popped Junior to strong attention. In short order, she raised her legs and tucked his legs under her legs and squirmed around so she was laying in his arms and her thigh was pushing hard against Junior.

"There, isn't that a lot more comfortable, Lee?"

"It sure is," he sighed and leaned over to kiss her.

Lee and Edith lost all track of the movie and time, until the lights went on close to midnight. They scrambled back to normal sitting, straightening their clothes. Both got in a lot of feels but Edith refused to let him play with her bare breasts or take her panties off, even though he got his hand inside. Lee had to redo some of his thirteen buttons when she had finally gotten hold of Junior. Lee ached.

"Edith, is there any place we can go so we can take our clothes off and have a good piece?"

"Lee, I'm a virgin. I won't sleep with any man until we are married."

"Really!"

With all that fingering, she thinks she is still a virgin?

"You mean no guy has made love to you?"

"Well, only what we did, and that's very nice. I like to do that."

Jeez, and I am really hung out to dry!

"So, when we leave here, you can walk me to my bus stop and say good-bye."

That was it.

Lee sulked.

She wouldn't even hold hands with him now. At the bus stop, she shook hands like the proper girl and wouldn't let him kiss her, either. He walked back to the ship and vowed never to speak a word of this to anyone. He'd be laughed out of the Side Cleaners.

Monday, June 27
Fort Lewis, Washington

A Bosun's Pipe shrilled Attention.

"All departments make ready to get underway." The Boatswain's Mate paused.

"Officers' Call, Officers' Call." He paused again.

"All Hands, Muster on stations."

The Chilton was preparing to leave US Naval Shipyard Bremerton for Fort Lewis, Washington, south of Tacoma. It was the Chilton's turn to load troops and cargo.

The Bosun's Pipe shrilled Attention. "The Officer of the Deck is shifting his watch to the Bridge."

The police whistle trilled. "Shift Colors, Shift Colors." Lee glanced at his watch.

Underway at 0831.

Stewart opened his cleaning locker and removed a broom, foxtail, and dustpan. He just knew that a lot of dust had collected on his Port 02 Deck since he swept it two hours earlier when the Boatswain's Mate had trilled Sweepers on his pipe. But orders were orders.

When he finished sweeping down and put those tools away, he took out a dirty rag, a relatively clean piece of toweling, and brightwork polish to polish all the chrome, brass, and copper fittings in his work space.

Stewart paused for a moment to enjoy the sight of houses and roads on the land on both sides of his ship as they moved slowly toward the main part of Puget Sound. He lit a Camel and began polishing the brightwork from the after end of his deck working forward.

Sixteen hundred soldiers with all their gear came aboard. Many six-by-six trucks and their assorted trailers were lifted aboard. Some artillery 75mm howitzers and their trucks were dropped into the holds, too. Number three hatch cover on the Mess Deck had two jeeps with radios and trailers tied down there. The Chilton took on a new look: she was much lower in the water now. Before the Chilton got to the Straits of Juan de Fuca, some soldiers were already puking their guts out.

The sea swells were fairly high but a nice distance apart.

That's got to come from a big storm way out in the North Pacific.

The Chilton took the deep swells on the port bow, causing her to lean right and left, as well as rising and falling. To the sailors, this was normal routine at sea. However, the soldiers were having a tough time of it.

On the Mess Deck, as everyone finished their meal, they took their tray, bowls, cups, and steel service to the scullery. Each item had a special spot to be placed. When that was accomplished, each tray had to be dunked in a garbage can with sudsy warm water between two wide brushes to remove food particles.

As one soldier leaned over to dunk his tray, the Chilton lurched up and to the left at the same time as a cross wave struck the ship. The soldier pivoted to keep his balance as the garbage can broke loose. The soldier fell into the garbage can backwards so his ass, belly and legs up to his knees were trapped in sloppy warm sudsy water. The can began sliding aft as the soldier screamed in terror. Soldiers and sailors scattered from his path as the can gathered speed. It hit a hatch transom and spilled its contents: soldier, water, and slop all over the deck.

The Mess Deck Master-at-Arms located the Mess Cook whose job it was to secure that garbage can, and took him aside for a private discussion.

Three days out from the West Coast, the amphibious convoy was attacked suddenly by Vought Chance F4U Corsairs from the Enemy Fleet's carrier. The Corsairs strafed the ships at mast height with blank .50 caliber machine guns.

"General Quarters—General Quarters. All hands, man your battle Stations. General Quarters." The General Alarm started clanging and gonging. Stewart ran for his G.Q. station as Pointer on Mount 44.

"Life Boat crew, man your boat on the double. Away the Life Boat."

They didn't call Man Overboard, wonder what that's all about?

Stewart's task, as Pointer of Mount 44, aimed the twin 40mm barrels up and down to track targets vertically, and would actually press the foot peddle trigger to fire the two guns when he and the Trainer agreed they were on target. Across the barrels on the right side of the mount from Stewart was the Trainer, a salty BM3 from WW2, who aimed the 40mm guns right and left, incensed that a *boot* was Pointer, and was loud in his anger about that.

The Gun Captain stood on a pedestal behind the guns. He had overall control of Mount 44 to make sure the four-round clips of 40mm ammo were delivered to each gun barrel loading slot, and to make sure the Pointer and Trainer were on the correct target.

A string of men called Loaders passed four-round clips from ammunition storage to the top of both barrels and jammed the clips down into their slots.

Stewart ran up, grabbed his life jacket and helmet, and slipped into his seat, strapping himself in. He reached over with his right hand and switched from Remote Control to Local Control, so the gun crew could control and exercise their gun mount. Testing to make sure the two barrels were moving up and down, he noticed several guys were staring off in the distance.

"Whatcha looking for?" Stewart asked.

"Two of those fighters collided and went in," answered the Gun Captain. The World War Two combat sailors had been quick to spot the planes and see the accident.

Xavier, the Gun Captain, a World War Two veteran of many air attacks at Iwo Jima and Okinawa, saw the accident and reported the collision over his phones. He continued to stare at the spot where the two planes had gone in.

"Didja see them go in?" asked Stewart.

"Yeah. One went in there and the other splashed there," pointing with both hands. He would continue to keep his eyes on the spots until the Officer of the Deck relieved him of that responsibility.

At sea, when someone goes overboard and you see the sailor, you keep your eyes focused on him because you may be the only one who can see him, and can direct the lifeboat to the man in the water.

"I didn't see any parachutes," said the right first loader, cupping his eyes against the sun.

"Let Air Guns know again," called Xavier. He was leaning way out over the gun tub and pointing his finger, as he spoke.

The telephone talker pressed his button and called. "Air Guns—This is Mount forty-four. Two of those fighters just collided, and splashed. We don't see anything on the surface. They musta sank."

"Mount forty-four—this is Air Guns. Roger, already been reported. That's where the lifeboat is going, to see if there are any survivors."

"Mount forty-four roger. Okay, Xavier, they've got the positions spotted." Xavier relaxed and shook his head as he blinked to relieve the strain.

The Chilton and two other ships pulled out of their respective convoy positions and headed toward the crash scenes. Three LCVP's—lifeboats of the three ships—slowly circled or moved back and forth over the gas slicks. There were no survivors.

JULY

July 1
In Convoy to Hawaiian Islands
U.S.S. Chilton APA-38

As Lifeboat crew member on an LCVP, Stewart held his normal position as Bowhook. Very boring duty, actually. Stewart used a lot of that time getting acquainted with the ET's, making his desires known. He also hung around when he was free to choose.

Elelctronics Technicial Chief Appleby smiled and spoke. "Stewart, enough of this idling around the door here. Put in a chit requesting transfer to the ET gang."

Stewart sucked in his breath. "Gee, Chief Appleby, do you really think there's any chance of it getting approved?"

"I'll certainly approve it and so will our division officer, Mr. Henley. That will give you a leg up for ET school when you ship over."

Stewart pulled a request chit from the rack in his compartment and filled it out, requesting interdepartmental transfer to the ET Division. He gave as his reason that he had originally intended to go to ET school but being an EV had stopped that effort. Stewart carried the chit up to Chief Appleby ETC for his signature and found him talking with the division officer, Lieutenant (Junior Grade) Henley. Spotting Stewart, the Chief interrupted whatever he was saying.

"Mr. Henley, this is Stewart, the man I was telling you about. Looks like he has a request chit already filled out."

"Have you checked his GCT and ARI scores yet, Chief?"

"Yes sir, 62 and 65. He only needs a combined score of 120 to qualify for school. And, sir, there are papers in his jacket that show he previously qualified for ET school when he enlisted last February."

"That's good enough for me, Chief." Turning to Stewart, he asked, "What do you have to say, Stewart? Is this an easy way to get out of being a Side Cleaner, or do you really want to become an ET?" Lt(jg) Henley peered closely into Stewart's eyes as he replied.

"Yes, sir, Mr. Henley. I was studying Radio Electricity in college when I was forced to join the Navy before I was ready to."

"What happened, Stewart?"

"Ran out of money, owed money to the college, and couldn't get credit or go on to the second semester until I paid my bills. Dad's only a Mustang Lieutenant and doesn't have enough to feed four mouths and pay for tuition and fees besides."

"Navy brat, huh?" he said in surprise. "Did you try for Annapolis?"

"Grades not good enough for that, sir."

Mr. Henley nodded and sat down. He initialed the chit and turned it over, writing an endorsement accepting Stewart to fill a needed ET striker's spot on their Watch Quarter and Station Bill.

Handing it back to Stewart, he said, "I'll do what I can to push this along."

"Thank you, Mr. Henley."

At Quarters for Muster the next morning, he handed the chit to Deak. Deacon Jones studied the chit for a few seconds, frowning and shaking his head.

"Stew, I can't let you go. I'm forwarding it disapproved to Chief Abernathy. You're too valuable as a Side Cleaner."

"Yeah, but Deak, anybody can clean, scrape, chip, and paint the sides. You don't need me that much."

Jones BM2, shook his head and stuffed Stewart's chit into his shirt pocket.

A little later Deak came down to the bottom of Cargo Hold Three where a bunch of sailors were making fenders for the boats.

"Stewart, Chief Abernathy wants to see you in the Chiefs' Quarters right now about your request for transfer."

Stewart put his fid down from where he was working on an end splice, wiped his hands clean, and began climbing out of the hold without another word. Coming to the door to the Chiefs' Quarters, he knocked and waited. A Chief's Mess Cook opened the door.

"Whatcha want?"

"Chief Abernathy sent for me."

The Mess Cook opened the door wide and pointed to Chief Abernathy sitting at a table. Stewart removed his hat and hesitantly walked across to the Chief. He had a funny feeling walking in there. His eyes darted here and there, taking in the Chiefs' Mess room.

So this is what it's like to be a Chief. Wonder if I'll ever make it here.

The Chief motioned for Stewart to sit down opposite him. Stewart's request chit, somewhat wrinkled, was on the table between them. Chief Abernathy pointed to it.

"You've been a busy boy, Stewart. Don't we keep you busy enough, you got time to hang around the ET shack with those pussies?"

"Chief, I was going to college to learn electronics when I joined and expected to go to ET school. I landed here instead because you can't get school as an EV."

"Yeah, well it so happens I agree with Deak. We can't afford to lose you just as you're getting ready to be qualified as an LCVP coxswain. I'm forwarding it disapproved." Stewart just looked at the Chief.

What am I supposed to do—thank him? Strike Two!

"Okay, Chief, is that all?"

"Yes, get back to work," he growled.

Two days later, Deak returned his request chit to him. His division officer, Lieutenant Commander Ambrose—*the First Lieutenant*, and the Executive Officer had disapproved his request for transfer to the ET gang.

"Stewart, You're too valuable an asset as a future LCVP Assault Boat Coxswain. We won't let you transfer to the ET gang," Deak said.

"Fine, Deak, I won't be shipping over on the Chilton, so scratch me as one of your assets." He glared at Deak. "Chew on them apples, Mr. Jones."

"You keep a cool tool, Stewart, or I'll put you on report for sassing me."

Stewart glowered at him a moment. "Deak, I really don't know if that would be good or bad, but you only have me for a few more months, then I'll be transferred to a receiving station where I can ship over and get my school. And, I don't think the Captain will be pleased at this outcome."

He and Deak looked at each other for a moment. "May I be excused to go back to work now, Deak?" Stewart asked politely.

Deak, angrily grunted as he pointed to the door with disgust. "Go!"

"Okay, Deak. Oh yeah—just so you know, I'm going to be spending most of my free time in the ET shack and Radio Room, unless they chase me out. Yeah, and call it *Off the Job* training. Should give me a little up when I get school after I leave the Chilton."

Deak looked at him, started to say something, shrugged and walked away.

Lee did spend nearly all of his free time in the ET Shack and Radio Room. This did not go unnoticed by Deak and Chief Abernathy. Lee did his work as a Side Cleaners as he should without slacking. He would not allow them to ding him for slacking off.

Slowly, he became acquainted with the radio and radar equipment the ET's maintained and repaired. He was not allowed to do any of the repairs but could follow along. His Olympic Junior College classes in Radio Electricity helped him in many ways.

For example, he still could read color codes for resistors and condensers to identify a failed component. Once in a while, he was asked to describe a problem and what he thought would correct it. He was allowed to "carry" bags for the ET's in their rounds and hold a Simpson Volt-Ohm Meter (V-O-M) where the ET could see it—even call out a reading or change a dial setting when it was inconvenient for the ET crouched under or behind an equipment bay.

Oscilloscopes were something else. Lee struggled with them.

0230, July 3
U.S.S. Chilton at sea
In convoy, nearing Hawaiian waters

As Port Lookout, Stewart's standing orders were to report any ships or aircraft approaching, objects on the sea, unusual coloration or turbulence in the sea and sky.

It was his second turn as a lookout on his third midwatch. Stewart was doing as he usually did as a lookout. He searched the water and sky from the bow around to the stern with his bare eyes and with the binoculars. There was no moon in a cloudy sky with stars poking through here and there. Even so, the heavens were so brilliant there was enough light to make out the ships running at Darken Ship over a mile away.

Phosphorous objects exploded into brilliant green alongside the ship's hull as the Chilton moved through the water. Every so often, even in the dark of the night, observers could hear and sometimes see dolphins rising, blowing, and diving along the bow. Flying fish commonly skittered along the surface before diving into a wave.

Suddenly, the clouds in the sky ahead of the ship turned bright yellow-green.

Is that a flare?

He raised his watchstander binoculars to the flare and studied it a second. Stewart continued to watch it as he reached up and pressed the microphone button next to his mouth.

"Bridge—this is Port Lookout."

"Bridge—Aye."

"Port lookout reports a very bright green light, a possible flare, two points off the port bow, high in the sky."

"Bridge—Aye aye." The Bridge 1JV talker passed this information to the Officer of the Deck.

"Bridge—this is Starboard Lookout."

"Bridge—Aye."

"Starboard lookout reports green flare dead ahead, approximate elevation thirty degrees."

"Bridge—Aye aye," answered the man who passed this to the Officer of the Deck.

"Very well," responded the Officer of the Deck as he passsed onto the Port wing.

"When did this appear, Stewart?" the OOD asked tersely.

"Just a moment ago, sir. That pale green light just suddenly appeared below the clouds, and lit up the clouds, Mr. Jorgenson."

The Officer of the Deck looked at it a moment longer with his binoculars. He let them drop to his chest as he reached down, pulled a handset from a box, pressed the buzzer, and waited.

"Captain, we have an unidentified green light in the sky ahead. Looks like a parachute flare but we don't hear the sound of aircraft engines—Thank you, Captain."

"Captain on the bridge," sang out the Lee Helmsman, as the Captain appeared on the bridge in pajamas, bathrobe, and slippers from his Sea Cabin. He took one look through his binoculars, and asked who had reported it.

"I did, Captain," Stewart said with pride. After all, that was his job: he was supposed to report any unusual sightings. It was the first time he had ever addressed the Captain.

"What did you see, seaman?" The Captain asked.

"Captain, it was just suddenly *there*." responded Stewart.

The Captain turned, raised his binoculars, and looked at the target.

The Junior Officer of the Deck, a crusty old Warrant Bosun, was looking at it now with his naked eyes. He started mumbling to himself. Over the quiet clear waters, the watch personnel clearly heard two nearby ships begin sounding General Quarters.

"General Quarters," called the Captain.

"Aye aye, Captain" answered the Boatswain's Mate of the Watch. Stepping to the 1MC, he raked his fingers across all the access levers to make sure everyone would hear the alarm.

"GENERAL QUARTERS! GENERAL QUARTERS!

All hands man your battle stations. All hands man your battle stations." He reached over and turned the red General Alarm crank clockwise until it stopped.

BONG BONG BONG BONG!

The JOOD was still mumbling, and then called out clearly to the Captain.

"Captain, I think that's Venus. It's a moonless night and Venus is at her closest approach to Earth in many years."

"Nonsense, Mr. Oaken, it can't be that bright," scoffed the OOD.

By this time, the Navigator who damn well better know the stars, puffed up onto the Bridge for GQ. The JOOD nudged him and pointed to the bright light. The Navigator looked where he was pointing.

"Christ, Bosun, Venus is terribly bright tonight, isn't she? Almost looks like a parachute flare. What's the excitement? Why are we at GQ? Good evening, Captain," said the Navigator, saluting, all in one breath.

The Captain acknowledged his salute with a nod, being uncovered as he was, and raised his binoculars to the bright, green light, again. The sound-powered phone talkers were reporting their stations manned and ready.

The Officer of the Deck reported, "Captain, the ship is manned and ready for battle in four minutes. Not bad in a peacetime navy at 0230."

The Captain dropped his binoculars and stared coldly at the Officer of the Deck silently for a moment.

"Secure from General Quarters. I will be in my Sea Cabin. You may continue to admire Venus, Mr. Jorgenson." The Captain continued to stare at the Officer of the Deck but said nothing else as the OOD shriveled under his stare. The Captain turned and disappeared behind the green curtain into his cabin.

"Captain off the bridge," sang out the Quartermaster of the Watch.

0420, July 6
Windward Oahu, Territory of Hawaii
USS Chilton APA-38

Two days later, the convoy arrived at its Hawaiian destination.

In the clear pre-dawn, the eastern horizon was already light gray; Venus, now pale, hung low in the west. The Captain appeared on the Bridge from his sea cabin in wash khakis. His Marine Orderly, in crisp dress blues, followed.

The Quartermaster of the Watch spotted him first and announced: "Captain on the Bridge." Then he turned around, glanced at the Bridge clock, reached for his fountain pen, leaned over his Rough Log, and entered that fact.

The Officer of the Deck turned to the Captain, smiling in the dim, red light of the bridge. "Fresh coffee, Captain?" he asked.

"Thank you, yes."

"Coffee for the Captain," called out his Marine orderly.

The Captain's Steward, in blue bellbottom trousers and white jacket without hat, came forward carrying a silver tray balanced on the palm of his hand. The tray held a small silver urn of coffee and a Mess Deck white mug on a silver tray, as the Captain preferred. Although silver cream and sugar salvers and silver spoon were on the tray, the Captain took his coffee the way it came from the pot.

In his Sea Cabin or Stateroom, or on his infrequent visits to the Wardroom, the Captain used cups and saucers. He frowned upon cups and saucers on the Bridge. He preferred to walk around without fear of dripping coffee all over the deck. His steward filled the mug two-thirds full and presented the tray to his Captain. Smiling, the Captain acknowledged his steward, "Thank you, Sanchez."

He lifted the mug to his mouth and blew gently. The steamy mist of fresh coffee drenched his nose. He looked around the Bridge as he took a couple of sips. He watched over the top of his mug as Sanchez finished wiping salt mist from his chair on the Port Wing. Sanchez done, the Captain walked out to his chair. He eased himself up into the leather, stuffed, swivel Captain's chair, settled in, and beckoned to the Officer of the Deck.

"Mr. Potter. Bring me up to date," he ordered quietly.

Without hesitation, Lt.(jg) Potter rattled off his report.

"Captain, we are steaming at Condition Three. Section Two has the underway watch. Our heading is one eight five true. We are making no turns except to maintain station. Convoy speed is zero, drifting on the wind and current. I make the depth under the keel, about four hundred fathoms (two thousand, four hundred feet). Distance to the landing zones is eight thousand, two hundred yards at one three five degrees relative. The convoy spacing is three thousand yards. Nearest ships are Bayfield, bearing zero four five relative at three thousand, two hundred yards; Union bears one eight oh relative at three zero five zero yards; Officer, Tactical Command (OTC) is in Mount McKinley, bearing two three eight relative at six thousand, five hundred yards. Boilers Two and Three are on line. The Main Generator is connected to Boiler Four. No signals are awaiting execution, Captain. We make sunrise at oh five thirty-two."

"Very well, Mr. Potter, I have the Conn."

The Junior Officer of the Deck called out, "The Captain has the Conn."

"I stand relieved, sir," responded Mr. Potter with a salute.

The Quartermaster glanced at the clock on the bulkhead, leaned over his Rough Log, and noted the fact the Captain had the Deck now.

"Where's the Boatswain's Mate of the Watch?" asked the Captain, looking around in the predawn darkness.

"Boatswain's Mate, aye, Captain?" responded Johnson BM2, coming across the Bridge from where he had been standing.

The Captain had full confidence in his amphibious operations staff to complete this planned exercise. Working at best speed under simulated combat conditions, the crew would take about thirty-six hours straight through to land the landing force, their combat equipment, and supplies.

"Johnson, sound general quarters, condition one able."

"Aye aye, Captain."

The Boatswain's Mate of the Watch walked quickly to the 1MC and flipped all selector switches down to ON. His left hand slid down the lanyard around his neck to his pipe in his shirt pocket. He pulled his pipe up, gripped it in his left hand, and raised the silver pipe to his mouth. He took three deep breaths, for this was a long call to pipe. He pressed the microphone button down, turned his head sideways by the microphone, and began piping General Quarters.

Once again, the Quartermaster glanced at the clock on the bulkhead and noted that GQ-1A had been sounded, in his Rough Log.

(Large capital ships—Aircraft carriers, battleships, and cruisers—had their own Navy bands, including buglers to play Navy orders such as General Quarters.)

Below decks, asleep in their bunks, the crew and troops turned restlessly when the first quiet crackle of an open microphone sounded. As the pipe began its mournful tune, the mad scramble began in the dark as officers, chiefs, and enlisted men leaped out of their bunks to dress and run to their General Quarters stations.

Troops began to dress for the ordeal ahead. Lights came on in the dark living compartments as Police Petty Officers turned light switches. The Master-At-Arms force took up their stations in passageways to insure proper traffic flow. UP and FORWARD on the Starboard side, DOWN and AFT on the Port side.

Johnson completed the long call.

"GENERAL QUARTERS! GENERAL QUARTERS! All hands man your battle stations. Condition One Able to land the landing force. Boat crews, man your boats." He reached over and turned the General Alarm crank clockwise until it stopped.

BONG BONG BONG BONG!

The General Alarm continued to sound throughout the ship for about two minutes, until the Captain called out, "Secure the general alarm."

Johnson, waiting for his General Quarters relief, quickly moved the brass alarm handle counter clockwise to its stopped position.

During amphibious operations, assault boat crews are dressed in olive drab dungaree pants and chambray shirts called Greens), gray helmets, and kapok life jackets. Just before they climb into their boat at the rail, they make a final run to the head, filled their canteens with water, grabbed K-Rations, First Aid kits, and toilet paper, to help them for their long period on the water. Most of them had extra cigarettes and some kind of reading material stuffed in back pockets.

In the economies of war, the amphibious warfare planners hope that (a) a boat will make it to the beach and (b) offload its cargo. In the savage ferocity of landing against a determined enemy, they hope the boat and crew will (c) survive one run in to the landing zone beach; (d) getting back off that beach is almost too much to hope. These flat bottomed boats are designed to drive through active surf and push onto the beach as far as possible, drop the ramp, and discharge sometimes unwilling passengers. Additional runs are pure gravy for the planners.

The element of surprise is therefore a cherished notion and prayer of the boat crews. These slow moving boats—at 6 to 8 mph—are easy targets for attacking aircraft and artillery fire directed from enemy emplacements on the beach. Mortars can reach out with deadly accuracy and smash P-boats hard on the beach. Machine gun and rifle fire are expected even before the ramps drop and troops dash out.

No one asked these boat crews to volunteer for this dangerous duty nor are they paid hazardous pay like fliers, flight deck crews, divers, and submariners. These sailors are selected based on ability to land and retract a boat. They are expected to just do a tough and frightening job. They don't get medals for five lucky trips between the beach and the ship, either.

After eight to ten hours in a roaring, bouncing boat, it is physically impossible to relax: muscles ache too much from countering opposing forces. Men try to wedge themselves in a corner and fall limp to roll with the P-boat's motion. That's not relaxation; it is exhaustion! If there are reserve boat crews, the active crew might get relieved to struggle back up the cargo net or Jacobs Ladder for a shower, clean clothes, food and a short nap.

P-boats are stacked three to a nest on a Whalen Davit, plus a fourth resting in a cradle on deck. A Whalen Davit has powerful electric motors to lift a boat up from its cradle into position, ready to begin its gravity slide down the rails and out over the side, for the drop to the water. A Boatswain's Mate, called the Davit Station Petty Officer, controls each nest of boats.

He receives orders through his sound-powered telephone talker, backed up by 1MC speaker voice announcements. The 1MC is a marvelous announcing system. Several switches let the announcer, usually the Boatswain's Mate of the Watch, select which areas of the ship will hear the next announcement. He can, for example, lock out all inside-the-ship speakers. This is good. The ship is constantly chattering commands to and about the boats.

0430, July 6
U.S.S. Chilton APA-38, stationkeeping
4 miles offshore, Territory of Hawaii

"Prepare to lower the landing boats," came from the topside speakers.

Alonzo, Boatswain's Mate, First Class (BM1), looked to the Electrician's Mate manning the Whalen Davit motor controller, pursed his mouth and raised his eyebrows in question to see if he was ready. The Electrician's Mate, Third Class (EM3), had the motor controller cover opened and AC power to the controller switched on. He smiled as he nodded to Alonzo. The Boatswain's Mate looked up to the lifting blocks above the LCVP in its cradle on deck. He raised his right arm to his shoulder and pointed his index finger to the sky.

There was a raspy growl as the winches tightened the cable and took a strain; the steel stranded cable snapped and slithered. The boat seemed to quiver a little, and then creaked as the lifting block pelican hooks attached to the boat's lifting rings began to lift. The blocks and their well-lubricated sheaves made no sound as they began to turn. Ozone mixed with the ocean air.

Down in the Engine Room at the electrical control board, an Electrician's Mate, Second Class (EM2), carefully monitored the voltage level and current flow meters. The electrical machinery operating the davits and cargo hold winches, placed heavy demands upon the ship's electrical generators.

In Fire Room Two, a Boiler Tender Third Class (BT3), scrutinized the Water Glass to make sure that Boiler Four had sufficient water for making steam. His Chief Boiler Tender (BTC), looked up at another gauge to make sure that steam was maintained at the correct pressure—PSI—to keep the Main Electric Generator from overloading, and thus dropping the ship's entire electric service for a few minutes.

This LCVP's blocks had become two-blocked—pulled together—as the boat was lifted up tight against the movable horizontal arm of the Davit. The lifting motor took on a deeper growl as the Davit arms holding the LCVP, creaked and moved upward in their tracks about a foot.

Alonzo clenched his fist and the motor stopped. Two Seamen (SN) handlers at each end of the boat reached up and pulled a quarter-inch thick flat, metal safety bar from the track and slipped it into its retainer. Until the two bars were removed, it was physically impossible for a Davit carrying a boat to slide down its cradled tracks and swing out over the water.

Alonzo still holding his clenched fist in the air looked at the two handlers to make sure the brakes were on. No talking was necessary. There was enough noise as it was. He looked to his telephone talker and nodded his head.

An oversized gray helmet protected the Seaman Apprentice (SA) telephone talker's head because he wore a particularly large headset with a huge sound-powered microphone pulled next to his mouth. A twenty-five foot long cable attached his headset to a jack box on the JA sound powered circuit near the motor controller. The talker pressed the microphone button on top of the mike:

"Control—Davit One."

"Davit One—Control, go ahead."

"Davit One—Request permission to lower P-boat eighteen to the rail."

"Control—Roger, standby. Davit Two has an electrical problem. It will be a few minutes, then we'll lower away together."

"Roger Control—One is standing by."

He walked over next to Alonzo, his long cable trailing behind him.

"Boats, they are telling us to standby. I heard Davit Two report their controller blew a fuse. It'll be about five minutes. The Landing Officer says he will lower all boats together."

Alonzo nodded, looked to everyone catching their attention, and raised both arms, fists clenched. He pointed at the two handlers, extended both index fingers toward each other and moving his arms together, signalling them to reinsert the safety bars.

After they completed that, Alonzo dropped his arms momentarily and then put both arms up with hands and fingers open wide. He twisted around both ways at everyone to make sure they understood. Then he dropped one arm, pointed to his wristwatch and showed five fingers with the other hand. Everyone understood they must wait five minutes—at least. The boat crew leaned back against the inner bulkhead to wait it out. They had gone through this before.

"Lower the landing boats to the rail!" came over the sound powered telephone circuit and 1MC.

Alonzo quickly raised both arms up with hands and fingers open wide, and whistled sharply to get everyone's attention. He pointed to the handlers and signaled them with thumbs pointing out and nodding his head, to remove the safety bars. When that was done, the handlers at the two brakes prepared to lift their brake control arms.

This was the big weakness in the Whalen Davit system. What mostly happened was that one end's pulley was faster than the other end. If the Station Petty Officer was not watching both ends carefully, the boat could tilt and jam the Davit.

Alonzo made sure both handlers were looking at him. He went to the ship's side and extended both arms away from his body with fists clenched. Each handler watched the fist closest to him. Now, Alonzo looked up to LCVP 38-18, let both arms droop to a 45° angle and extended both index fingers, something like a jitterbug dancer would do.

Each handler lifted up his brake handle keeping both eyes fixed on Alonzo. Now Alonzo closed and opened his fingers to put on one or both of the brakes as the LCVP slid down the track to the end. The Davit tilted, rotating outward over the ship's side placing the boat in position to drop by gravity to the sea below. Alonzo clenched both hands for a moment until the boat stopped rocking. Then he extended both fingers.

The weight of the boat responded to gravity and both cables unwound from their drums. The sound was something like the old Pacific Electric Red Cars running between Long Beach and Los Angeles, when they started up. When the boat's coaming was even with the 01 deck, he clinched his fists again, and nodded to his telephone talker.

"Control—Davit One."

"Control—go ahead."

"Davit One—request permission to load crew on P-boat eighteen."

"Control—name the crew, Davit One."

The telephone talker pivoted around and looked at the crew to identify them.

"This is One—Jones BMSN Coxswain, Bailey FN Engineer, Stewart SA Bowhook, and Hendersen SA Sternhook."

"Davit One this is Control—Very well. Permission granted to load boat crew on P-boat eighteen. Report when the crew is safely aboard and their gear stowed."

"This is Davit One—Aye aye, sir."

"Boats," called the talker. "The First Lieutenant says go ahead and load the crew and their gear."

Alonzo nodded and looked to the crew: "Jones, load your crew."

The four walked to the ship's side where the temporary railing had been removed. Alonzo checked them carefully. "Dogtags, guys," he said.

Stewart pulled his dogtags from under his skivvy shirt so Alonzo could see them. They had their white hats folded in one pocket and a standard navy issue jackknife in another. Later, they could remove their helmets and wear white hats turned down as protection from the sun. Each man had a full canteen of water.

A small barrel of fresh water, eight K-rations, a couple of rolls of toilet paper, and the Combat First Aid kit were stowed in the engineer's compartment. The crew put on their life jackets and fastened all ties, straps, and stops.

While Alonzo was checking, the two handlers used boat hooks to pull the knotted safety lifelines out of the P-boat onto the deck. From the 01 deck, it was about thirty-five feet down to the water.

The boat crew held on to the lifelines, as insurance, as they stepped across the void and jumped down into the boat. Stewart had to move rapidly to make his checks before Alonzo started to lower away to the water. He pulled the forward two lifelines in and inspected the Bow quick release hook mouse. Then he cut away the mouse twine on the forward hook with his jackknife.

A hook is moused when twine was wrapped around the hook in such a way as to keep the tripping mechanism tied down in the hook. The weight of the P-boat kept the hook in place now. As soon as the boat hit the water, tension was removed and the quick release could be tripped (yanked). Hendersen did the same at the after end of the boat.

Finally, Stewart took the Sea Painter from one of the Davit handlers and fastened it inside the boat. The top of the sun was just below the horizon. In a moment, they would get the first stab of light from the sun.

Meanwhile, Bailey moved the battery switch to ON, turned on and listened for the exhaust fan, and carefully checked his engine for fuel, fumes, and oil level. Then he inspected the sand filters to make sure they were empty. He waited until Jones looked up.

"Okay Jones, check your magnesyn and magnetic compasses, horn, and panel lights."

Jones waved at him and leaned over the control panel. There was a squawk as Jones tapped the horn. He pulled a switch. The panel's lights glowed softly in red. Everything looked good. He looked down and set the magnesyn compass, and looked over his right shoulder at Bailey in the pale predawn light.

"Yep, everything checks out here. How about you?" Jones asked. Bailey held up a forbidden can of ether in case the engine didn't want to start. He had opened the engine housing port side hatch where he could splash a few drops of ether on the air cleaner, if needed.

"We're ready," he said after he felt around in the predawn light for the water keg, K-rats, and first aid kit.

Jones unlocked his steering wheel, while pushing down to make sure it was all the way down. The transmission forward-reverse gearshift/throttle lever was in neutral for starting: the throttle handle—shaped like a child's red flyer wagon handle—was turned and locked to the Start position. Jones looked forward to the 'Hooks. "Stewart, Hendersen, checks?"

Stewart stooped over and lifted the plywood deckplate, grunting with the effort, to make sure the drain plug was screwed in tight. Down on his hands and knees, peering down to the inner keel, his helmet fell off, clunking against the hollow wooden deck.

He felt around the dry bilges in the dimness of dawn, found the plug and screwed it in tight. With his head below the deck plate level, he felt like he was inside a seashell listening to the waves. Refitting the deck plate into its slot, he stomped on it to make sure it was seated, then went forward to the bow ramp, recovered his helmet and put it on.

Stewart checked the port and Hendersen checked the starboard side to make sure the bow ramp clamps were locked, both cable reel ratchets were locked, and the running lights were off. They each waved at Jones to show they were ready.

From boarding 'til completion of launching, tasks took less than two minutes. Jones, the coxswain, was boat commander. Once they were free of the davit, everyone and everything aboard was his responsibility and subject to his orders. But at this moment, Alonzo was still in charge.

"Okay Alonzo, we're ready," Jones called out. Alonzo nodded and smiled back at Jones.

"Right. Time to wait for the word from above," he called down to Jones. He tapped the telephone talker on the shoulder.

"Control—Davit One."

"Control—Aye."

"This is Davit One—Peter Eighteen crew is aboard, ready to lower away."

"Control—Roger, standby until all boats are ready."

"Davit One—Wilco."

"Gotta wait for all boats to be ready, Boats," he told Alonzo. Alonzo nodded and continued to stand next to Peter Eighteen.

On deck—away all boats!

Alonzo looked around, checking the handlers, then signaled with two fingers down. Four boats began their drop amidships—slower than the average elevator, two on the starboard side and two on the port side, amidship outsde of the main superstructure.

Hendersen, Bailey, Jones, and Stewart lightly held their lifelines. If they gripped them too tightly, the descending boat would leave them dangling in the air.

A slithering, moaning sound spread as the drums unrolled under dynamic braking to control the rate of fall. Steel cables creaked and snapped as they wove through six sheaves, unwinding. The hand brakes were only to stop the boat. The boat crew moved their hands down, knot by knot on the lifelines, as the boat approached the water.

Jones dropped his safety line first, pushed the primer button three times, and pressed the starter. The diesel caught with a roar. Jones left it there for a moment to make sure he had a solid engine, then throttled back to idle after goosing it a few times.

Bailey checked his gauges—and looked up to nod at Jones that all was well. Alonzo was still in charge. He clenched his fists when the boat was just above the water to stop descent for a final check.

"Standby to release the hooks on my command," Jones yelled to Hendersen and Stewart. Peter Eighteen was swinging away and back to bump the ship's hull opposite the Chilton's roll from side to side. Fenders were out to protect Peter Eighteen and to keep from scraping the ship's gray paint scheme.

The engine exhaust echoed off the side of the ship and the water just below. The crew looked down at the waves to see what kind of action they were going to have. The waves were high enough that a few slapped against the bottom. Stewart checked to see if the Sea Painter was set for release inboard and free along the ship's hull. This small line held the P-boat fast to the ship.

Jones looked up at Alonzo and gave him a thumbs up. Alonzo leaned back and signaled the handlers to release the brakes. Hendersen and Stewart faced Jones with their hands on the quick release lines. Not tight, but like holding the reins of a horse. They could see they were going to be first in the water.

They hit the water with a splash and immediately began bouncing around.

"NOW!"

Hendersen and Stewart yanked down on the release lines and the large, heavy rings dropped. Immediately, the Davit blocks and tackle began retracting to clear the P-boat, growling as it pulled. It would be another five long minutes before the next P-boat was ready to be lifted out of its cradle. Alonzo waved the boat off.

"Stewart, let go the Sea Painter."

Thank God I've got good sea legs.

He staggered across and crashed into the Port side of the boat as it tossed, pitched, and rolled and pulled out the fid with a flourish so everyone topside could see it was pulled. The Sea Painter fell away and was immediately yanked up to be fastened to the next P-boat.

The Sea Painter had been looped around a cleat inside the open boat. The end of the line had an eye splice. As it was looped around the cleat, a loop of the line was pushed through the eye splice. A pointed, hard wooden pin, called a fid, was slipped through the loop to hold it fast. Very fast release.

Jones pushed the forward-reverse lever and throttle into forward and gave a little clockwise twist to the throttle for more RPMs. He turned his horizontal steering wheel right and cautiously pulled away from the boat ahead, and away from the ship. Peter Eighteen was free.

"Get those fenders in," Jones called out.

The 'Hooks leaned over the side and pulled them inboard. Hendersen and Stewart helped each other with the rings and cables. Hendersen held up the forward deck plate as Stewart staggered around, dragging the forward ring and cables into the bilges, still attached to their anchor bolts. They both jumped up and down on the deck plate to make sure it was locked into place. The deck had to be clear and stable so the assault troops wouldn't bust their asses. Then Stewart went aft to help Hendersen store the tackle on the after deck plate.

"Peter Eighteen Peter Twenty-one, proceed aft to the starboard quarter and circle until called."

As soon as the crew heard their number—Eighteen—they all turned toward the ship, cupping their ears and listening in case Jones couldn't hear the orders. But he heard and acknowledged with the semaphore letter "R" for Roger—meaning I understand what you said—by extending both arms straight out sideways at shoulder height from his body. The crew would do that a lot today. All boat crews had to know rudimentary semaphore signals and international flag hoist signals.

Jones ducked down low and unclamped his steering wheel shaft. Straightening up, he pulled the wheel assembly up as high as it would go—about three feet—and reclamped the shaft. Jones jumped up and stood in perfect balance, albeit precariously, with his left foot on the port side of the boat coaming and his right foot on a wooden separator between his tiny 3 foot by 4 foot 'topless cubicle and the Engineer's topless compartment. In this position, Jones could see the ocean waves and, more to the point, where he was going.

Eighteen had been ordered to the right rear of the ship and would move slowly in a clockwise circle with ten other P-boats from the Starboard side until all P-boats had been unloaded from both sides of the ship. The same number of P-boats would be on the port quarter, circling counterclockwise. The three command and control boats, including the Captain's Gig if used on this mission, would be the last unloaded.

The ship was also unloading the LCM's—M-boats or Mike boats. They were stacked in cradles on cargo hatches; four forward and four aft of the superstructure. Big electric winches and cargo booms with one very large and oh, so deadly hook, were used to lower them over the side into the water. Once the quick release hook was snapped, the Coxswain steered away from the ship with two individually controlled diesel engines, and went into its own circling pattern on the starboard bow or on the port bow with other Mike boats.

While this had been going on, the Fort Lewis soldiers climbed out of their berthing holds, ate an early breakfast, grabbed their combat packs, and walked to prearranged stations along both sides of the ship. At these station, large rope cargo nets with 1 foot by 1 foot mesh had been attached firmly to the rail and dropped over the side down to the water line. Horizontal 4 by 4's attached to the cargo nets kept the nets away from the hull, thus permitting combat boots a toe-hold. The soldiers formed four lines in front of each net. No soldier approached the bulwark or got on the net until a boat was alongside, held by a sea painter.

"Peter Eighteen, Peter Eighteen—report to Station Yellow Five—report to Station Yellow Five."

The 1MC sounded very weak and hollow way out where the P-boats were circling.

Jones waved an "R" and peeled off, increasing speed as the boat cleared the circling P-boats.

"Stewart, Hendersen, get those fenders back out on the port side."

They waved and both seamen put two over the port side. These fenders were boat bumpers that would soften the constant bumping and reduce the amount of paint scraped from the ship's side while holding position at the cargo net.

During inclement weather when work could not be accomplished on the weather decks, coxswains and 'Hooks often could be found in the bottom of Number Three Cargo Hold. They practiced marlinspike seamanship by manufacturing their own boat fenders from worn out six-inch hawsers. They used hacksaws, fids, quarter-inch line, and muscle work.

When a boat was called, the coxswain continued circling until his boat came around pointing forward and parallel with the ship. He peeled off by going straight ahead to the named station on his side of the ship. A sheet metal panel hung over the side at each loading station showing its station number and color to reduce confusion.

Circling off the bows, the M-boats went along side the main cargo hatches for combat cargo. They were more cumbersome to handle than P-boats, so they had more room to maneuver.

There were five loading stations on both sides of the ship. During Darken Ship hours, it was tough working by starlight and little else. Some stations handled only troops. Stations where the hull curves in were reserved for cargo only. Other stations handled troops or cargo according to the combat load. After combat personnel loading had been completed, both Port and Starboard accommodation ladders would be lowered to accommodate passengers in small boats traveling between ships.

0500, July 6
LCVP-38 #18
Alongside USS Chilton APA-38

Stations Yellow Five and Six, amidships in the superstructure—with accommodation ladders—were not used for troop loading, even though they were the most stable loading stations on the starboard and port sides.

While the troops needed stability, using the accommodation ladders would be too slow. For that reason, the troops had practiced on wooden walls festooned with cargo nets into fake boats below at their home camps or forts.

This time, rocking and rolling, cold, the steel wall was festooned with cargo nets at forward stations Three and Four at Cargo Hold Three, and stations Seven and Eight at Cargo Hold Four. The cargo net swayed away from the ship and slapped back against the hull as troops climbed down the net. At the bottom, each man encountered the difficult task of placing their boots inside a small boat that was bouncing around a lot. At some point, their feet would touch the floor of the boat and they had to let loose of the cargo net.

Troops had to be reminded constantly to hold onto the vertical lines. If a man held the horizontal lines of the net, the man above might step on his hand. This could cause him to jerk his hand out, lose his grip with his other hand, and fall into the sea between ship's hull and landing craft. For the untrained landsman, it could be a terrifying, and perhaps, fatal experience.

"Stewart, secure the Sea Painter as quick as you can."

Jones was just reminding Stewart of his next task. The coxswain had to know everyone's job from memory. They didn't have the time for check off lists. This time, a trip alongside was easy because Boat Eighteen is the first boat alongside a station. They didn't have to thread their way between boats arriving and departing the ship's side. Jones slipped up to Yellow Five and gave a quick squirt of reverse just as Stewart caught the heaving line monkey fist when it dropped into the boat.

A monkey fist was a weight about the size of a small monkey's head. The dark hemp twine woven around it was suggestive, looking like a monkey's head. A woven line is part of the monkey fist. It, in turn, was attached as a downhaul for the Sea Painter.

Stewart pulled the Sea Painter in as fast as he could. Hendersen was standing by with the fid. As the boat bobbed around like a cork in water, they grabbed each other and the cleat. A quick loop and pass through, and the Sea Painter was attached to the boat.

"Watch out guys, here goes the heaving line," Stewart called out.

The crew looked up anxiously; they didn't want it bouncing off their heads. He gave the end of the line a couple of twirls and let it go on the rise. A boat handler caught it the first time and pulled it in, and the crew relaxed.

Jones and Bailey kept the boat in position. Hendersen and Stewart grabbed opposite sides of the cargo net, lifted the net from the water and pulled the bottom inside the boat. Steward and Henderson grabbed and hung on to each side to reduce cargo net motion as the troops climbed down. It was their job to help get the first troops into the boat.

As the troops came down, the crew had to worry about another hazard: falling objects, such as troops, rifles, helmets, or other gear. Besides their packs and rifles, the troops were temporarily wearing kapok life jackets. Beachmasters would collect the life jackets for return to the ship.

The two line handlers guided the troops' feet onto the top edge of the boat and encouraged them to jump down to the floorboard three feet away. After the first line of troops was in, they helped their buddies come off the net. As more weight was added to the boat, it sank deeper into the water and tended to bounce less.

When the last of the troops were in the boat, the crew counted noses to report their counts to Jones. He agreed, made a megaphone of his hands, and called up to the Loadmaster above:

"Thirty-six troops."

"Correct, set your magnesyn compass to one three five degrees heading from the Chilton to the beach," the Loadmaster called to Jones.

Jones reached down to the strange magnesyn subpanel that looked like a compass with a boat silhouette instead of a needle, set his compass steering by twisting the black knurled knob until the bow of the boat pointed to one three five degrees, and gave the Loadmaster a thumbs up and got a wave-off in return. They were cleared.

"Stewart, let go the Sea Painter."

Stewart checked above to make sure those line handlers were ready to pull the Sea Painter up before he pulled the fid. Stewart couldn't take a chance of fouling the Sea Painter in their screw. Jones engaged Forward and more throttle than when the boat was empty. The boat with a flat square bow, weighted down with thirty-six men and their equipment —three-and-a-half to four tons—pushed hard against the water and lurched away from the ship, jolting against each wave, slapping water up and into the boat. A breeze began to pick up, forming choppy water. The bottom of the sun no longer touched the sea.

"Peter Eighteen, Peter Eighteen—rejoin the starboard quarter circle—rejoin the starboard quarter circle."

Jones reached out with an "R". Eighteen staggered through the water, jolted by every wave hitting the flat bow.

Jones headed back to the circling position with other loaded and not yet loaded P-boats. Sea spray, driven by the wind, whipped across the boat, stinging eyes and wetting everyone. The P-boat was down to twelve inches of freeboard now.

Twelve inches away from being swamped.

Hendersen and Stewart joined Bailey and Jones in the after wells. It was a bouncy ride caused by waves of other boats, swells from a storm many miles away, and choppy surface from the rising morning breeze. In a few moments, the troops were miserable. Some were already heaving their guts out. Others were swearing at puke that suddenly appeared on their battle gear.

Boat Eighteen crew was amused by their discomfort. As Stewart scanned the soldiers, he looked back to one that seemed to be smiling at him.

Holy Shit! That's Larry Jensen. Son Of A Bitch!

He leaped back into the well deck and worked his way through the soldiers and grabbed his buddy by the arms.

"Damn, Fella, I heard you were on your way to Japan to the First Cavalry. What the hell are you doing here?" Then it hit him. Larry had been aboard since Fort Lewis.

Larry whinnied his usual laugh. "Mom said she talked with you a while back. As usual, she got things wrong when she gets excited. You know her."

"Yeah, but damn, Lar', didn't you know this was my ship?

We could have had some good times together when I was off watch and not on my cleaning station."

"Mom never did get back to me with your address. I didn't know you were here until I passed you on the cargo net."

"Well, that's too bad. We'll just have to fix your Mom somehow when we get back together in Bremerton again."

"Yeah. Remember the time we scared her with the elk head?" They laughed together.

"The story is, I got drafted and sent to Basic in Texas, then back to Fort Lewis. And here I am, in your boat, about to hit the beach. Now, that's a story both our folks will like. After this is all over, I'll be shipped to Japan."

"That's something else you don't know, Larry. Dad got orders to the East Coast. Got no home up on Magnuson Way now."

"No shit, Lee? Where's home, then?

Lee pointed down. "The Chilton. From now on, I just visit the folks whenever we both happen to be in the same port."

"Wow! No home to go to. Hey, honestly, is this boat safe?"

"Oh shit yes, Larry. The toughest part is after you charge up the beach—wish I had a camera for that."

"Wanna get together after this is all over, Lee?"

"Hell yes. I know we're going into Pearl for three days and I got liberty two of those days for sure. How about you, Lar'? I got a story to tell you about my last liberty in Bremerton. Ran into Edith."

"Edith?" A big grin spread across Larry's freckled face. "You mean Edith cockteaser Zimmerman?"

"That's her!"

"Fergit it. I been there and didn't score either."

By now, the two high school buddies, and next door neighbors, were leaning back against the side, shoulders touching, just like old times. Stewart saw a sergeant looking at Larry with something akin to annoyance on his face.

"Maybe we ought to cut this short, Larry. Your sergeant is staring at you. Let's meet on the beach under the Banyan

Tree in front of the Ala Moana Hotel—that's on the beach side, not the street side. Try every day at 2PM for a half-hour. How's that sound?"

"Sounds good to me, Lee. Go do your stuff."

Lee and Larry looked at each other one more time, punched each other on the shoulder, and smiled. It was so good to see a friend. Stewart turned away and wormed his way back to the break.

"What was that all about, Stewart?" asked Jones.

"That's my best buddy from home—Bremerton. We went to high school together. Lived next door. After I joined the Navy, he was drafted and ended up at Fort Lewis. Talk about your small worlds."

Jones nodded. "Take the wheel from Hendersen. Stay in the circle, Stewart."

"Aye aye, Jones."

He clambered over the barrier and relieved Hendersen. Every so often he caught Larry watching and grinning at him.

How can I keep a straight face with that damn fool grinning like a banshee at me?

He grinned back, happy to see his buddy.

Jones let Hendersen and Stewart practice being coxswain by letting them steer in a circle while waiting for the remainder of the P-boats to load up. Of course, that did not mean holding the wheel in one position. The waves and breeze constantly pushed and pulled in different directions. Course adjustment was an ongoing thing.

Each wave of P-boats, consisting of eleven boats, was under command of an officer. They were still waiting for their wave commander to join their circling P-boats. He, the wave officer with a portable radio, joined the last boat—Peter-23—to be loaded.

When all boats were loaded and circling again, the wave officer reported that fact to the ship who released the wave to the Beach Control Vessel for landing.

Ensign Donnely climbed on top of the plywood engine and stood with bent knees, swaying, pitching, and tossing in equilibrium with the boat's reaction to the waves. His coxswain handed him the Handy-Talky, turned on, with the antenna extended.

> **"HANDYMAN THIRTY-EIGHT—THIS IS HANDYMAN THIRTY-EIGHT DASH ONE— OVER"**
>
> **"HANDYMAN THIRTY-EIGHT DASH ONE —THIS IS THIRTY-EIGHT—OVER"**
>
> **"THIS IS HANDYMAN THIRTY-EIGHT DASH ONE—WAVE ONE IS READY TO PROCEED—REQUEST PERMISSION TO DEPART—OVER"**
>
> **"THIS IS HANDYMAN THIRTY-EIGHT— PERMISSION GRANTED—OUT"**

Ensign Donnely handed his radio to the coxswain and looked at all the other P-boats to make sure he had their attention. He extended his right arm vertically for a moment, then brought it down horizontally in front of him, almost losing his balance. On that, his coxswain cranked his wheel a half turn clockwise, breaking out of the circle, then brought the wheel back to the neutral position.

His circling wave peeled off and followed him, in column formation, toward the Beach Control Vessel. When all eleven P-boats were stretched out in a column, he stood up and pumped his arm vertically twice. He looked down to his coxswain.

"Okay, Edwards, full ahead now," the ensign ordered, and dropped into the engineer's compartment where there was marginally more space.

"Aye aye, sir."

The run to the Beach Control Vessel at 1800 RPMs took thirty-five minutes. Upon arrival and the report to the Beach Control Vessel, the wave officer climbed back onto the engine housing and signaled his wave back into a circle, waiting for the Beach Control Vessel to signal the Chilton's Wave Officer. He looked at his engineer and beckoned him closer.

"Son, stand that sign post up where Beach Control can see who we are," he ordered the man slightly older than he was.

"Aye aye, sir," he answered with amusement.

The Beach Control Vessel function is to control movement of the landing craft. It is stationed at the Line of Departure to start each wave of boats in the proper sequence. The Beach Control Vessel had the Operation Miki Operation Order, listing the content and source of each boat to be in each wave. The Beach Control Officer must know the order in which specific waves were supposed to be released to land on the beach.

At the beginning of an assault on any beach before the Beachmaster is established, the Beach Control Officer ordered landing craft waves to advance to the beach. When the Beachmaster landed and established his foxhole base, he would coordinate with the Beach Control Officer using radio or semaphore, advising what or which kind of material or personnel were required next in the pipeline to the beach.

Several waves circled near the ship, waiting their turn to be ordered to a beach. The boats arrived from widely separated ships. It was extremely difficult to time the order of boats arriving at the jumping off point. In the swing of things, some waves arrived there out of order for any number of reasons.

The Beach Control Officer must identify each wave correctly and release specific waves of boats to specific landing beach zones, at the proper intervals, with lessons learned from World War Two in the Pacific. The Beachmaster, already established on the landing zone, knew the needs of the landed troops, and told the Beach Control Officer what they needed now.

The Beach Control Vessel radioed Eighteen's Wave Officer the release to move out.

> "HANDYMAN THIRTY-EIGHT DASH ONE THIS IS EAGLE—OVER."

> "EAGLE THIS IS HANDYMAN THIRTY-EIGHT DASH ONE—YOU ARE LOUD AND CLEAR—OVER."

> "THIS IS EAGLE—YOU ARE RELEASED TO BEACH GREEN THREE. CARRY OUT YOUR ORDERS—OVER."

> "THIS IS HANDYMAN THIRTY-EIGHT DASH ONE—GREEN THREE WILCO—OUT.

The Peter Eighteen crew saw the Wave Officer clamber up and stand on the engine housing of his P-boat and signal his wave to increase speed and follow him in column formation. He waited until all the boats acknowledged his two simple semaphore signals, and peeled off slowly at 1200 RPM.

The Wave Officer jumped down into the Engineering space and pulled out his landing beach chart. He needed to find Green Three. Locating it, he knew where to point his wave.

Once again, he stood up and used his arms to signal the eleven boats to make a right flank turn. As they acknowledged and executed the command, his boat circled back and assumed the center position with five P-boats on either side of his P-boat.

When all boats had accomplished that and were in a reasonably straight line, he pumped his arm up and down. The wave of P-boats increased speed to 1800 RPM, maximum standard speed. He studied the shoreline ahead. The wave was less than a thousand yards from the beach. Speed had ever so slowly increased to maximum velocity. At 500 yards, he pumped his arm up and down vigorously. In quaint 'Gator Navy parlance, that meant put the throttles to the fire wall and haul ass for the beach.

All eleven engineers reached down and flipped a lever on the throttle linkage, just after the coxswain dropped the throttle to idle. The engines rev'd to battle speed, 2250 RPM.

Jones dropped down to the deck and let his wheel drop to the bottom. Until the boat was safely retracted from the beach, he wanted closer control of the wheel, gear lever-throttle and to stay out of the way of bullets flying their way. Bailey squatted, ready at the engine to assist with anything.

The troop platoon leader standing with his back to the ramped bow yelled out:

"LOCK AND LOAD — SAFETIES ON."

Sergeants checked their men and equipment. There were snaps and clicks as clips were inserted into rifles, and safeties snapped on. The rifles were raised to port arms. The troops began to crouch down.

Hendersen and Stewart made their way forward to the bow ramp. As they stepped forward, they called out and waved to the miserable troops to move back away from the ramp. The more weight aft, the higher the bow, the further up on the beach Jones could drive. They crouched down next to the ramp locking levers and released their winch's ratchet latches. They waited tensely for Jones's screamed command to drop the ramp.

Jones timed his move with the waves. He wanted to ride the back of a wave if he could. He definitely did not want to ride the front of a wave! A P-boat tilted forward in high waves could possibly slam into the ground below the wave, and pole vault upsidedown. The usual problem was to be pushed just a little out of a straight run, and broach sideways, parallel to the waves.

Peter Eighteen began to tilt like it was climbing a hill and the diesel engine labored harder. Did the engine have enough power to stay there? The engine roared faster as cavitation began. There was a heavy bump at the rear and the boat leveled out, a grinding sound and the boat began to scrape, slide and bump to a stop. The propeller raced in cavitation. Jones yelled:

"NOW!"

Stewart and Hendersen reached out to lift their ramp locking levers, looked back at each other, nodded, and lifted the locking levers together in one swift motion. There was a zipping roar as the two cables slipped out of their winches and the steel ramp smashed in the churning surf. Jones yelled:

"GO GO GO GO!"

He rode his horizontal wheel with one hand and the gear lever-throttle with the other. As the troops ROARED and raced out, the boat lifted from the rear and tried to slide forward while the surf surged past. Jones battled the surf with wheel and throttle for another moment. If he continued to slide forward, there was a chance the boat's steel ramp would cut down some of the troops from behind, like a scythe.

Four "enemy" fighter planes appeared out of nowhere going balls to the wall. If Stewart had known they were coming, he might have been able to hit them with a rock, they were that low. Two strafed the boats on the beach with blanks, and two strafed the troops just beginning to move off the beach into the jungle with blanks. Both pairs, with ear shattering engine roars and multiple .50 caliber machine guns, fired their guns. Then were gone. Just that fast!

Stewart only managed a quick glance recognizing two Grumman F6F Hellcats and two Chance-Vought F4U Corsairs, though. One LCM managed to return fire with their 20mm's blanks. The P-boats were unarmed.

The troops cleared the well deck, splashing through water heading for the dry sand ahead. Stewart watched Jensen charge out with his M1 rifle at high port arms. Jones pulled the gear lever throttle back through neutral to reverse, momentarily twisting the handle counter clockwise to reduce the engine to idle. As the surf action lifted the stern, he goosed the engine with savage twists clockwise momentary for high RPMs to break suction between the bottom and the sand, to begin retraction from the beach.

As the surf passed, Jones dropped from high RPMs but kept the pressure on. If his reflexes were slow or he misjudged his moves, Peter Eighteen would broach sideways to the line of boiling surf and oncoming next Wave —or if Peter Eighteen's engine quit, the boat would turn parallel to the surf—broaching—and could turn over.

If hit in real action, the crew probably wouldn't care. Bailey was hanging on for dear life and watching the oncoming surf and the next Boat Wave as Jones struggled. He shouted warnings Jones of surf about to hit the boat, and where the next Wave of landing craft was. The boat began to move backward, jarring, and bouncing off the beach. Waves of water splashed over the transom, drenching Bailey and Jones.

Jones needed his concentration to keep Eighteen lined up perpendicular to the surf. If the next Wave of landing craft was too close for Jones to attempt maneuvering, he had to hold up before retracting from the beach. Otherwise, he could back into an oncoming loaded boat with disastrous results. There were only seconds left before the next Wave would close with the surf. If there were enough time and space, Jones would start retracting from the beach watching the surf with great care.

Hendersen and Stewart had their hands full. They started cranking their ramp cable winches as soon as the last ground pounder stepped off the boat. The winches were located outboard on each side's coaming. Two winch cranks, inside against the hull, were used to wind the heavy, metal ramp back up against the hull.

The hardest part they faced was cranking the ramp up above horizontal so the water flowed off. As many times as Stewart had done this, cranking the ramp up above horizontal was the hardest work of all. Eighteen jolted up and down as the surf passed the boat rushing to the beach.

Eighteen tilted forward and the bow jerked hard against the bottom as Stewart strained to hold onto the crank and keep his footing without banging against the side too hard. He turned the crank at a steady pace. He knew he would be really bruised before the operation was over.

Stewart couldn't afford work gloves and the ship didn't provide them. His hands blistered, the blisters broke, tore off, and his hands stung with the salt water.

Why the fuck aren't there electric winches to pull this bastard up?

Already drenched with saltwater and constant surf splash, his arms were like rubber, his hands were aflame with salt stinging his broken blisters, and his chest heaved in agony.

Hendersen and Stewart yelled in cadence as their cranks reached the top of the circle. If they lost their rhythm of lifting evenly, one carried the full load of the ramp alone until the other could catch up. There was no stopping or resting. They had to pull the ramp up tight against the hull facing and latch the ramp to seal out the water before Jones could stop backing and move forward against the bow ramp.

Going forward with an open ramp would drive the P-boat under water. Stewart's breath was ragged and there was a stitch in his side as he heard the last click. They could ratchet their cranks no further. Hendersen held his crank hard back, holding the ramp hard against the boat front so Stewart could reach over the gunwhale, outside the protective shell, and lock his own ramp latch. Then he staggered to the other side, reached over and locked Hendersen's ramp latch.

A Wave of P-boats roared past Peter Eighteen on both sides, heading in to Green Three landing zone. In a state of near collapse, the 'Hooks make their way back to the after wells. Hendersen and Stewart knew the pain would almost disappear before Peter Eighteen joined up with the other boats.

Bailey began hand-pumping water out of the bilges with a handheld billy pump as Stewart and Hendersen latched the ramp. Surprisingly little water entered from the open ramp. Most of the water was from surf over the transom. Bailey never could figure out why an electrical pump wasn't added to those boats since swamping water was part of the action.

While Bailey pumped the bilges, he checked the engine temperature and saw it was beginning to climb.

The salt water intake sand filter is probably clogged. Time to switch tubes.

A long plastic tube filtered the incoming salt water to keep beach sand out of the engine. Two tube filters were installed in a mechanism.

Bailey reached out and threw a lever. The clean sand filter was now in line with the cooling salt water. Bailey would clean the sand-clogged filter after they cleared the beach area.

Jones had been watching for the ramp to be sealed against the sea. He had been steadily retracting from the beach as rapidly as the boat moved and the incoming waves permitted. He knew surf water would come aboard over the transom, but by judicial use of the throttle, he could reduce how much came aboard. It was a miserable, splashing event. Special splashboards installed on the transom to stop surf from joining the crew inside barely did as designed. As Peter Eighteen retracted, Jones and Bailey were soaked to the skin by the surf.

The next Wave plunged past. Now seaward of the surf, Jones turned the wheel hard over. Just before the P-boat reached right angles to the beach, he shifted forward, cranked the wheel full opposite, and twisted the throttle to high rpm's to clear the landing zone. Straightening the wheel, he headed out toward the designated rendezvous.

Eventually, their formation would return to the Beach Control Vessel to learn where to pick up the next load. They might go back to the Chilton or off to another APA or one of the cargo ships—AKAs. It just depended on what had to be unloaded next. The ground pounders and their fighting gear were supposed to come ashore by the numbers. Bailey continued to pump the bilges. At length, Jones cleared the path of the oncoming waves.

"Stewart!"

Stewart, still panting and trembling from his exertion, twisted his head back to see what Jones wanted. Jones beckoned him to take the wheel. It was a struggle to get back on his feet and clamber over the well deck partition to the coxswain's pit.

"Bring us around until the magnesyn compass points to the stern. That's the course back to the Chilton. Then, steer toward the Control Vessel. Stay out of the path of incoming landing craft. Let me know when we are about one hundred yards away from the Control Vessel. Got it?"

"Aye aye, Jones, I got it," puffed Stewart, still breathing hard.

Jones stepped onto the engine cover, tiredly pulled off his gray helmet and held it by the straps before dropping it into the pit. Jones bounced and jolted this way and that in the near shore wave action as he checked Peter Eighteen for seaworthiness. He pulled his folded white hat from a back pocket, snapped it open and pulled it down on his head to shade his eyes. He checked to see how his engineer was doing. Bailey was just about finished pumping bilges and very much as tired as the rest of the crew.

"Hendersen, you watch for the other Chilton boats from our wave so we know where to form a circle."

Hendersen nodded. Jones got down and laid out spread eagle on the warm engine cover to dry off in the sun; he pulled the white hat over his face. Meanwhile, Stewart extended the wheel to its highest level and pulled himself up to steer the boat and find the most comfortable speed to get Eighteen to the destination.

Hendersen spotted two P-boats behind them with the big white letter 'L' on the front of their ramps. He thought another one was ahead but couldn't be sure. Stewart brought Peter Eighteen to the destination in about twenty minutes and joined the other P-boat ahead, already circling, which turned out to be Chilton's Peter Twelve. Stewart decided he had enough.

"Henderson!"

Henderson looked up from where he was resting. Stewart pointed to Peter Twelve.

"Follow that boat until the rest of the Wave joins us."

Hendersen nodded and took Stewart's place. Stewart jumped into the wet, sandy well and flaked out with his white hat drawn over his head.

Maybe a little rest will do.

Hendersen circled with the other Chilton boat until the Wave Commander in Peter Twenty-three joined with three boats, and continued to circle until all eleven P-boats were present. The Wave Commander radioed the Control Vessel for new orders. After the Beach Control Officer radioed the response, the Chilton Wave Officer signaled 'follow me in a column formation at half speed.' Breaking out of the circle, he pointed the Chilton boats at Monrovia APA-31 for the next load.

Peter Eighteen made several more trips to the same beach landing zone. Jones had Stewart as coxswain of the boat until time for battle speed. On the last two runs, Jones coached Stewart all the way in and out, taking his place on the crank. Then the Beach Control officer split up the Chilton wave into independent, as-needed, assignments. Peter Eighteen was returned to the Chilton.

The sun was halfway to the western horizon as they approached their ship.

> **"Peter Eighteen, Peter Eighteen—tie up to the after Starboard Boat boom for refueling and relief. Report to Chief Abernathy on the fantail."**

The crew was too tuckered out to smile. Stewart stood up on the engine cover and signaled "R" with his arms.

They climbed over the Taffrail one by one and stood there on the rock solid deck. In reality, the Chilton gently rocked in the breeze and waves, but after eleven and a half hours in a P-boat, it was like solid ground. The skin on their faces was stretched tight from sunburns and puckered from dried salt spray. Their uniforms were soaked with salt, crusted dry. Jones waved his crew in to lean against the After Deck House to wait for the Chief. All four were exhausted.

Chief Abernathy arrived and looked them over. "God, you guys look like shit! Any problems to report?"

They all shook their heads as the Chief checked each one for a problem to explain.

He smiled. "Okay. Go directly to the Mess Deck and enjoy a steak dinner. You deserve it. Then drop by SickBay for some of their sunburn shit. After that, have a hot shower and hit the pad. We'll wake you around 2400 for night runs to the beach."

Jones stared in horror at the Chief through bloodshot eyes.

"Are you shitting me, Chief? I've never landed on a beach at night before."

The Chief looked at Jones with a slight smile. "Jones, there's a quarter moon and starlight to help your vision. The Wave Officer does the navigating and even if you get separated, the boat's compass and magnesyn will get you there and back. The Tin Cans are going to be firing Parachute Flares over the landing zones all night long. Now go eat and rest up. You'll get all the hot poop tonight."

2355, July 6
Station keeping off Windward Oahu
Operation Miki
U.S.S. Chilton APA-38

Stewart felt Alice tugging his blankets again so June and Alice could watch each other being nailed to the mattress. Not ready for that, he pulled them tighter around him. But a voice came through his sleep demanding his attention.

"Stewart—Stewart," a voice whispered. "Wake up. It's almost midnight and Peter Eighteen crew assembles on the Mess Deck in fifteen minutes."

Stewart opened his eyes into the red nightlight darkness and tried to blink the scratchiness away. He flipped his blankets out of the way and grabbed the bunk chain by his head.

Lordy, what a hardon. Maybe I can fix that in the shower.

Pivoting outward and downward, around his elbow, he landed lightly on the steel deck despite shouting and screaming muscles all over his body. Stewart couldn't believe he could be so stiff and sore. He stumbled into the Head and took a fast cool shower and painful shave before donning a clean set of greens. This time he loaded his pockets with Camels, Zippo, and lighter fluid.

Eyes still scratchy, he wandered into the red nightlight darkened Mess Deck where the late night boat crews were assembling for another meal and instructions.

How about that! They're offering little steaks and eggs for Mid Rats. This is going to be one tough night!

Stewart looked around and confirmed his thoughts. No one was smiling. Everyone was eating or just drinking coffee. He pushed a tray down the steam line, filled up, and joined the rest of the Eighteen crew at a table. No one had anything to say; heads down and eating.

"Let me have your attention, please."

The people turned toward the Landing Officer to learn what he had to say. He held his fist up with the index finger extended.

"First off, this will be a bitch the first time you land tonight —that is precisely why this trip is necessary," the officer said chuckling at his own little joke. No one smiled or chuckled back.

"Renquist—are you here?"

"Here, sir," came the response. A Second Class from Second Division stood up and waved his hand. The Landing Officer waved him back to his seat.

"Renquist is the ONLY P-boat coxswain to have made a night landing. That was during the Okinawa campaign on Charlie Blue Three beach. Nowadays, he drives a Mike boat. This situation is much the same throughout the 'Gator Navy. We need experienced LCVP and LCM coxswains." He looked around at each crewmember to make sure he had their attention. The second finger popped out and he waved it around so everyone could see his fingers.

"Second. No troops. Your boats will be loaded with cargo nets of boxed supplies. The Beachmaster will have stevedores unload the cargo. You are going in with the tide. That means you should not get hung up high and dry to wait for the next tide." You could feel the tension ease. Not having troops or cargo to mess with made life a little easier—not easy—but easier. He dropped his arm and picked up his coffee for a sip. Placing the cup back on the table, he continued without showing any fingers.

"Third. Our boats will operate only to and from the Chilton in this training phase. We don't want boats heading off for China during the night. Make damn well sure you set the magnesyn properly and cross check with compass bearings to the beach and return to the Chilton." Crews were beginning to nod as they saw how this thing would be fitted out.

"Fourth. Each Wave consists of four P-boats and one M-boat. The Wave Officer will be in the M-boat. Since night operations are so goosey, five boats will occupy the same wave front as eleven did during the day: plenty of room to maneuver. You don't run to the beach until the previous wave is out of the picture. Same applies to the wave following you." People were beginning to stand and stretch sore muscles. He held up his hand with all fingers and thumb extended.

"Finally, several 'Hooks have made initial qualification runs on Silver Strands and Camp Pendleton. If you feel competent, this is a great opportunity for final qualification. Let your coxswain and Chief Abernathy know before you board your boat."

Stewart hesitated because he still wanted to go to ET school. He mentally shrugged, leaned over and tapped Jones. Jones nodded. Hendersen hadn't qualified yet, so he wouldn't be permitted to try out tonight or tomorrow.

"I'll let the Chief know, Stew," grinned Jones.

"Any questions?" asked the Landing Officer, looking around. "Okay, man your boats." The crews headed aft to the Boat Booms.

Peter Eighteen was circling empty off the Starboard Quarter. Jenkins and Henderson, the 'Hooks, were leaning against the engine compartment. Bailey and Jones were sitting on the fantail with their feet dangling in the well.

Stewart had the wheel. He was surprised at how well he could see the ship in the starlight, quarter-moon, and distant star shell parachute flares. He was shocked at how difficult it was to judge distance in the dark. After two runs to the beach, Chief Abernathy told Jones to observe Stewart on the next run. An addititonal sailor came down the Jacob's Ladder, and joined the crew as replacement Bowhook.

"Peter Eighteen, Peter Eighteen—come alongside Station Red Three—come alongside Station Red Three."

Stewart turned and nodded at Jones. Their destination was the starboard side, forward of the superstructure at cargo hold three.

"Red three. Will you roger that, please, Jones?"

"Aye aye, Stewart."

Jones picked up his portable signaling lamp with an amber lens cover and aimed it at the Chilton's superstructure. An amber glow reflected off the waves as Jones flashed the letter 'R'—short long short—to the ship. Peter Eighteen rumbled slowly around the circle until parallel to the ship. Stewart twisted the throttle wide open to squirt out of the circle, then throttled back to 1300RPM.

In the beginning day operations, the Landing Officer brought boats along side starboard Stations White One, Red Three, Yellow Five, Green Seven, and Black Nine, according to the load requirements. The Port Stations were assigned the same colors but with even numbers, such as White Two.

The small cargo holds at Stations White One/Two and Black Nine/Ten were emptied before all the M-boats had departed on their first run. Then boat booms were swung out at those stations under the steep curvature of the ship's hull. Hereafter, refueling and repairs took place at Black Nine and Ten. White stations One and Two handled P-boat carpentry repairs and P- and M-boat storage.

In night operations, troop stations Yellow Five and Six were not used. That left Stations Red Three and Four, and Green Seven and Eight, opposite the two primary cargo holds, on either end of the superstructure.

In the shades-of-gray light, Stewart saw the boom swing out over Red Three with a full cargo net.

"Jenkins, Hendersen—fenders out—then get back into the engine compartment."

Stewart wanted them safely out of the way as the cargo net dropped into the well deck. He watched, with Jones's hand on his shoulder, as Peter Eighteen slapped its way slowly under the cargo net. Just as he threw the lever in reverse, Jones squeezed his shoulder. Stewart knew his timing had been correct. Peter Eighteen slowed to a stop, pitching and rocking in the reflected wave activity close to any hull.

Topside, he could see the cargo boss—another Boatswain's Mate First—signaling the net down by pointing his arm down and motioning up and down. The heavy cargo net hovered just above the deck plates as the cargo boss judged the P-boat's up and down motion. Suddenly, as the boat reached a high and started falling off, the cargo net came down rapidly, landing in the well deck just before the boat bottomed out in the wave trough.

"Jenkins and Hendersen, pull the pelican release and get the hell out of the way."

The two 'Hooks scrambled over the cargo net. Jenkins, bigger than Hendersen, grabbed the hook's ball weight and attempted to hold it still. Hendersen grabbed the pelican hook's release line and jerked it. The cargo net ring fell away from the hook. They scrambled back to the engine compartment fearfully watching the big hook.

Topside, the cargo boss had already signaled the winch operator to bring up the hook. As soon as the hook cleared the well deck, the cargo boss looked down at the P-boat and waved them off.

Stewart, who had been holding station by manipulating transmission and throttle, pushed the lever into forward and twisted the throttle. He turned the wheel slightly to the right and stood up to check for other boats. Bailey and Jones had been watching, too.

"All clear, Stewart," called Bailey.

Stewart nodded and dropped back down into the coxswain's compartment. Turning the wheel more to the right, he increased the throttle and watched as the rpm's built slowly toward 1300 RPM. As Peter Eighteen came around, they saw the other boat leaving Green Seven. Two more P-boats and one M-boat still had to be loaded. Stewart regained the Starboard Quarter circle and slowed down to wait it out.

The M-boat lumbered its way into the circle. Before completing one full circle, a strange pale blue light above its tall cockpit began flashing Morse code.

What the hell's that all about?

Then he remembered from the other two trips.

Jones spoke. "Stewart—that's a numeral one and means follow me in column formation."

"Okay, give him a roger, Jones."

"Aye aye, Stewart."

Stewart nodded as Jones stepped back and sat down again. Stewart watched as the M-boat plowed straight away from the Chilton. He jumped up, pulled the wheel to its highest position, and strained to see the whole wave.
Only one boat behind him.

Same process, different methods. Again, a numeral one as the wave left the Beach Control Vessel. The P-boats struggled with 1500 RPM as they closed to within five hundred yards of the beach. Another signal: this one meant turn flank right. The other boats were visible in the pale green light of the parachute flares.

He could see the trees inland but still couldn't see the surf. Jones moved up behind him to assist—just in case— but didn't say a word. This was Stewart's trip unless he got into trouble.

The Wave Officer flashed increase speed to 1800 RPM. Stewart tried to stay cool.

Where's the fuckin' surf?

Now, the Wave Officer called for 2250 RPM.

"Bailey—Battle Speed."

He watched as Bailey reached in to the governor latch. Stewart dropped the throttle to idle and Bailey disengaged the governor. Stewart savagely twisted the throttle full and looked up to find the surf.

There you are, bastard. Now I can see what's going on.

Fresh star shells burst overhead.

Oh shit. An M-boat is broached right in my path.

He looked right and turned his wheel while frantically sounding his horn. The outer P-boat crew heard, saw him coming, and moved farther right. The surf was just ahead.

He jumped down into his well and dropped the wheel. Quickly, with his hand on the throttle, he scanned the water on both sides to pick up the waves before they broke.

There's one.

A snap look at the beach, and back to the wave as he reduced throttle.

Come on bitch, ease back into the wave—slowly now—slowly—GOTCHA—now just a little more throttle.

Stewart had Peter Eighteen just hanging back from the very edge of the comber. He jerked the wheel slightly left as he watched the dark beach looming up fast.

A little more right rudder.

The jolt and grind caught him off guard. Eighteen bounced off the sand and continued toward the beach. He gunned it as the boat began to slide forward on the sand and lurched to a stop.

Oh shit, I forgot. Where's Jenkins and Hendersen?

Stewart looked wildly around for the two 'Hooks.

Of course—they know their jobs.

The two were standing near the ramp waiting for him to give the word.

"NOW!"

The ramp dropped with a splash. Two stevedores in greens from the Beachmaster hopped onto the ramp and into the P-boat. Once again, the special jeep drove right onto the boat as water swirled around Peter Eighteen. One of the stevedores grabbed the hook on the jeep's short jib boom, passed it through the cargo net eye and back around its cable. Holding the cable taut, the stevedore looked at the jeep driver and waved his hand toward the shore. The driver took up the slack and the stevedores jumped out of the way as the jeep began to drag the cargo net and all its boxes of combat goods into the surf and up onto the sand.

Stewart assisted by going into reverse as soon as the jeep cleared his ramp. Jenkins and Hendersen were in position to begin cranking as soon as the net cleared the ramp.

Stewart, with hands on wheel and throttle, squinted into the shifting darkness behind him. There was no sign of the next wave of boats. He had Peter Eighteen in reverse with steady pressure on. The cargo's weight tilted the stern up so surf could easily surge under, lifting the boat. The jeep's four wheels spun and slowly pulled the cargo net clear of the ramp. Peter Eighteen's bow leaped upward as the cargo net cleared the ramp, forcing the stern into the sand. The crew was battered around for a moment. Suddenly Jones yelled, "Look out Stewart. You're turning into a broach!"

Stewart whipped his head around to orient his view and discovered the last bounce moved the bow off the perpendicular line.

Jesus H Christ, this is going to be tough.

He cranked the wheel and began goosing the throttle to realign the boat. She slowly came around as Jones hovered to push Stewart out of the way.

Come on bitch. Come on around. There you go, now let's get off this fucking beach.

Stewart had one hand on the stiff wheel and the other hand on the throttle.

Slowly, Peter Eighteen bucked its way back through the surf. The salt water, splashing over the transom, had drenched him completely and his eyes stung. Lee leaned his head into a completely wet sleeve and tried to wipe his eyes. Squinting, he checked alignment as Peter Eighteen made a final bounce and cleared the surf line.

Adrenaline had pumped Stewart 'til he was shaking all over. Jenkins and Hendersen had gotten an assist as the cargo net bounced off the ramp. They got a few fast turns. The ramp was already latched securely. Stewart kept backing a few more seconds to make sure of his position. Then he cranked the wheel over, waited for the turn, and changed to forward gear.

The P-boat gathered speed and bounced out of the inner line of waves.

I made it!

As Eighteen headed out, Stewart spotted the next wave waiting and crossed their front to get out of the way.

No need to hurry. Two more boats are still retracting.

"Hendersen!"

Henderson twisted his head back to see what Stewart wanted. Stewart beckoned him to take the wheel. He watched as Hendersen struggled to get back on his feet and clamber over the well deck partition to the coxswain's pit.

Stewart ordered, "Bring us around until the magnesyn compass points to the stern. That's the course back to the Chilton. Then, steer toward the Control Vessel. Stay out of the path of incoming landing craft. Let me know when we are about one hundred yards away. Got it?"

"Aye aye, Stewart, I got it," puffed Hendersen, still breathing hard.

Stewart stepped onto the engine cover, tiredly bouncing this way and that in the near shore wave action as he checked Peter Eighteen and the crew. He pulled his folded white hat from a back pocket, snapped it open and pulled it down on his wet head to keep it warm. Then he checked to see how Bailey was coming along. He just about finished pumping bilges and was very much as tired as the rest of the crew.

"Jenkins, you watch for the other Chilton boats from our wave so we know where to form a circle." Jones grinned to himself as he watched Stewart go through identical motions he had gone through.

He learns good, Jones thought.

During Operation Miki, the boat crew spent nearly thirty-three hours in Peter Eighteen, landing troops and cargo from four APAs, four AKAs, and one AKL.

1200, July 8
Under the Hammerhead Crane
Pearl Harbor, T.H.

The Chilton tied up in Pearl Harbor for three days of liberty, before returning to San Diego. Large transports would carry the soldiers to Japan, and the AKA's would carry their equipment.

Stewart had liberty the first two days in Pearl. He was eagerly looking forward to a rowdy liberty with Larry Jensen. As promised, Stewart made his way to the Ala Moana's Banyan Tree and sat drinking Cokes. The beach was loaded with girls baking in the Hawaiian sun as they watched all the service men. But that's all they did—watch. Some of the girls wore two-piece bathing suits, even showing their navels!

At 2:45PM, Larry hadn't shown up, so Stewart left the beach to tour Waikiki. Disappointed by the high prices, he headed back to the ship in time to eat dinner and watch a movie. He signed up for a pineapple field and factory tour for the next morning. He would be back in Waikiki in time to meet Larry at Two PM.

Again, Larry wasn't able to make it. For a while, Stewart had thought about taking a ride on one of the outrigger canoes until he found out it cost twenty-five dollars. Eventually, he caught a bus back to the Main Gate at Pearl Harbor and walked back to the Chilton.

It was a point of pride—seamanship, if you will—to be able to hold a mug of coffee in the crook of your index finger without spilling a drop. Didn't matter if you were standing still, or as you walked along a passageway, or about the weather decks, during storm conditions, flexing your knees, hips, and spine like a downhill skier as the ship pitched, tossed, and turned.

During a big storm when Stewart was off duty, he loved to take his coffee and sneak up as high as he could on one of the weather deck bridges: usually Sky One, the highest open bridge for Flag Commands when they were aboard. The regular Watch Crew did not take kindly to someone enjoying their drudgery, and the officers did not take kindly to someone looking over their shoulders.

Stewart loved being at sea. The fact that he was never—ever—seasick probably had much to do with that feeling. He really liked the sting and smell of sea spray, the taste of salt in the spray, the smell of burned fuel, and the shock absorbing balancing act as he walked on deck or down a passageway. It was embarrassing when the ship lurched unexpectedly and coffee splashed on his dungarees and the deck.

A solid, windy storm with high, rolling waves was just great. Stewart watched the bow dig deep in the trough of a wave, and then rise up as the sea begrudgingly parted; he could feel the power of the wave in his knees, as the ship began to lift slowly, then faster, up, out of the trough.

Reaching the top of the wind-blown wave, the ship creaked and groaned, hesitating as she quivered and slowly dove, smashing into the next trough, digging in as the sea tried to bury the ship.

Once in a while, a really large wave would loom up out of the horizon. Then he hung on tight. Stewart tried counting large waves on the theory of sevens. Every seventh wave was supposed to be larger. The Seventh Seven was supposed to be a real monster.

Not true.

Stewart's first four months in the Fleet passed quickly and he began thinking ahead because in February 1950, it would be time to ship over. There was never any question in Stewart's mind of whether he would ship over: the big question was, how was he going to get to go to ET school at Great Lakes Naval Training Center.

Stewart didn't want to ship over on the Chilton because he was not about to become a Boatswain's Mate. Ever since his request chit for transfer to the ET Division had been disapproved, he knew that was exactly what Boatswain's

Mate Second Class Deacon Jones, Chief Boatswain's Mate Abernathy, and Lieutenant Commander Ambrose had in mind.

He already had learned this proud and venerable rating was so overcrowded, his chance for advancement beyond BM3 was tight, and beyond BM2 almost nonexistent. He was afraid he might be forced into accepting something he did not want. It was his life the Navy was messing with.

SEPTEMBER

The Chilton and her sister ship the Bayfield, received a new assignment from the Navy Department. Not directly, you understand. The Secretary of the Navy, seeking to balance the needs of the Navy throughout the world, decided to transfer two attack transports from the Pacific Fleet to the Atlantic Fleet. He made his desires known through channels.First, the Joint Chiefs of Staff, thence to the Chief of Naval Operations (CNO).

In turn, the CNO nodded to his staff and they contacted Commander, Amphibious Forces, Pacific Fleet in San Diego, California, (ComPhibPac) to determine which two transports would make the move to the Atlantic Fleet. Commander, Amphibious Forces, Atlantic Fleet (ComPhibLant) in Norfolk, Virginia, was kept advised through the flurry of messages that moved throughout the Navy Department. ComPhibPac asked his three Amphibious Groups for recommendations.

ComPhibGru Two nominated Bayfield and Chilton. Thus, after some thought, in a twinkling of an eye, Bayfield and Chilton had a new homeport: Norfolk, Virginia, and a new Amphibious boss: Vice Admiral Fahrion, ComPhibLant.

Among other things, Bayfield and Chilton would proceed together from San Diego, California, south to transit the Panama Canal, east across the Gulf of Mexico and the Caribbean Sea, and north to Norfolk, Virginia. It was further ordered they should arrive in time for Thanksgiving.

In an old tradition, all hands were asked if they would rather stay in the Pacific Fleet or stay aboard their ships and move to the Atlantic Fleet. If those who would rather stay could find someone of the same rate, doing the same job and would like to swap, the Navy would make great efforts to insure those transfers would be approved.

Of course, personnel swapping ships did so at their own expense, after both Commanding Officers and their higher Commanders approved of the mutual transfers. Chief

Abernathy chose to stay and finally found a swap with Chief Neal of the Noble APA-45.

After this phase was well along, all married personnel who opted to stay aboard the Chilton and Bayfield were made aware of a grand experiment. Those families whose Navy men were Petty Officer Second Class or higher, or lower rank with more than four years of service, could accompany their sponsor, a Navy man or Marine, aboard ship to the ship's new home port, bag, baggage, and car. If this experiment worked satisfactorily, the Navy stood to save a considerable amount of money now spent on moving families about.

NOVEMBER

November 10
Broadway Pier, San Diego
U.S.S. Chilton APA-38

Those who wanted to go were loaded with all household goods and effects aboard, including POVs (Privately Owned Vehicles). Families of enlisted men and chiefs were housed together in troop officer quarters (the men remained in their bachelor bunks or quarters); officers' families were in their husbands' staterooms, roommates having been moved temporarily to other quarters. Automobiles and household effects were stowed in the Combat Cargo holds. Families ate at special times in the Mess Deck, Chiefs' Mess, Warrant Officers' Mess, or Commissioned Officers' Mess.

All hands, including the Side Cleaners, prettied up the ship before the day both ships would depart San Diego. A lot of people would be present. On that special day, the Commandant, Eleventh Naval District, headquartered in San Diego, the Commander, Amphibious Forces, U.S. Pacific Fleet, in San Diego, the Mayor of San Diego, and many friends were at the Broadway Pier to see the two ships depart, a very festive occasion.

The first day out was like any commercial ocean liner. All the standard drills—plus General Quarters—were conducted because the families had to know where they were expected to be. For example, during the Man Overboard drill, all families reported to their sleeping quarters to be counted.

Preparing to abandon ship was extended because the families had to figure out where their LCVP was located and how they would board at the rails—never done with troops. Even though the planners had foreseen the problem, it was still awkward fitting the life jackets to young children. Lunch ran a little late the first day at sea.

The bachelors aboard almost never saw the dependents unless their cleaning or watch station was nearby. Lookouts on duty between sundown and sunrise began reporting suspicious activity and noise in the deep shadows of the gun tubs within their view. A few couples had been seen casing the gun tubs before sundown.

Never claimed, a Gunner's Mate upon entering his 40mm gun tub cleaning station one morning, found a pair of panties hanging on one of the 40mm muzzles.

Passage from San Diego to the Panama Canal was relatively quiet. Some of the women found out their electrical appliances, such as AC/DC radios and hair dryers, were not allowed due to the amount of radio noise they produced. A few who tried to use their record players gave up without having to be told. As the ship rocked through its three axes, the 78 and 45 rpm needles were skipping or bouncing from groove to groove.

After several single men knocked their heads, tripped, mashed fingers, and even broke one leg, the Executive Officer was forced to issue instructions to the accompanied married men that their wives and teenaged daughters could not lay out on deck in their bathing suits. Too many accidents were caused to men who were not allowed to stare but couldn't help their natural healthy appetites.

Just before arriving at Balboa, Panama Canal Zone, the Chaplain conducted a poll to determine how many of the crew had ever been through the Canal. He was surprised to learn that only nine sailors had been through the Canal, plus one wife on a hospital ship when she had been a Navy Nurse during World War Two.

Half the crew was allowed liberty in Balboa; the other half on the Atlantic side at Cristobal. Since he had a choice, Stewart opted for Balboa. The Command decided to let the single men off the ship before the dependents because the dependents would be spread out while the sailors would disappear in a hurry.

1200, November 17
U.S. Naval Station Balboa
Panama Canal Zone

Stewart had a full payday minus a trip to the Ship's Store for a carton of Sea Store cigarettes. He kept his money in a billfold, which he jammed into a tight front pants pocket of his Whites. Saluting the Colors, he ran down the gangway directly onto the gray Navy bus and immediately regretted running because of the high humidity. He was drenched suddenly with sweat.

The Panamanian bus driver drove them through the gate separating the Republic of Panama from the fenced off U.S. Canal Zone. A light breeze blew steadily in from the Pacific Ocean. It was a beautiful day with piercing blue sky patched with towering white and dark gray clouds. Lush foliage of every size, shape, and shade of green, and very tall palm trees with light gray trunks that looked like concrete were everywhere. Splashes of red, yellow, orange, and blue flowers boldly shouted their presence. Colorful birds, screaming and cawing, flew everywhere. There was a perfume in the air something like cinnamon. Honeysuckle, orange blossoms, and gardenia filled the nostrils to the exclusion of all else.

White three story buildings, surrounded by carefully manicured lawns that came right to the edge of the pavement, lined the boulevard.

Man, I've never seen anything like this before. This is certainly different from Hawaii.

He sat comfortably in the bus with his elbow hanging out of the window as he gazed about studying the new scenery.

He was not too hot because his sweat wetting his uniform acted to cool him.

Wonder why the first floor of those buildings are car port garages, instead of having two story houses and separate garages?

The bus slowed to a smooth stop and the driver stood up, looked at the sailors with a happy face, and spoke with very good English, "Okay sailors. Bus be here every hour on the hour until midnight for ride back to your ship. After midnight, you take taxi."

"Shoeshine, sailor? You like a shoeshine?" Several boys were clamoring for attention as the sailors got off the bus.

Lee shrugged. "How much you want, kid?"

"A nickel, you gimme a nickel, yes?"

"Okay." Lee lit a Camel as he watched the boy.

"You have cigarette for me, too, sailor?"

"Nah, you're too young."

"My sister. I take you to my sister. You like her. Only five bucks. You like a screw for five bucks?"

"Just shine my shoes, kid."

Wonder if he's really peddling his big sister?

He patted his front pocket.

Yep, the pack of rubbers is there.

In two minutes the kid had put something on each shoe tip to make them shine and that was it. Lee strolled off, enjoying the sights and sounds of old Balboa. At the next corner, boys rushed at him with their shoeshine boxes. One skidded on his knees in front of Lee and grabbed a foot.

"Hey sailor. You need a shoeshine. Only a dime."

"Nah, Kid, I just got one for a nickel."

"But your shoes are dirty now and that's extra work to make them shine. Only a dime, sailor."

Lee looked at his shoes, discovering the boy had something on his hands to dirty both of his shoes. He frowned and wondered if this was going to happen all over Balboa.

I'll leave them alone; otherwise the next guy is going to charge me a quarter.

"Get away, kid. They don't need a shine." Lee walked off rapidly, as the boys shouted angrily in Spanish at him.

Colorful downtown: tiny streets with very narrow sidewalks, taxi horns blaring loudly at every corner as a substitute for brakes, iron work balconies—some black, others green, and more boys with shoeshine kits and dirty fingers to make you get a shine.

Girls in every doorway in a variety of sleezy blouses, t-shirts, bare midriffs, shorts, billowing skirts and nearly no skirts at all; some of the girls not so clean looking.

Bars with very tall ceilings and slow turning fans. The only light came through from doors and windows. Empty bars—no music.

Occupied bars—loud music. Beautiful potted flowers hanging on walls all over the place. Police in white uniforms and pith helmets stood in the middle of every intersection.

Special deals on every kind of merchandise, mostly rings and watches, everywhere along the streets and corners; lots of restaurants to fit your pocketbook. No age limit on drinking.

After a few drinks of rotgut, Lee was ready when George Bailey walked up and sat down at the bar next to him.

"Hi, Lee. How about it? Bunch of us guys are going to take a taxi to a special house in the country, choice of many girls. The cabbie keeps talking about Frenchy Frances, the triple threat that is such a hot number. We need one more guy to cut the taxi price down."

George, you're not going to talk any girl out of a free piece of ass down here.

Lee picked up his change, cigarettes and lighter off the bar, and followed George out to the taxi. Lee recognized the other guys but not their names. They cheered when George dragged him over to the taxi.

They rode along a dirt lane for twenty minutes until the driver pulled up in front of a large, high wooden gate with barbed wire across the top.

Keeping them in or keeping us out?

The cabbie honked three times and waited. The gate began to slowly move inward, dragging on the dirt.

The two-story house sat on a rise, surrounded by tall trees filled with gaudy, squawking birds and screaming monkeys. The wooden house looked to have a wide veranda on all four sides. It wasn't in the best of shape but he didn't think it was going to collapse today. A coat of paint would have done wonders to that bare gray wood but he noticed the veranda screens were copper, new and tightly stretched.

Oh yeah, this is Yellow Fever and Malaria country. That's why our shots were brought up to date before we left 'Diego.

Inside the main room, things were just as drab.

"Hey guys, these women are all native Indians, except that red head sitting by herself," said George.

"Isn't that Fearless Francie?"

"Frenchy Frances, Stew. Get it right. Frenchy Frances. She takes it in all holes."

Frenchy overheard their low voices and tried to put on a big smile. Getting up, she stepped out of her shorts and vest, and stretched, turning slowly around. Then she walked toward the group of sailors.

The effort was wasted. She was a very old woman, probably in her thirties. Her thin boobs hung down—almost far enough to throw over her shoulder, she was overweight, and had needle marks on her arms and legs. A guy would have to be awfully hard up or very drunk to try her on for size.

"Hi boys. Wanna give me a whirl? A good fuck, a blow job, and a shot at my brownie for fifteen dollars."

No one would touch her with a ten-foot pole. Each of them moved out of her reach, grabbed the nearest girl, and headed upstairs. Lee's light brown female with a round flat face and straight black hair and small boobs was ten dollars. He couldn't begin to guess her age but felt she was a teenager. She grabbed his hand and took him upstairs to a cot draped with mosquito netting. Wasted effort; he just couldn't get it up with her, even though she tried with her hands and mouth.

He was dressed and sitting on the veranda sipping a Panama beer when the last of the guys came downstairs. Lee was ready when a taxi appeared with another group of guys from the ship. He had nothing to say to the new bunch coming in. He had nothing to say to his own group either.

This had been a wasted ten bucks.

Transiting the Canal took several hours. Stewart's underway cleaning station was a section of the 02-deck weather deck on the starboard side. He had a foxtail broom, a dustpan, swab, pail, hard soap, and a piece of toweling. Luckily, Stewart had no bright work to polish on this station.

In this position all day, he got to watch the Lock operation, the Culebra Cut, and the mooring near Cristobal or Colon, while the other half of the crew took liberty.

1730, November 25
USS Chilton APA-38

U.S. Naval Operating Base, Pier 4
Norfolk, Virginia

The Chilton and Bayfield arrived from San Diego, California, this morning and tied up to Pier Four. A Navy band met them and played many marches and songs until all the dependents had left the ships for previously arranged temporary quarters. Their husbands would be responsible for removing all personal gear within a couple of days of arrival. Meanwhile, the Chilton would remain tied up there while the dependents' household goods and cars were unloaded into the adjacent warehouse.

Standing at Quarters for entering port, the crew learned things would be a little different at Naval Operating Base (NOB), Norfolk (commonly expressed by sailors as No-fuck). All hands topside would wear undress blues, regardless of the hour or work detail. This created havoc with everyone's work routine. Side Cleaners, for example, would wear undress blues over the side while painting.

The reason for this revolting development was flying at the truck of a strange looking amphibious command ship, the U.S.S. Mount Olympus AGC-8. A blue flag with three white stars fluttered in the miserable breeze!

This Vice Admiral liked his amphibious fleet shipshape; so much so he was inclined to send messages to a ship's Amphibious Group Commander inquiring into the reason he had spotted a sailor in dungarees on this ship or rust on that ship.

Yonder 'Mt O' was tied up exactly opposite the Chilton where the Admiral could stare across at them. The Captain decided he wanted the ship to look shipshape, immediately.

The five Side Cleaners, led by Deak, left the gangway and walked rapidly in the dim light of scattered pier lights to the head of Pier Four for their first Norfolk liberty. They were in Dress Blue Able with flat hat, Peacoat, and gloves. The Side Cleaners had had to work over the side until beyond dusk before they could secure for the day and clean up.

As a group, they had eaten aboard because it was so late. Now, they were on the way to Main Street to hoist a few. Everyone was over twenty-one except eighteen-year-old Stewart, but they thought they could find a quiet place to sit and relax together.

A big cab sat in front of the Fleet Landing just inside the gate, so they grabbed it. The Negro driver looked them over, especially Deak.

"Where to, sailors?"

"Take us down to Main Street to a quiet place where we can relax, no questions asked," said Monroe.

"Okay, and where do you want to go, Boats?" the driver asked, looking at Deak.

"We're all together," said Stewart.

Shrugging his shoulders, the cabdriver responded. "Okay, Main Street it is."

Everyone flashed their ID and liberty cards for the Marine Sentries at the gate.

The cabbie drove out, turned left, drove several blocks to Granby, and turned right. As he drove, he kept watching the sailors with a worried look; he didn't want to get into the middle of a problem. So he said nothing. Downtown at Main Street, he let them off and pointed to all the clip joints along the street.

They walked along, absorbing the sights and sounds of Main Street, Norfolk. They looked through the windows; every place seemed loaded with sailors at the bars and tables. Finally, about four blocks along, they found a place that had a few civilians and a couple of sailors.

They went in taking off their hats and smiling tentatively as they did. They were in new territory. The words came harshly.

"Hey you—nigger—what the fuck do you mean, coming in a white man's bar? Get your black ass outa here before I bounce a bottle off'n your head!" yelled the man behind the bar.

Five heads snapped to the bartender. Their ears couldn't believe what they were hearing. The five kept coming in off the street but formed into an arc as they looked around.

"What are you talking about, man? This is a sailor and a friend of ours. We just want to hoist a beer and have some peace and quiet."

The bartender stepped to the end of the bar and lifted the flap, coming toward them fast. He carried a short baseball bat like a billy club.

"Get his black ass out of this bar before I club him and call the cops to take him away. We don't allow niggers with white folks around here." He raised his baseball bat, making for Deak. Monroe stepped in front of him and crouched, cocking his left fist.

"Don't even think it, asshole, or I'll jam that club up your brownie."

Deak reached out and touched Monroe. "Come on, there's gotta be other places we can go without this kind of business," called Deak, softly.

They began to back out of the bar followed by the bartender and several of the patrons. There was a squeal of tires and the sounds of car doors opening and slamming. The Chilton sailors turned around and faced two policemen holding night sticks in their hands. The bartender rushed up behind Deak and tried to hit him in the head. Monroe grabbed the baseball bat from him.

"I told you, asshole, what I was going to do if you tried that." Monroe whirled him around and started to jam the baseball bat at his ass.

"FREEZE. DROP IT RIGHT NOW, SAILOR."

They looked back at the policemen who had drawn revolvers but kept them pointed down. The puzzled and now scared sailors didn't know which way to turn. Monroe, still holding the bartender, dropped the baseball bat with a clatter.

"Officer, we don't want any trouble, but this bartender attacked us before we had a chance to say hello. He threatened Deak inside, and just now started to hit him with that baseball bat. That's when I took it away from him. I didn't want Deak getting hurt by this asshole."

The lead policeman looked carefully at each of the five sailors then pointed his chin at Deak.

"What are you doing, trying to go into a white man's bar, nigra? I'm afraid I'm going to have to arrest you and lock you up."

Stewart looked at the others, stepped in front of Deak and faced the policeman.

"Hey wait, officer. We're the injured party. Why do you want to arrest us?" asked Stewart with some heat.

"We aren't arresting you, kid. We're arresting that nigger sailor that's hiding behind your skirts."

Stewart's armpits started pouring water and his belly was pounding. He was scared but this was bullshit. He had seen it as a young teenager in New Orleans during World War Two. He stared at the officer.

"Looks like you're going to have to lift my skirts to get to my innocent shipmate—officer."

The sarcasm was not lost on either policeman. Their hands went down to their holsters again when a black van screeched to a stop behind the police car. Doors slammed open and closed as two Shore Patrolmen raced over. The senior patrolman was a Chief Torpedoman (TMC); the other a Boatswain's Mate Second Class (BM2).

"Jeez, Charles, do you always have to do sailors this way?" chuckled the Chief. He saw the confrontation immediately.

"Nah, only with the tough bastards. I don't think these guys have had a drop to drink either. That's what makes it bad. But I'm going to take that white sailor and the nigger behind him."

"Before you do, can I talk to them a second?"

"Yeah, but it ain't going to do any good, Chief. They went too far."

"All right sailors, ID and liberty cards, NOW," demanded the Chief Shore Patrolman, while snapping his fingers with a loud crack. The five hastily handed them over. The Chief and his running mate checked them thoroughly.

"The Chilton, huh? How long you guys been in town?"

Deak looked left and right, then spoke, "Chief, these guys work for me—Side Cleaners. We haven't been in Norfolk more than half an hour, as long as it took in a cab from Pier Four to here."

"You guys off that ship that just got in from 'Diego with all the dependents on board? Big write up in the Ledger Dispatch today."

"Yeah, Chief, that's our ship. We had to do some touch up over the side before we could come ashore. Everyone else got early liberty at 1300."

"You boys been in the South before?"

"No, Chief, and I don't think I like what I see, either," Stewart grumbled.

"Shut your mouth, Stewart, before all these fine gentlemen shut it for you. Okay sailors, listen well. Apologize to the bartender and patrons, right now. You done wrong and I'll explain later. Then turn around and apologize to these police officers. They are good people and doing their job. Maybe, just maybe, they won't arrest you, then."

The Chilton five heard him with widening eyes. But as one, they turned to the bartender and his patrons and apologized. Deak, hating every second, even took off his hat and nearly blubbered over them. Monroe politely handed back the baseball bat, carefully watching the bartender, and letting the bartender know with his eyes, he better not swing at Deak, police and Shore Patrol, notwithstanding.

They turned around, gritted their teeth, smiled at the officers and apologized to them profusely. The civilians laughed and catcalled in the background. The police and Shore Patrol let them squirm for a minute. Charles, the lead policeman, turned to the Chief.

"Okay, you can have them, Chief, but you better cut 'em in fast before they get in a heap of trouble around here."

The police got into their squad car and drove off. The Chief herded them into the back of the S.P. van and drove down the street, around the corner, and stopped near a big bus stop. The Second Class opened the back of the van and motioned them out. The Chief waved them over in front of him where he leaned back against the hood.

"You guys are lucky. We've been doing this for Chilton and Bayfield sailors all afternoon. Your lack of Southern culture and charm shows. Now, I'm going to tell you the rules, and like 'em or lump 'em, they are the rules written on the Stars and Bars of the Confederacy. So as you hear them, don't blame me. I'm just passing it along. I mean, after all, it's only been eighty-five years since the North put down the Southern Rebellion, know as the Civil War. Right?" They all nodded.

"Rule one above all else, Jones. Negros and Whites don't mix nohow, nowhere, notime, when you are off the ship and bases. Negros aren't treated very well over here. These Southerners say they treat Negros equally. However, there are separate facilities for Negros. Like drinking fountains, usually very dirty. Toilets, always filthy. Bars, restaurants, balconies in movies, and hotels. Gas stations, if you have a car.

"And for God's sake, when you get on a bus, watch for the sign in the back. You can't even sit together on the bus. Negros go to the back of the bus. Obey that bus driver like your life depended upon it: it may! Don't mess with white men. If they tell you to get out of the way, do it before they ask.

"Boats, don't *EVER* get caught looking at a white woman or bumping into one. You may just disappear. I shit you not. Now, you guys should be able to enjoy some cools ones— except you, kid.

Ah horse piss!

"So, use the slop chute on the base, and ship's parties, that sort of thing. Now, stay out of trouble and get lost."

What the Chief told them shocked and hurt all of them. Even though Deak had his ass on the line just like everyone else on the ship, he wasn't good enough.

Well, screw the South.

DECEMBER

The Ivan Stewart Residence
8364 Chesapeake Street
Norfolk, Virginia

Stewart had a place to go in a town renowned—even worse than San Diego—for its miserable treatment of sailors. Stewart's Dad was on a ship stationed in Norfolk, and his family lived in Norfolk. Back in Bremerton on the Lex II, Dad had requested his new duty be in the Pacific, not another aircraft carrier, and certainly not one to be decommissioned and mothballed.

His new orders, as Chief Engineer, to report to the U.S.S. Siboney CVE-114 in Norfolk for duty was disgusting. When he reported aboard, Lieutenant Stewart discovered the Siboney was scheduled to be decommissioned. She would be placed in mothballs at the Naval Shipyard, Philadelphia. Young Stewart had sense enough to hide his face at the dinner table when his Dad told him that story.

7:00PM, December 12
The Gregory Miller Residence
12-401 Deal Blvd, Apt 3C
Norfolk, Virginia

Lee had a blind date.

Rosalie Waters, his mother's friend of many years, was also a Navy wife. She was acquainted with the Miller family, a nice family, across the street from her house. Their niece, Bobbie Sue Miller, was visiting while looking for a job in Norfolk. Bobbie Sue didn't know anyone except her aunt and uncle, and the older Navy couple across the street. She wished she were back in Winchester, West Virginia, with all her friends.

Susan Miller was complaining to Rosalie over coffee that Bobbie Sue was driving her nuts. She needed a man to distract her, preferably a Christian man who would not try to have his way with her.

Rosalie thought for a minute, and smiled.

"Think I have the answer," she said as she got up from the kitchen table, walked purposefully into the hall, and called her old girlfriend, Wilma Stewart.

"Hello?" Wilma asked.

"Hi, Wilma, Rosalie here. Can you come over for coffee and a bear claw? I have something to talk about."

"I was about to go to the Commissary, but that can wait. Be there in ten minutes."

"That's great. See you then. Bye."

As Wilma drove away in their new 1950 Ford Fordoor sedan, she wondered what Rosalie had in mind.

The ladies sat at the kitchen table enjoying the last crumbs of their bear claws. Rosalie had suggested to Wilma that Lee needed some female companionship in this town, notoriously unfriendly toward sailors. Lee had met 'Irish' Waters the first time his Dad had taken him aboard the Saratoga in '39.

Susan mentioned that her niece Bobbie Sue had cabin fever and needed male companionship. From a couple of letters Wilma had received from Lee, she got the impression he was now a sailor through and through. She wondered aloud if this was a good idea, sic'ing Lee on this nice girl. Bobbie Sue should take his mind off trying to get ET school for the moment.

"I'll spring it on Lee when he drops by for dinner tonight. Do you think Bobbie Sue will go out with him tonight?"

"Strike while the iron's in the fire, I always say," said Susan. "She's due home about 3:30 this afternoon. I'll tell her to get prettied up for a blind date tonight—and threaten bloody mayhem if she refuses."

Susan snickered and looked at Wilma. "What about Lee? Do you think he'll go along with the plan?"

Wilma grinned her Cheshire grin.

"He'll do anything to drive the new Ford. Lee'll be there. Besides, I know he hasn't had a date since he arrived last month. After that run-in with the police on Main Street, he hasn't gone downtown."

Lee pulled up in front of the Miller's house and turned off the ignition. He got out of the car and walked to the Miller's front door.

The lights were out, so he looked at the apartment complex across the street. There were a sprinkling of Christmas decorations already showing in apartment windows.

That's right. Mom is buying a tree tomorrow and I am supposed to help decorate it.

He waited for the right moment in traffic, and dashed across the street and began looking for apartment 3-C.

He heard the doorbell buzzing somewhere in the apartment and then steps walking quickly to the door. It opened, and he was looking at a very attractive girl. She had green eyes and very deep auburn hair that curled around her shoulders. A smattering of freckles covered her narrow face.

Not too bad, Lee, not bad looking at all.

Then she smiled a big toothy smile showing; that was a mistake. Her teeth were discolored and twisted. If that wasn't bad enough, she had two large buck teeth.

"Hi. I'm Lee Stewart and you must be . . ." He left it hang there.

"And I am Bobbie Sue Miller from West Virginia. How are you tonight? Won't you come in?"

Hey, he's pretty well put together, but I wish he were in civilian clothes instead of that uniform.

"Have you met my aunt"—she pronounced it 'ont'—"and uncle?"

"No, I haven't," said Lee. He looked aside at the couple approaching the front door where Bobbie Sue and Lee stood.

The man stuck his hand out for Lee to shake. "Hello, Lee. I'm Greg, and this is my wife, Susan. Looks like you've already met Bobbie Sue." Susan was looking him up and down. For the life of him, Lee couldn't tell if she approved or not.

"How do you do, Lee? Please call me Susan," she said as she continued to shake his hand. "Rosalie has told me all about you, Lee. Come on in and sit down for a few minutes. Then, you can tell us your plans for tonight with Bobbie Sue."

Greg and Susan sat on the overstuffed yellow sofa-bed and Bobbie Sue and Lee were in matching overstuffed yellow chairs facing the sofa, but at an angle so they could continue to size each other up.

Lee cleared his throat, thankful that his mother had slipped an additional twenty dollar bill in his hand with the keys to the car. "Well, not knowing Bobbie Sue, I made some temporary plans that can be changed." He turned directly to the girl. "Bobbie Sue, do you like Italian food?"

"I don't know, Lee. I've never been to an Italian restaurant before. Did you plan to go dutch?"

Shocked, Lee said, "No, I didn't. I made reservations at The Blue Grotto. Can't think of a better way to get acquainted than over dinner, can you?"

"Well, no, but I didn't expect that on a blind date." Lee looked at her, flicked a glance at the Millers, and stood up.

"Bobbie Sue, would you like to go to dinner at The Blue Grotto with me tonight?"

She laughed. "Since you ask so nicely—yes. I'll just be a minute. Have to get my coat and hat."

Lee watched as she disappeared into her room.

Susan spoke up. "Lee, why didn't you wear your civilian clothes?"

Lee looked puzzled. "First of all, I don't have any civvies. I'm not allowed to have civilian clothes aboard ship. Second, this Dress Blue uniform is considered formal enough to wear to black-tie occasions." Susan nodded acceptance and didn't say anything more. She saw that Lee was put off by the question.

Bobbie Sue appeared in her coat and feathered hat. Lee opened the front door for her and looked back at the Millers.

"We should be back well before midnight, folks."

At The Blue Grotto, Bobbie Sue had three glasses of burgandy to go with her dinner. As a result, she was feeling a little gayer than earlier. She had pouted when Lee had to show his age and do without wine. Bobbie Sue had not been aware that Lee was only eighteen. Not knowing her age, he was a little defensive when he said he would turn nineteen, January fifteenth. Shocked, she didn't let on she was nearly twenty-four.

Lee checked the bill their waiter had left. Her linguine with clam sauce, the wine, and his sea bass in sour cream sauce came to $11.24. He carefully added $1.25 as a tip, and they left. The temperature had dropped and snow threatened to shorten their first evening out.

He started the engine and moved the temperature control to hot without turning on the fan yet.

"Brrrr, it's cold in here," she called, huddled next to her door with her coat wrapped tightly around her.

"Why don't you slide over here and I'll hold you in my peacoat until the car warms up."

She gave him a sideways glance in the near dark. "Can I trust you?" Lee unbuttoned his peacoat and held it open. Bobbie Sue quickly slid across the seat and snuggled up as close as she could get with her head on his shoulder. He wrapped the peacoat as far around her as he could.

The engine was beginning to race, so he tapped the pedal. Immediately, the engine idled back to that tinny Ford motor sound and rumbled quietly. Still holding her, Lee leaned forward and turned the fan on high to warm the car. Leaning back, she snuggled a little closer and murmured "Thank you, Lee, that was a very nice place to take me on our first date." She stretched up and barely touched her lips to the corner of his mouth.

Lee cleared his throat. "Can we try that again?" Bobbie Sue buried her head in his chest. A muffled no was his answer.

For twelve bucks, all I get is a little peck?

He was still considering that answer when she started speaking.

"When we have gone out together enough times, we can go steady. Then, you can have as many kisses as you want, Lee."

"Jeez, not even good night kisses?"

Her head popped up, eyes wide. "Lee Stewart, what kind of a girl do you think I am? We just met a couple of hours ago. No, you can't have a good night kiss until we have dated a while." She straightened up and folded her arms across her chest.

Do I want this?

"And you know what else, Lee? Once we're engaged . . .

Wait a minute!

"I'll let you have all kinds of nice liberties—only with your hands, of course."

She certainly has my life planned out. No thanks, lady. Time to take you home.

He leaned over and kissed her forehead. "Gee, thanks, Bobbie Sue. You've really given me encouragement. I'll get you home so Susan and Greg don't think badly of me."

She nodded and smiled sweetly.

She doesn't get it!

6:30PM, December 13, 1949
The Ivan Stewart Residence
8364 Chesapeake Street
Norfolk, Virginia

Seaman Apprentice Lee Stewart sat cross-legged on the living room floor in his Mom and Dad's house, a Camel cigarette dangled from his mouth. The steam-heated apartment was so stuffy he had pulled his jumper off and wore only his dress blues trousers. The rest of his uniform—neckerchief included—were on the sofa on top of his inside out folded dress blue jumper; wallet, Camel cigarettes, Zippo lighter, loose coins, and his handkerchief were gathered in his upside down white hat. Besides, this was his folks' home and he didn't have to be on his best behavior.

No civvies though.

When his civilian clothes and effects were sent home from Boot Camp in San Diego to his mother, she had gathered up all of his clothes and washed, pressed, folded and put them back in a suitcase.

First time Lee showed up at his folks' house in Norfolk, his mother brought out the suitcase with all the stuff he shipped home from Boot Camp. Opening it, he stared at its contents. He remembered stuffing everything that wasn't issued at Boot Camp back in a suitcase to be shipped home in Bremerton, Washington.

But his Mom had obviously been in the case. Too bad: he tried on the cord slacks and jeans but those didn't fit him anymore. He didn't even bother trying the shirts. Boot Camp had changed his physique for all time.

Besides, Lee lived aboard ship where enlisted personnel were not allowed to have civvies, even if there was room to store them. He planned to visit one of the tailor shops or locker clubs that populated the streets just outside the Main Gate at the Norfolk U.S. Navy Operating Base. He needed to pick up a pair of jeans or slacks and some kind of shirt.

His Mom and Dad met the ship when it arrived at Pier 4, Naval Operating Base a few days ago. He was sleeping over at his folks' house tonight. His father, Lieutenant Ivan Stewart, USN, promised to drop young Stewart off at the Chilton in the morning, at least at the head of the pier, before going on to his own ship, the USS Siboney CVE-114.

What was left of Mom's special Tom and Jerry batter sat on the kitchen table: bottles of bourbon, brandy, and scotch, surrounded by empty mugs, guarded the batter. Several of their friends had and would be stopping by for Christmas cheer. Steam rose from hot water simmering on the stove.

His Mom, Wilma Stewart, said she didn't mind if Lee had a few Tom and Jerrys tonight. It was a special night while the three of them decorated the house for the holidays. After all, he was in the Navy and nearly nineteen. It didn't take a sharp eye to see the family resemblance. His mother's dark blonde hair and blue green eyes and his father's somewhat square head with wavy hair and height were passed to Lee.

"You know, Mom, you ought to break loose and buy new lights," suggested Lee. "Trying to find the dead light in this series string is for the birds." Lee wore his fine blond hair in the military crew cut style. As usual for a young man, his clean-cut features had a scattering of blackheads and pimples that teenagers endure.

He and his father had two known good Christmas tree lights and were working in from both ends of the string of colored lights, unscrewing one and screwing in the good one, looking for the burned out lamp.

"Maybe I will when the after-Christmas sales begin. Wouldn't you two be smarter if you used that good string to test all the lights on that one? What if there were two or more burned out?"

The senior Stewart looked at his son and grinned wryly. "What do you say we start over and do it like your mother says, Lee?"

Lee nodded in disgust.

"Lee, I forgot to ask you—how was your date with Bobbie Sue last night?"

Lee laughed aloud, looking at his mother, hanging ornaments on the other side of the tree.

He moved his head and frowned as he tried to remove his cigarette glued to his lower lip.

"She's a mantrap, Mom. In a few weeks, I can kiss her goodnight. Her schedule has us getting married next summer. But thanks for letting me use the car. Your new Ford is really neat."

"You going to see her again?"

He made a rude sound and his Dad snickered.

"You tell your buddies, Rosalie and Irish, they got to do better than that if they want to stay on my good side, but thank Rosalie for her effort. I did appreciate the try. Did you meet Bobbie Sue, Mom?"

"No, but I saw a recent photo of her. I thought she was a good looking gal, Lee."

"Then, you missed her smile. That ruins everything; really bad teeth. Not even sure I want to kiss her. Anyway, I shook hands at the door and came home."

"Lee, you and I better have another Tom and Jerry, and I'll tell you how I met your mother," chuckled his Dad.

She looked through the Christmas tree at them with amusement. "Yeah, and you and Lee can toss a coin to see who sleeps on the sofa and who sleeps on the floor, if you do."

Lee looked back and forth at his Mom and Dad, wondering what that was all about. She slipped to the table to make three more Tom and Jerrys. The batter was almost gone.

"I'll mix a new batch of Tom and Jerry batter. Then, I think we ought to sit down and reflect upon this Christmas."

Sitting there listening to Christmas carols on the 78-rpm phonograph, sipping on her Tom and Jerry, Lee's mother thought of something and looked at Lee.

"Lee, how about that money you owe Olympic Junior College? Are you ever going to pay that off?"

Lee nodded. "Already done, Mom; all of it. Not only that, I took the United States Armed Forces Institute (USAFI) first-year college level examination and passed it."

"That's wonderful!"

"Yeah. Sometime in the next year, I plan to take the second-year college level exam after I hit the books for a while. The Second Year exam is a lot tougher. Most colleges accept the USAFI scores to meet their entrance requirements and some colleges even give credit for two years."

"Then, you'd only have two years to do for your Bachelor's Degree?"

Lee nodded at his mother again.

"That's grand. Keep it up."

Lt. Stewart looked at his son thoughtfully. "You know, Lee," he said, "with two years of college credits according to USAFI, you just might qualify for OCS."

Lee looked at his Dad grimly. "Not quite so, Dad. I checked with Personnel. According to them, OCS requires two years of campus time, not USAFI."

His Dad sipped his Tom and Jerry and shook his head. "I didn't know that. Keep trying, son. Just keep trying."

Lee was happy to be with his folks. This was a night to remember. Here he was, sitting with them, smoking and drinking a Christmas Tom and Jerry, relaxed and kidding around. It was the first time he had been treated as an adult instead of a high school teenager, one who could be kidded, and be part of serious conversations.

It was not always this way. The closer Lee had drawn to his eighteenth birthday, the more strained the relations with his mother. Dad, in the Navy, was away most of the time. That meant his mother decided most family values and she kept a very tight rein on her son.

December 25, 1949
The Ivan Stewart Residence

8364 Chesapeake Street
Norfolk, Virginia

Mom had asked if Lee would like to invite some of his friends on the Chilton to Christmas dinner. Lee invited Deak and the other three remaining Sidecleaners home for Christmas dinner. They didn't really connect that his Dad was in the Navy until they went to the closet for their peacoats and hats to return to the ship. His Dad's bridgecoat with Lieutenant's bars on the shoulders was hanging among theirs.

JANUARY 1950

January 25
U.S.S. Chilton APA-38
NOB, Norfolk, Virginia

With less than three weeks before the end of Stewart's Enlisted Volunteer hitch, Deak said he wanted to talk to him.

"Get a cup from the coffee shack and I'll meet you up on the Foc'sl," he said and walked forward looking over the Port side as he went.

Stewart got a cup of coffee, walked forward checking over the Starboard side as he went, and joined Deacon Jones, BM2, who was sitting on one of the wildcats. Stewart checked to make sure the white paint was dry and sat down on the other one.

"What's up, Deak?" he asked. Stewart pulled out a Camel and lit up. Deak was in a talking mood and he was pretty sure what was coming.

"Stew, it's time to shit or get off the pot. Are you going to ship over or get out?"

Oh boy! This is going to be some tough shit.

"If you ship over, the Captain will make you Seaman for shipping over."

Hmm! That's a break.

"Second, if you don't fuck up, in six months you can take the Fleetwide Competitive examination for Boatswain's Mate Third—BM3."

Damn, that's new.

"The way you stack up against the other guys here, you might make it first, almost surely the second time around." Deak took a drag while he stared at Stewart.

"Also, next week you are going to be named a qualified Assault Boat Coxswain, as a seaman deuce." "This ain't bad for a kid just turned nineteen last week. What say, Stew?" Then he took a sip of his coffee while continuing to watch Stewart.

Ah, crap!

Lee stirred reslessly on the wildcat and sipped his coffee. Took a drag on his Camel and squinted at Deak.

That's what I was afraid of. The Chilton is dangling a couple of big carrots in front of me to keep me in and on board.

Many sailors, even a chief, had left and were leaving because of the big pay loss Congress handed to service men and women a few months ago. Deak had already lost his BM3 assistant and Leading Seaman to the Hardship Discharge operation. But that would be the end of the line.

Even as a real junior seaman, my chances of advancing to Petty Officer Third were fairly good. However, beyond that to BM2 and BM1: very slim to non-existent, and slim was over the hill. I want ET school at Great Lakes. Right now, I'm simply a sailor with no specialty. But if I accept the offer, I'll never see ET school. This conversation was grim and going to be worse.

"Look Deak, I want to go to ET school, you know that. I could have been striking for ET right now if my request to transfer to the ET Gang had been approved, and I would have shipped over on board. If I ship over on board, I'm going to ask for ET school. All my grades and the special electronics test will put me in ET school in a couple of months."

"If you ask for ET school, Stew, the Captain is going to forward it recommending disapproval because you are needed here and are a qualified Assault Boat Coxswain, now in short supply. Also, if you ask for school, the Captain is not going to make you Seaman just to have you say thank you very much, good-bye!"

"Instead, it's fuck you very much, is that it, Deak?" Suddenly, Stewart's coffee turned sour. He got up and walked over to the side and looked down. His Side Cleaner crew was still leaning into the hawser forcing the camel to wedge the ship outward from the pier. It was very slow but you can move a ship.

Before the next storm arrives, we have painting to do.

"Deak, do I tell Personnel I want to transfer to the Receiving Station, or do you?"

"Stew, they won't let you do that. The only way you're going to get off this ship is to go for discharge."

Deak, the ever-smiling sailor, was not smiling. He stubbed his cigarette on the bottom of his shoe, threw the butt over the side, and walked away.

Stewart sat down on a bitt and watched Deak walk away. He knew he just lost a good friend and counselor, saying effectively that being a Boatswain's Mate wasn't good enough for him. That wasn't it, really. He wouldn't be able to advance through the ranks like his Dad had done if he became a Boatswain's Mate because there was no room at the top. He felt like throwing his coffee mug over the side.

Cripes.

BM1's were taking the test for BMC knowing even before they sat down to take the test, not one BM1 would advance to Chief Boatswain's Mate in the entire Navy, maybe for several years.

They did it just to keep up the practice against the day some BMC billets would reappear. Stewart also knew that Deak wanted him as his assistant. Deak had already talked him into staying in the Side Cleaners instead of going to the First Division.

It felt good to be trusted with a P-boat. However, this is not a career.

He walked aft to the Personnel Office. Stewart knocked on the closed door to Personnel. It wasn't that many months ago he came aboard and knocked on the door to check him into the ship's complement. Now he wanted out.

The top half opened and Quinn, the Yeoman First looked at him in surprise.

"Hey Stewart, I was just going to send for you to sign your new shipping articles. You want to do it now?"

Stewart's belly tensed up knowing this was not going to be a pleasant interview. He didn't know why they were sure he was shipping over. He looked grimly at Quinn.

"Deak has been dreaming too much, Quinn. I'm not shipping over on the Chilton."

Quentin looked at Stewart in surprise but quickly recovered.

"Stewart, do you know that Jones spent a lot of time convincing the First Lieutenant to advance you to Seaman and change your primary Navy Job Code to Assault Boat Coxswain? He really busted his balls for you, shitbird."

Stewart sighed.

This was not going to be easy.

He looked at Quentin straight on, eyeball to eyeball.

"No, I didn't know that, Quentin, but that cuts no ice. There is absolutely no future in being a Boatswain's Mate. First time you order a BM3 test for me, I'm locked in. I want to go to ET school. The Captain won't let me go. I quit."

When he finished, it was Quinn studying the top of his dutch door. He knew Stewart was correct.

"I thought you were a lifer, Stewart.   Out of curiosity, what are your plans?" Quinn asked.

Stewart shrugged. He had given thought to that and had worked it out.

"After I check into the Receiving Station over there, I'm going to march up to Personnel breathing fire and say I changed by mind, I want to ship over if I can go to ET school. They aren't going to send me back to the Chilton. When I take my reenlistment leave, I'm checking into Pier 91 in Seattle. That's about as far as I can get from good ole Nofuck Virginia."

Quinn nodded. "Come see me Monday for your checkout chit, Stewart." Stewart nodded and walked away. He had a long weekend to spend with his folks and break the news.

FEBRUARY

February 3, 1950
U.S. Naval Receiving Station,
Norfolk, Virginia

It wasn't that Stewart was shunned. Since he kept mostly to himself, only Deak, Chief Neal, and Jones BMSN really knew him. Since they believed he was double-crossing them, there were no good-byes. He stopped by Personnel with his packed seabag and gym bag to pick up his records and orders.

He knocked on the upper half-door. It swung open with Quinn's questioning face looking at him.

"There you are, Stewart. You know the drill. Keep a clean nose and maybe you will get ET school. At least, I do see your point."

"Thanks Quinn. You're about the only one talking to me, so I'm ready to leave."

Stewart heaved his seabag to his shoulder, grabbed his gym bag with records and orders, and walked to the After Quarterdeck. The Quartermaster of the Watch copied his orders into the rough log and took one copy of his orders for the record.

Stewart picked up everything and turned to the Officer of the Deck, saluting.

"Sir, I have been transferred to the Receiving Station. Request permission to leave the ship."

"Permission granted, Stewart," the Officer of the Deck, an ensign, replied returning his salute. "Good luck in civilian life."

Stewart nodded, turned aft to the Colors, saluted, and left the ship. Off the brow, he set his seabag down and looked at the ship. Deak was watching him and Stewart waved. Deak turned away without responding.

I guess that's that!

Stewart checked into the Receiving Station Norfolk about ten blocks from the Chilton. Fortunately, it was only a few steps on to the bus, and a few more steps off the bus at the Receiving Station, a beautiful steam-heated brick building. The next day Stewart dropped by Personnel and announced he had changed his mind. He wanted to ship over for six years, in exchange for going to ET school in Great Lakes; he would take his thirty day reenlistment leave at his Home of Record, Bremerton, Washington.

Only two changes to his plan: the Personnel Yeoman said Stewart couldn't make his requests for duty assignments until after he reported in from shipping over leave.

Well, I can live with that, I guess.

Since he was going back to Bremerton, he would report into the Navy Receiving Station at Pier 91, Seattle, for processing and assignment. Stewart didn't see any problem with that. That was also good because it meant he would report to school from the Pacific Fleet and would return to some ship in the Pacific Fleet.

The Barracks Master-At-Arms looked at Stewart, incredulously. "You're a Seaman Deuce and you're shipping over for six years? You are out of your rabbit ass mind, kid!" He knew Stewart had slipped around the bend. Stewart was the only man to ship over in a week that saw literally hundreds of sailors being discharged for hardship because Congress had given the Military Services another 'pay raise'.

Because of the infamous congressional pay revision in July 1949, the Armed Forces began to have federal income tax withheld from their meager pay. Married men really felt the crunch of the changed pay, and many career sailors left the service, even some that had shipped over just a few days before the bill passed.

There were so many sailors getting out on Hardship Discharges in the Norfolk area that all hands waiting for hardship discharge were moved into World War Two temporary wooden 'X' barracks down by the Naval Operating Base piers. The 'X' barracks, long due for destruction, hadn't been torn down owing to lack of funds. Instead, the 'X' barracks were reactivated in January '50 to handle the hundreds of men being discharged. The regular Receiving Station Barracks could only accept twenty-five or thirty transient sailors at a time.

Horror stories were coming out of the 'X' barracks. Most of the toilets stopped up and spilled over. Wash basins' plumbing didn't work. No steam heat in a very cold January and February. Cold water showers.

Just maybe Stewart wasn't out of his rabbit ass mind. Captain Brown's ship, the U.S.S. Missouri BB-63, had just gone aground on Thimble Shoals.

The Receiving Station was ordered to stop discharging the men. Help was needed on the Missouri. Dischargees began offloading stores and ammo from the Missouri: your rate didn't matter. As a future civilian, you were now a grunt: squat and strain, sucker! Discharges were delayed about one month as they worked on barges or deep in the bowels of the Missouri, or learned to splice hawsers together.

On the other hand, Stewart, that silly fucking Seaman Deuce who didn't have enough sense to come in out of the rain, was relaxing in establishment brick barracks with steam heat, hot showers, great single level bunks with 4-inch mattresses, highly polished linoleum decks, and liberty every night.

The soon-to-be-discharged personnel stood in very, very long lines to eat breakfast and evening chow, and to carry box lunches out to the Missouri. Stewart ate with Station Personnel, going to the Mess Hall with 'head-of-the-line' privilege.

Just have to bide my time until Personnel gives me my Ruptured Duck pin, Honorable Discharge, DD-214, back pay plus travel pay to Home of Record (Bremerton, Washington) and then swear me in for a six-year tour of duty.

For nearly two weeks Stewart was a sightseer with no duties. He roamed the Naval Operating Base piers looking at the great battleship New Jersey, several beautiful heavy cruisers, the big aircraft carriers, and the 'Gator Fleet. He didn't get to the destroyers and submarines because they had their own base, the Destroyer Piers and Submarine Piers, somewhere else.

When that became boring, Stewart visited the library and read books. Too young to drink, his evenings were spent in the Barracks playing pinocle, going to the Station Theater to see a movie, or visiting his folks. His folks would like him to stay with them but to do that, he had to sleep on a lumpy sofa. With only a few dollars in his pocket, the City of Norfolk was not on his list of places to visit.

0845, February 15, 1950
Personnel Office
U.S. Naval Receiving Station
Norfolk, Virginia

Finally!

"Stewart, Lee H. Lay to the Master-At-Arms office." He got off his bunk where he had been reading an old magazine and walked a dozen steps to the window.

"Stewart here."

"Okay Stewart. We're going to start processing you for re-enlistment. If everything is up to snuff, the Personnel Officer will swear you in late this afternoon. Okay?"

"Great."

"Good. First thing you do is lay out your bag for inspection."

"Aw crap, is that really necessary?"

"Yep. We have to make sure you have a complete bag upon discharge and re-enlistment. Any shortages must be replaced this morning. If you are short of money, your pay record will be docked for the amount you are short. Any questions?"

"Yeah. Where do I spread it out?"

"No sweat. This isn't a drill field, Stewart. Lay everything on your bunk. We just need to count. Any items at the cleaners, show us the ticket. Call us when you're ready."

At least I don't have to get down on my hands and knees to place everything just so, like in Boot Camp.

Stewart turned his seabag upsidedown on his bunk and shook everything out. It took about fifteen minutes to sort everything for the MAA to check.

"Hey Boats, I'm ready."

The Boatswain's Mate First looked at Stewart, set down his coffee cup, and got up. He grabbed the clipboard with seabag form on it and strolled out to Stewart's bunk.

Unbeknownst to Stewart, the Boats had already checked everything off and signed the form. But he made the motion of counting Stewart's bag.

"Okay Stewart. Everything is shipshape. At 1330, report to Personnel."

Stewart sighed in relief and began repacking his seabag. He would be ready to leave as soon as he was sworn in, and paid.

At 1330, he was sitting next to the Personnel Yeoman going over his record while Stewart began signing papers. The formula for reenlistment bonus for a six-year contract worked out to: 6 years times $60 per year for $360.00. Travel to Stewart's home of record, Bremerton, Washington, 3183 railroad miles @ 5¢ per mile, gave him the princely travel sum of $159.15. Stewart also had his final pay and unused leave on the books. He was ready to leave Norfolk with a resounding $581.65, in traveler's checks and cash: a nice, tidy sum in February 1950.

Stewart's official discharge paper, the form DD214, showed that he had not earned any service ribbons, medals, or other commendations. He had kept his nose clean, with 4.0 Conduct. Stewart had completed 0 years, 8 months, 14 days of sea duty. Further, he completed Practical Factors for Seaman with a grade of 3.92; and had taken Navy Training Courses for Seaman and Boatswain's Mate Third Class, with grades of 3.96 and 3.87, respectively.

Stewart was eligible for advancement to Seaman when recommended, and when he passed any command's Seaman Examination, but not as long as he was an USN-EV. As Stewart was reenlisting, his DD-214 remained in his Service Record. His enlisted Navy status changed from USN-EV to USN.

Yea!

Since the Chilton had not put in a recommendation for advancement to Seaman because he left the ship to be discharged, he was not advanced upon shipping over.

At 1345, he stood at attention in front of the Personnel Officer and repeated the vows he had made when he first joined the Navy in Seattle on February 15, 1949. This time, the Personnel Officer shook his hand and congratulated him on a fine decision.

February 15, 1950
Re-enlistment Leave
Norfolk, Virginia

Lee had gone to his folk's house the night before to have dinner and say good-bye. It was a misty-eyed occasion, for they did not know when they would see each other again. They sat around the kitchen table talking about his plans and the near future. He wanted to see Washington, D.C., and New York City before taking military hops to NAS Sand Point in Seattle. He would be in touch when he arrived at the

Naval Training Center, Great Lakes, near Chicago, Illinois, for ET school.

Stewart had learned he could hitch a ride in a Navy plane at NAS Norfolk to NAS Floyd Bennett Field in New York City. Stewart had 'scoped out his travel plans carefully to conserve his money. He wanted to visit New York City and climb the Statue of Liberty's arm to the torch, go to the top of the Empire State Building, see Times Square, and visit some of the other fine places.

In New York City, Lee discovered he was old enough, now nineteen-years-old, to drink liquor. At the U.S.O., he received a ticket to a musical and enjoyed a good evening of that. Watching his wallet carefully, staying at the Abraham Lincoln Hotel, and walking a lot, he managed to go to the top of the Empire State Building, climb the Statue of Liberty up to the torch, see the Rockettes, and walk around Times Square: all the sights he had planned. When Lee was ready to leave New York City, he went back to NAS Floyd Bennett and hitched a ride to NAS Anacostia in Washington, D.C.

Lee used another couple of days sightseeing around the Capitol. There were so many things to see. In one day, Lee managed to go to the top of the Washington Monument and walk down the stone stairs, visit the Lincoln and Jefferson Memorials, and visit one of the Smithsonian Museums.

He got to visit the House of Representatives in the Capital Building and meet his Congressman, even though he wasn't old enough to vote yet. Stewart was thrilled to salute President Harry S. Truman who doffed his hat to him, as he arrived at the White House in his limousine.

At Bolling Field, Stewart checked in at Operations and signed up for an air hop toward Seattle. Completing that, he found his way to the PX cafeteria. He enjoyed a good deluxe hamburger, potato chips, and coke for lunch, and struck up a friendly conversation with an Air Force Captain sitting next to him.

Finished with his lunch, Stewart leaned back and sucked in his breath to pull out his wallet tucked under his blue trouser waistband. Checking the slip, he laid a two-dollar bill on the counter to pay for lunch. The Captain spotted the bill and cleared his throat.

"Sailor, would you mind terribly if I exchanged that Two Dollar bill for two one-dollar bills?"

Stewart wondered if the Captain had gone round the bend. He smiled, "No skin off my teeth, Captain. Go right ahead."

Still the same money.

The Captain laid two ones on the counter and carefully picked up the Two Dollar bill and placed it in his wallet. Stewart picked up one of the dollar bills and left the other one to pay his bill and leave a dime tip. Leaning back, he slipped his wallet over the top of his trousers.

The Captain looked at Stewart with a serious expression on his face. "I'm saving them for my daughter's college fund," in way of explanation. "You catching a flight here?" He asked Stewart.

Stewart nodded as he sipped his coffee. "I'm trying to get to NAS Sand Point in Seattle."

The Captain acknowledged that with a big smile. "How would you like a ride in a B25 as far as Wright-Patterson Field?"

"Captain, I'd get in trouble with that Sergeant at the Flight Desk because there is a big sign . . ."

"I know all about that sign," the Captain interrupted. "Would you like a ride or not?"

"Well, yes sir, I would," smiling with a broad grin.

"Good. I'll take it up with the Sergeant. You grab your duffel bag and meet me over by that door," he said pointing to the double doors to the flight line.

"Aye aye, sir," responded Stewart, automatically.

The Captain glanced at Stewart and smiled at the unusual reply. Then he walked over to the Flight Desk as Stewart headed for his seabag. He watched the Captain talking with the Sergeant. Suddenly, the Sergeant straightened to attention as the Captain leaned forward into the Sergeant's face, forcefully tapping his manifest. The Captain turned, looking for Stewart. Finding him, he beckoned and Stewart threw his seabag over his shoulder and walked up to the Desk.

"Sailor, I don't even know your name, but if you will give it to the Sergeant, he will happily include it on my manifest and we will be on our way." Turning to the Sergeant, he said, "Isn't that right, Sergeant?"

"Yes sir, Captain."

Stewart gave the required information to a glowering Sergeant and trotted after the Captain. The Captain, his copilot, engineer, radio-gunner, and tail-gunner, with Stewart tagged as a waist-gunner, walked forever along the flight line until they reached their B25. He was amazed an Air Force Captain would go to all that trouble just because he let him take his two dollar bill in exchange for two ones.

What kind of people does the Air Force breed?

Stewart got off the B25 after an ear-shattering ride, late at night in the middle of freezing Ohio. Lucky him, a few minutes later Stewart was on the manifest of a Flying Boxcar, used to drop paratroopers. The temperature was in the teens on the ground and got colder after the plane got to altitude. All the passengers complained how frigid it was. The plane commander, from the warmth of his heated suit, suggested the passengers exercise. He hastily changed his mind when all the passengers began running back and forth, upsetting the plane's trim.

Eventually, Stewart rode in a Naval Air Transport Service (NATS) R4D to NAS Sand Point, Seattle, Washington.

Lee Stewart immediately caught a bus across town to the waterfront and boarded the silver ferry, Kalakala, back to Bremerton and checked into the YMCA. Lee was eager to look up his old friends and classmates from high school and college again.

People had moved away, and with those left, he just didn't fit in. Lee took the bus up to Eastpark where he had lived. It was eerie looking at his old house at 179-F Magnuson Way, because different people and kids lived there now.

He went next door and knocked. Mrs. Jensen answered the door and swept him into her arms, crying happily. She and Mr. Jensen fed him dinner, asking about life in the Navy. Larry had written about the wild meeting on the landing boat he was on, and their plans to get together in Waikiki after the war games.

Unfortunately, the soldiers were quarantined at Schofield Barracks for about a week, while they were issued new gear for severe winters and got shots for the Far East. Then they boarded the transports and headed for Japan.

Larry's mother gave Lee Larry's new address and told him that Larry was heading for an Army camp somewhere in Hokkaido, Japan. Lee hated to say goodbye and promised to write them with his new address.

Back downtown, he stepped into the Downtowner Cafe for some coffee and spotted another friend in Air Force blues at the counter. Lee walked up behind him and shook his rotating stool. Bill Stuart, turning, caught the Navy uniform and started to growl.

Lee smiled at him, took his white hat off and bowed low. "Hey, Bill, how's the Air Force?"

An uneasy waitress turned away, smiling. She understood that two hometown boys just found each other.

"Air Force is fine. It's Bremerton, I don't understand anymore," he growled. Bill stood up and squeezed Lee's shoulders.

"Damn, you look good, Lee. Navy seems to be treating you okay."

Lee and Bill had coffee and pie and teased the waitress unmercifully after they introduced themselves. She thought they were brothers, or at worst, cousins.

"Well, Lee, what do you want to do for the rest of the evening?"

"You know, I bet I can get us free tickets to the Roxy again." They marched arm in arm around the corner and down the street much to the amusement of passersby. At the Roxy, his old boss had come back for a visit and gave them complimentary tickets for their entire stay in Bremerton. Thanking him profusely, they went into the darkened theater and sat where Lee had sat down the last time he was here.

"Hey Bill, the last time I was here, Edith Zimmerman came in and we went back up by the projection booth to play around. Lots of good feels but nothing else."

"You're puttin' me on, Lee. Edith Zimmerman? Couldn't get to first base with her in school."

"Well, I tell you, we had a hot time of it playing stink finger and such until the lights came on."

"Yeah, well where did you sit, wise guy?"

"Hey, Bill. No shit. Less than five minutes and we were petting pretty good."

There is absolutely no way to prove this to Bill, dammit. He just knows this is another sea story.

Lee looked back at the screen.

A couple of minutes later, he glanced at the figure coming up the aisle.

"Holy shit!" he gasped, and nudged Bill. "Speak of the devil, here's Edith. You want to play? I don't want another case of lover's nuts from her."

Bill looked at him and at the girl coming closer. "Sure. Can you introduce me?"

As chance would have it, Edith sat down immediately in front of them. Lee waited for her to settle down.

"Hey, Edith, how's it going?" She whirled around in her seat and looked at him.

"Oh, for God's sake, it's you again, Lee. Got room for me up there?"

"Sure. Let me move over a seat and you can sit between Bill and me. You know Bill Stuart, don't you?"

Edith turned to Bill and looked carefully at him. "Nooo, I don't think I do, Lee."

"Edith. Now you've done it. My feelings are hurt. I sat ahead of you in Lit 2A in Mrs. Frazier's class."

Edith moved her head closer to Bill and looked again. "Oh, God, I do remember. How are you and what are you two doing here?" She looked back and forth between them.

Lee realized two things: She was wearing exactly the same thing as last summer, and she either needed glasses or wasn't wearing them. "Listen folks. I'm tuckered out and want to go back to the Y and crash. You two stay here and enjoy the movie. Good to see both of you again."

Stewart checked out of the Y after three days in Bremerton and headed for the Navy Receiving Station at Pier 91 in Seattle. He didn't see Bill Stuart again.

1335, February 26, 1950
U.S. Naval Receiving Station Pier 91
Seattle, Washington

The Yeoman First Class studied Stewart's orders and leave papers.

"Stewart, you can't stay here or eat chow here while you're on leave."

"I understand that. I'm checking in off leave, Quills. Ready to go to school."

"But you still have nineteen days to go on your thirty day shipping over leave. You sure you want to check in, Stewart?"

"Yeah, it's advance leave anyway. Don't know anyone back in Bremerton anymore."

The Yeoman nodded and tore open Stewart's records. "It says here your Home of Record is Bremerton." He looked at Stewart questioningly.

"Dad's in the Navy, too, and the family is living in Norfolk now. Can I change my Home of Record to there?"

"Sure, we'll take care of that here. Take this slip to the Master-At-Arms in the barracks. He will assign you a bunk and work detail while you're our guest, Stewart. Come back tomorrow morning after 0800 muster. Then, we'll have our interview to see what we can do for you."

Stewart nodded, threw his seabag over his shoulder and headed out the door.

Never pulled liberty in Seattle. It's going to be a while before my orders to ET School come in. We'll just give 'er a whirl and see what happens.

He crossed the street and entered the barracks.

A smiling Master-At-Arms took his check-in chit and studied it. "You just passing through, Stewart?"

"Yeah, gotta go through Classification but hope to get ET school."

"Well, let's just see what kind of temporary duty we have for you, Stewart."

Oh shit!

"Here it is. Yes indeedy, the Mess Deck Master-At-Arms has been hollering his head off just for you." He grinned at Stewart's look of disgust. "Shouldn't take you more than a half hour to check in at the other places on this list. The good news is, uniform of the day for transients is dungarees, except Dress Blue Able for liberty."

"Able?"

"Yeah. Flat hat and peacoat."

"I thought I'd never use it again."

"Then, you better go on liberty so you can try it out. Mess Cooks liberty doesn't start until 1800, Stewart."

Stewart figured he would be here for less than a month, maybe way less, depending upon which class he was able to catch. All the personal lockers were six feet tall with room to hang coats. He rapidly emptied his seabag and stowed the empty seabag, bottom up for his shoes to rest on.

Wearing dungarees and white hat, he trotted around in the rain, getting his chit signed off. Reporting back to the Barracks Master-At-Arms, he found out that in addition to every thing else, he would stand a seabag inspection tomorrow at 1000. It didn't matter he had stood bag inspection less than three weeks ago. That was there and this was here.

0830, February 27, 1950
Classification Center
U.S. Naval Receiving Station Pier 91
Seattle, Washington

Stewart sat in the straight-backed oak chair next to the Yeoman's desk, watching as Ichien YN1, went through Stewart's personnel jacket.

"Okay, Stewart, it says here you entered the Navy from Bremerton, February 15, 1949, expecting to go to ET school following Boot Camp. Is that correct?"

"Yeah, Ichien. It should also show that I completed all of the tests to qualify for ET school."

"They are here, too. You still want to go to ET school?"

"I sure do."

"Okay. We will list that. However, according to the rules, you must also select your three choices of sea duty, a place for shore duty, and a place for overseas duty."

"Oh, hell. Just put down anything. I want the school."

"Oh, no, Stewart. You do that, not me," and he extended the form to Stewart to fill in the blanks.

Stewart selected destroyers in San Diego, Long Beach and Pearl Harbor; San Francisco for shore duty; and Canal Zone for overseas duty. Of course, he wrote ET in the blank for school. Then as he started to hand it back to Ichien, Ichien spoke up and said, "You gotta sign it, too, Stewart, to show those are your own selections."

He did so. "Is that all there is to it, Ichien?"

"That's it," he responded with a smile. "We'll call you when your orders come in. Meanwhile, you're free to go on liberty every night until they come in—you mess cookin'?"

"Yeah, worse luck."

"Well, don't worry. It shouldn't be too long."

Stewart stood up and stretched. He nodded to Ichien, lit up a cigarette, and headed for the Mess Deck.

I still got that damn bag inspection at 1000.

MARCH

U.S. Naval Station Tongue Point
Astoria, Oregon

U.S. Naval Station Tongue Point is situated on Oyster Bay behind Tongue Point on the Columbia River, about three and a half miles upstream from downtown Astoria, Oregon. Naval Station Tongue Point's mission is to maintain a Reserve Fleet of mothballed amphibious ships, mostly cargo ships, LSTs, and other craft

During World War Two, Navy amphibious patrol bombers, the Martin Mariner PBM amphibian and Consolidated Catalina PBY-5A amphibian, flew from Tongue Point on anti-submarine patrols. They often coordinated possible sightings with blimps from NAS Coos Bay, Oregon. As a Naval Aviator, the current Executive Officer kept up his monthly flight pay hours by flying his Commanding Officer to NAS Sand Point in Seattle, as well as to other air bases.

U.S. Naval Station Tongue Point was desperate. Green ET3, the only Electronics Technician on the base was due for Honorable Discharge in June. Green's assignment was to maintain and repair all military electronic equipment at U.S. Naval Station Tongue Point. That critical job included radar, radio transmitters and receivers, antennas, and associated signaling lines all over the Naval Station and the large Reserve Fleet.

Letters, messages, and several phone calls to Commandant Thirteenth Naval District, District Personnel Office in Seattle, finally produced results. The Bureau of Naval Personnel (BuPers), Washington, D.C., would send a recent graduate of the ET school at the Naval Training Center, Great Lakes, near Chicago, Illinois, to U.S. Naval Station Tongue Point, Astoria, Oregon for duty.

Machine Accounting in BuPers sorted their machine card files looking for a recent graduate of the Electronics Technician school, who was still waiting for assignment. A machine card dropped into the slot. That night, BuPers transmitted a message to U.S. Naval Receiving Station, Seattle, Washington.

0915, March 1, 1950
U.S. Naval Receiving Station Pier 91
Seattle, Washington

"Now hear this—Stewart Lee H, Seaman Apprentice, lay to the Personnel Office on the double—Stewart, Lee H."

"Yaa Hoo, my orders are in!" Stewart screeched. Mess cooking at a Receiving Station didn't turn him on anyway. The Mess Deck Master-At-Arms waved at him, acknowledging he heard the announcement, too. Stewart raced out to the Transient Personnel window, puffing as he arrived.

"Hi, I'm Stewart, Lee H. You called for me?"

"Oh yeah, good news kid," said the old Yeoman Second Class. "You're going to Naval Station Tongue Point in Astoria, Oregon, for duty." He was smiling as he gave Stewart what he thought was pretty choice news.

Stunned, his belly began aching. Stewart asked, "Tongue Point? What the fuck happened to ET school?" The Yeoman gave him a frosty stare.

"Don't know anything about that, but this is where you're going." Desperately, Stewart tried to get out of it.

"But they guaranteed a space in ET school, and I specifically said I did not want shore duty."

The Personnel Yeoman leaned out the dutch window toward Stewart and glared. "Stewart, you're going to Tongue Point. BuPers ordered you to Tongue Point by name. Take this goddamned checkout slip around and be back here with your fuckin' bag and baggage in two hours. You have to catch the noon Greyhound Bus to Portland. Now get your ass in gear."

Stewart was miserable. It was classic: the fickle finger of fate had just fucked him again: just like at Boot Camp and on the Chilton. The purple shaft having been jammed in and rotated, benignly pulled out and moved implacably along.

0945, March 2, 1950
U.S. Naval Station Tongue Point
Astoria, Oregon

A Blue sign with Gold lettering proclaimed this was the Main Gate of U. S. Naval Station Tongue Point, Astoria, Oregon. Stewart grimly reached up and pulled the buzzer cord. He had been either riding buses or waiting for a bus since noon yesterday. He was tired and grimy with bloodshot eyes, and needed a shave. His Dress Blues hadn't seen the inside of a dry cleaning plant for a long time.

The Astoria city bus stopped at the Main Gate and the driver looked at Stewart in his mirror. "Enjoy your stay," he said grinning, as he opened the bus back door. Stewart grimaced in return, pulled his seabag against his belly and shuffled along the aisle, stepping down and off the bus.

A Seaman Guard on duty at the gate watched Stewart walk up from the bus stop and waved him to the Gate House. "Welcome to our little home on the river," he said sourly. "Go on in the Gate House. The Petty Officer of the Guard will log you in and get a ride for you."

Stewart nodded grimly and trudged onward. He carried his seabag and orders into the Gate House, and dropped the seabag on the deck. A Machinist Mate Third Class, (MM3), put down the comic book he was reading and looked up at him.

"Hi, I'm checking in for duty. Where do I go?" asked Stewart, with a friendly smile and warm voice.

The petty officer got up from where he was slouching, came over to the counter, and stuck out his hand. Without a word, he pulled Stewart's orders from the envelope and studied them. He picked up the phone, dialed three digits, and waited for someone to answer, studying Stewart while he waited. "You look like shit, you know that?" he said conversationally. Then he turned to his phone.

"This is Martin, Machinist Mate Third Class, Petty Officer of the Guard at the Main Gate. I've got a SA for Ship's Company up here. You wanna send someone for him?" He listened, then hung up. Martin picked up Stewart's orders to read them again. Then he wrote Stewart's name and other information from his orders into the logbook. He looked up and spoke his first friendly words to Stewart, pointing to a bench.

"Have a seat there, Stewart. Someone will be along shortly."

A gray Dodge van drove through the gate and made a u-turn, stopping next to Stewart. "Throw your seabag in back and pile in, buddy."

Doing as instructed, Stewart hopped in the front seat and watched as the van drove slowly down a long hill, around a three-story building, and pulled up to a yellow brick building and stopped.

"This is our barracks. The Mess Hall is at the other end. Go on in there to the Master-At-Arms shack. He'll fix you up with a bunk and locker, and direct you to Personnel."

Stewart nodded and got out with his gear. He stood looking at the two-story barracks for a moment as the Dodge disappeared around the corner of the building. The air was damp and smelled of the river. Turning, he could see a line of mothballed LST's and other ships riding at lines of mooring buoys in the bay. Shrugging, he grabbed his gear and reported to the M.A.A. shack.

"What's your name, sailor?" The Master-At-Arms held a stubby pencil over an index card, waiting.

"Stewart, Lee H."

Finished writing on the card, he headed out of his office, beckoning Stewart to follow him. He stopped by a double bunk half way along the long barracks. "This upper bunk is yours," he said, and slipped the index card into a holder on the end of the bunk.

"This is your locker," he said, pointing to a six-foot tall, single door locker. "Everything you own, including civvies and seabag, goes in here. There's locker inspection once a year with plenty of notice. Better yet, no bag inspections."

Stewart managed to smile at that. If there was anything worse than a locker inspection, it was a bag inspection. He'd already had five since he left Boot Camp a year ago.

"For right now, throw your seabag on your bunk and get over to Personnel in that three-story building."

Stewart looked where he was pointing through a window and nodded.

"Sheriff, can I get cleaned up first? Been on the road for almost 24 hours. I need a shave and a shower, and I know my dress blues look like shit."

The Master-at-Arms thought about it for a second. "Nah, they just want to get a new head count. You'll have plenty of time after you get checked in. Now, take off to the Admin building. Personnel will direct you to all the places you need to go to get checked in."

Gonna have to get used to long walks around here. Not like back on the Chilton.

With orders and sealed service records in hand, Stewart opened the white door and followed the printed white signs in the long hallway to Personnel. A Yeoman looked up as Stewart leaned against the counter and dropped his records on it. He looked around at the office and saw only the one Yeoman.

"Hi, I'm Stewart. Checking in for duty."

"Be right with you, Stewart. I'm Swensen. Why don't you grab a cup of coffee there in the corner while you're waiting?" The Yeoman Second Class in undress blues was friendly and talked with him as he opened the envelope and pulled out his Service Jacket, Medical Record, Dental Record, and Pay Record.

"Thanks, Swensen. You the only Yeoman here?"

"Only three of us. One is on leave; the other is in Sick Bay. Not much to do anyway. I see you still have the old-fashioned jacket. Well, we'll fix that up in a jiffy."

He handed him a blank check in slip.

"Fill out the top portion of this. You are in Ship's Company, Communications Department. Then I'll give you a little map to find your way to all these offices."

It was not at all like checking in aboard ship. He spent the rest of the day walking around to the various departments around the base. Some civilian lady in the Communications Office on the Second Deck had initialed for the department where he would work. Stewart finally got all the check off spaces initialed and returned to Personnel.

Swensen got up and carried his coffee cup over to the counter where Stewart stood waiting. "Okay, Stewart. You have the rest of the day to get your gear stowed and take care of other personal matters. Our work uniform around here is Undress Blues, without neckerchief, and with white hat." He watched Stewart to make sure he understood. "After 1600, undress blues is still Uniform of the Day on the base. If you have liberty and are going ashore, wear civvies or Dress Blues." Swensen looked Stewart up and down, frowning at his dirty dress blues. "By the way, we lucked out. The base has a cheap dry-cleaning service. Don't have to take things into town. Another good thing, the Navy Exchange stocks some civvies you can buy."

That's a break.

Stewart nodded and knew his dry cleaning bill would have been high until he could afford some civilian clothes.

"If you have the duty, the uniform is undress blues with neckerchief." The Yeoman took a sip of coffee and continued. "You can forget your dungarees. The only time you could possibly wear them is if you're on a dirty work detail, and I don't think your duty assignment involves dirty work."

Stewart looked at him in surprise.

What the hell am I going to be doing?

"Even then, you need a dungaree Pass signed by your Chief. If someone catches you in dungarees without a pass, you're on Report for being out of uniform—okay?" asked the Yeoman with raised eyebrows. Stewart nodded understanding.

"Report to the Naval Station Communications Department for duty tomorrow during Quarters for Muster."

Communications Department? What the hell am I going to do there?

"That's tomorrow morning at 0745 in back of this building. Don't worry, Communications is the only department back there. You won't get lost. Just report to the Chief who is expecting you. He'll tell you what to do."

Stewart nodded, smiling, and walked to the barracks about two hundred yards away.

"Sheriff, is there an iron and ironing board available around here? I'd like to dress up my undress blues and neckerchief, if possible."

The Master-at-Arms smiled, "Gimme your ID Card and I'll loan you the community gear. You getcher ID Card back when you turn in the iron and board.

Stewart carried the gear to his locker. He pulled a couple of wash cloths out and wetted them both, wringing them damp dry. Armed with two wire hangers, he pulled two sets of undress blues out of the locker. With a wash cloth between the iron and uniform, he steam-ironed them to get rid of any wrinkles from being rolled in the seabag. He hung them inside out in his locker and pulled out a couple of white hats and his neckerchief.

Looking at them critically, he decided they would pass inspection.

Okay, I will look sharp tomorrow at Quarters and am set for a couple of days.

"Okay Sheriff, here they are. Can I have my ID Card back?" asked Stewart. "Now, where is the dry cleaning shop?" Getting directions to the other end of the building, he turned in his blues, returned to his bunk and waited for evening chow call.

I'll look for the library tomorrow.

0745, March 3, 1950
Rear of Administrative Building
U.S. Naval Station Tongue Point
Astoria, Oregon

In the morning, Stewart turned the corner of the Admin Building and saw a division lined up for Quarters. He walked up to a Chief who welcomed him with a shit-eatin' grin.

"Fall in, Stewart. We'll have some coffee after Quarters and talk about your duties here."

"Thanks, Chief."

In spite of duty on the Chilton, he still felt uneasy when a Chief talked to him.

"All right sailors, listen up. Our new man here is Stewart. He's going to be working with Green. You'll have a chance to talk with him later."

Stewart liked the friendly smiles looking his way.

Maybe things won't be so bad here after all. I wonder what Green does?

After Quarters, Stewart followed everyone to the Communications Room and hastily accepted a cup of coffee thrust at him by one of the Third Class Radiomen. Everyone seemed to have a particular job to do, so Stewart decided to stand until the Chief was ready for him. The Chief began talking as he inspected Stewart.

"People will be straggling in here until 0830. Look around if you want."

What was that strange look on his face all about? The Chief doesn't like something about me. Now what?

He rapidly stole looks at his uniform and shoes to see what upset the Chief. Stewart had gotten a haircut day before yesterday up at Pier 91, so that wasn't it. He shaved just an hour ago just before breakfast but felt his face just to make sure.

I wonder what's wrong this time?

He looked around with interest. Stewart had checked out the ET and Radio Shack spaces on the Chilton and recognized some of the equipment. There were several different kinds of radios. Each one had a neat little metal speaker attached to it. He could see two Morse code keys in little cubbyholes under each radio. A typewriter sat bolted to a sliding tray in its typing-well below two radios. He knew this was a communication position where radiomen operated on radio circuits. Communication positions lined the entire wall but only two appeared to be active since there was paper in both typewriters, and none of the other positions even had typewriters. As Stewart looked at them, the Chief ambled over with a coffee mug crooked in his finger. He had a friendly smile on his face.

"Stewart, have you any idea what you're looking at?" he asked. Stewart still did not know the Chief's name.

"No, Chief, except these are some kind of radios." He pointed to the paper in the typewriters. "These are some kind of logs because I see timed entries."

"We call those receivers, not radios, Stewart, and those times are Greenwich Mean Time the Navy calls Zebra Time. Why did you call them radios? Don't you know what they are?"

Stewart, puzzled by the question, shook his head and looked at the chief for clarification. Far as he knew, a radio was a radio. What's the difference? The chief had a curious look on his face that made Stewart feel uneasy again. Before he could answer, a Lieutenant Commander walked in, looked him over, and stood frowning while he drew a cup of coffee.

"Stewart, this is Mr. Bowser, Head of the Communications Department, and our Division Officer."

Stewart didn't know whether to salute or shake hands. Instead, he shyly nodded his head.

"Pleased to meet you, sir."

Mr. Bowser nodded and walked into his office.

An older man with rounded, stooped shoulders, wearing clear, plastic-rimmed Navy glasses, walked in carrying his lunch in a paper bag, casually waved to everyone, and sat down at the main desk in the corner.

His hair, what was left of it, was neatly trimmed. He took his time settling into his swivel rocker, fussing with odds and ends on his desk, and putting his brown bag lunch in the bottom right drawer. The Chief waited patiently while the civilian went through his morning ritual. He put his hand on Stewart's back, nudging him toward the older man.

"Stewart, this is Mr. Ned Wetter, a retired Chief Radioman. He is a civil servant who is in charge, under Mr. Bowser. The rest of us come and go, but he is always here. That's why he is so important. Always address him as Mr. Wetter. Okay?"

In the meantime, Mr. Wetter stood and extended his hand in greeting. Stewart shook hands and smiled.

"Chief Nevil didn't quite say it right, Stewart."

So that's his name.

"You take orders from him. I'm just a technical advisor to handle all the radio traffic."

A woman's laughter sounded behind the door and Stewart turned to see to whom this new voice belonged. Chief Nevil spoke up, still chuckling.

"Stewart, this is Helen, the Comm Officer's secretary." Stewart nodded and smiled faintly. She was the sharp-faced brunette who had initialed his check-in chit the day before. Her voice was full of laughter and she was smiling as she spoke. "You best be careful. Ole Ned Wetter is boss here, even the Chief quakes in his boots when he speaks."

Wetter snorted and picked up his pipe. "You'll just have to get used to some of these jokers in here, Stewart. I'm just a poor, innocent civil servant trying to make a buck." That brought on chuckles and laughter from all points.

Some more men in undress blues walked in to begin their morning activities. The Chief beckoned one of them.

"Stewart, this is Green ET3, our only Electronics Technician. You are going to work for him."

Aha! Maybe that's it. There aren't any vacancies at ET school, so the Navy sent me here to begin striking for ET until a slot opens at Great Lakes. I'll have a leg up on the other students in my class at ET school.

Lieutenant Commander Bowser motioned to Chief Nevil and Green to follow him into his office. He sat down at his desk and waved to Green to shut the door.

"What's wrong with Stewart, Chief? He's only a Seaman Deuce. Hell, he doesn't even have an ET's striker badge on his jumper," questioned Bowser.

"I don't know, Mr. Bowser. He wasn't using the correct terminology a few minutes ago when we were talking about the receivers. Called 'em radios. But he knew what the logs were all about," replied Chief Nevil.

"Well, what the hell are we going to do with him? Green here is leaving us in less than ninety days. This kid has got to be checked out on all of the equipment—I mean all of it—before I permit Green to leave."

Green flinched. "Excuse me, sir. On June 12th, I am a civilian and you can't stop that. I'm outa here!"

"I know that," Bowser snapped angrily. "But think how long it took to get a replacement ordered in here—and look what they send us!"

Chief Nevil raised his hand and Mr. Bowser nodded at him. "Sir," the Chief suggested, "let's have Green give him some kind a test to find out what he knows. That way, we'll have an indication of how bad things are."

"Good idea. Green, write up a test with fifty questions. Mix it up. The kind of thing an ET School grad ought to know. Don't use multiple choice. Also, give him some practical exercise to test his equipment knowledge with various kinds of gear here on the base—you got that?"

"Yes, sir. I think I can have it ready for tomorrow morning, sir," affirmed Green.

"Good. Chief, you and Green administer this test tomorrow."

"Aye aye, sir." Chief Nevil motioned to Green and they left the office.

They stood stirring their coffee and looked at Stewart across the room. The Chief looked at Green.

"You think you can put together a good test before tomorrow morning, Green?"

"Yeah, Chief. Got plenty of vacuum tubes, resistors, chokes, capacitors, and the like down in my ET shack. I can test his knowledge of their purpose and some test equipment easy enough."

"Well, that isn't enough. Make sure you get him out to the hanger Control Tower on that Collins Auto-Tune transmitter. That's going to be his meat and potatoes, as many problems as you've had with it."

"Right Chief. Can I go home now and write the written part? All my books and material are there."

"Yeah, go ahead. If something horrible happens, I'll give you a growl to come on back. Otherwise, see you here in the morning with Stewart's written test."

Stewart had no idea he was in a world of hurt. He was only a SA. They knew most ET school grads came out as ET3. The ET school command promoted the top five percent of a graduating class of SA's or SN's to ET2 in appreciation of their electronic knowledge. In response to their lack of skill, the bottom ten percent became designated ET strikers at the SN level: ETSN. Stewart was a SA without an ET specialty badge. They needed to find out just how much Stewart had learned in ET school at Great Lakes.

The next day, the Chief pointed at Stewart and crooked his finger. Stewart came over to his desk.

"Yes, Chief?"

The Chief handed him several sheets of paper. "Stewart, the Commander wants to find out how much you learned at ET school."

Stewart sucked in his breath in shock. "Hey, wait a minute, Chief. I haven't gone to ET school yet. I shipped over in Norfolk and reported in to Pier Ninety-one off shipping over leave. I just put in for ET School. I was waiting at Pier Ninety-one to go to Great Lakes for training."

What's going on here?

Stewart began to panic and back away from the Chief's desk, palms out toward the Chief, shaking his head. He hadn't cracked any textbooks in over a year.

"I see." He shrugged. "Well, take the test anyway."

The Chief doesn't believe me.

"Chief, you don't understand. I'm not an ET. I don't even know why I was transferred here."

The Chief was pissed. He didn't like being interrupted. His mouth looked as if he just tasted shit!

"Stewart," he growled, pointing at a desk, "get over there now and take that fucking test. No more words. Just do it!"

The results would have looked better if Stewart had closed his eyes and dive-bombed the answer sheet. Two questions were on physics and he got them right. The remaining questions were about specific Navy equipment. He didn't have a clue how the named equipment functioned and hadn't the foggiest idea what they expected him to do with or to it. The whole exercise was bizarre.

His college Radio Electricity courses more than a year ago had not prepared him for this! Oh, to be sure, he recognized condensers, inductors, resistors, and some of the vacuum tubes types, even if he did not know their function. He blanked out from tension and could not remember the color code for resistors and condensers, either.

The big practical test was a horror.

> Tune the LR Frequency Meter to 2498kc/s. Connect the LR to the Collins Auto-tuned transmitter and zero-beat the oscillator to this frequency in AM mode on channel 07; load the transmitter on the vertical cone antenna and determine output wattage. Switch the transmitter to Remote and notify the Comm Center that the Collins is ready on Channel 07.

Stewart did not understand the instructions at all. This was followed by a tsk, tsk, tsk'ing from Green as he corrected the answer sheet. That was nothing compared to a one-sided screaming match in the Comm Officer's office with closed door. Stewart was his target.

"Stewart, how in hell did you manage to graduate from ET school? You must have been a crummy student. You didn't even make ETSN, much less ET3! You're not even designated as an ETSA striker."

He wouldn't let Stewart speak. Not only had he not gone to school, but also they were treating him as though he had flunked out of ET school. Fearfully, standing at attention, Stewart interrupted:

"I didn't get to ET school, sir. I was waiting at Pier Ninety-one in Seattle for orders to ET school when they sent me here—to this place, sir."

"Goddamit, you're lying to me. You flunked out of school," he shouted.

At that, Stewart angrily leaned forward and said: "No sir, I am not lying, sir. I have not been to ET school yet. I requested ET school as part of my shipping over deal, sir," Stewart answered, spacing each word carefully, as he watched him.

Stewart was afraid of this idiot, but was also getting mad at the unfairness of it all. Lieutenant Commander Bowser was red-faced and still yelling at Stewart.

"If you're lying, you're in deep shit."

Hey, what the hell, I'm already swimming in it.

The Comm Officer whipped around and pressed a lever on the Intercom.

"Personnel—Communications," he rasped.

"Personnel, aye. What can we do for you, Commander?"

"That new kid you sent us—Stewart?

Kid? Why does he have to call me kid?

"He claims he has not gone to ET school or graduated from ET school. I want to know when he graduated from ET school and with what grade."

"Standby, sir, I'll have to pull his service record."

There followed a long pregnant pause in which the Communications Officer glared at Stewart and Stewart stubbornly stared back.

"No, sir, Commander. There's nothing in his record to indicate he's been to ET school. Hell, he hasn't enough time in the Navy to have been there and back, sir." Stewart's Division Officer glared at the intercom, then glared at

Stewart, tight-lipped and red-faced, and tersely ordered, "Come with me." He dashed along the passageway and down the ladder to the Main Deck, and headed off to Personnel, with Stewart trailing behind him.

There are no floors, ceilings, halls, stairs, or walls in the Navy: only decks, overheads, passageways, ladders, and bulkheads.

The Comm Officer opened Stewart's service jacket. His original pre-enlistment test results, the page with his quarterly marks on the Chilton, and training course study results, his DD-214, reenlistment papers, and orders to Tongue Point, were acco-fastened to Stewart's file folder. There wasn't much there after one year.

His duty assignment request sheet, filled out at Pier Ninety-one for ET school, destroyers, shore duty, or overseas duty was still in the jacket, dated about one week previous. Lieutenant Commander Bowser glared at the yeoman.

"Where are his orders from NTC Great Lake, ET School? This doesn't show his attendance at Electronics school." The Comm Officer wasn't really that bright. Swensen, Yeoman Second Class, stared at him for a moment. He patiently took him through Stewart's one year, one month career.

"Well, why was he ordered here as an ET grad?"

"Someone fucked up, sir."

The Comm Officer didn't calm down but at least Stewart was out of the frying pan for the moment. Now he was pissed at the yeoman.

Mother Goose, was this the way it was going to be here?

Stewart was miserable. His life had gone behind a cloud. He was a non-designated seaman apprentice assigned to work for Green ET3, as a trainee. As Stewart trailed him in bewilderment around the Station, he began to make some sense of what Green was trying to teach.

Occasionally, they worked together in the Comm Center on some receivers or controllers, or wiring. Mostly, Stewart did exactly what Green told him to do, responding without knowing what he was doing. After he broke one of the Collins Auto-tune clutches, Green wouldn't let him touch that anymore. He watched the radiomen at work and liked that.

Mr. Wetter liked to have one of the radiomen put Morse code on a speaker so he could listen to it across the room at his desk, like music—LISTEN TO IT. He didn't write it down. He just 'read' the code as it came over the speaker.

"Burns," Lee asked one of the RM strikers. "What's that all about?"

"He's reading the news, Stew. Ole Wetter can read code in his head. He doesn't have to write it down or type it. That's how he gets his news everyday. It's Mackay Radio out of San Francisco, with United Press."

Now, that's class.

Infrequently, he could catch a letter, not very often though.

Stewart gave his next move a lot of thought. He had refused the Chilton's offers in favor of ET school and landed here. The Comm Officer wouldn't talk to him or even acknowledge his presence, not to mention send a letter to the Bureau of Naval Personnel and say they had fucked up, and a replacement for Green was still required, or that Stewart was still requesting ET School. Stewart decided a trip to Personnel was important.

Stewart came to the Personnel office counter and waited until Swensen noticed him. Still only Swensen in the office. "Swensen, I got a problem."

"Okay, shoot. Whatcha' got going?" He asked with raised eyebrows.

"I think you realize the Comm Boss would like to take me out to the middle of the Columbia and tell me to swim for shore."

Swenson grinned at him. "It does seem that way."

"And, I don't think he will approve my request to go to ET school." Swensen nodded agreement.

"I was wondering, what are advancement opportunities as a Radioman? If they are good, I'm going to ask to change from ET striker to RM striker. Otherwise, I'm just going to sit here for two years as an SA, if the Comm Boss has any thing to say about it."

"That might be a good move, Stewart. There is a critical shortage of Radiomen in the Fleet now. If you can cut the mustard, all you have to do is pass a test to advance through the ranks." Swensen hunched over his coffee cup and squinted through Stewart's cigarette smoke. "As a matter of fact, your boss and the Exec are trying to figure out how to drop you from the books as an ET, so they can order an ET."

"Okay, Swensen. Thanks for your help." Swensen smiled and turned back to his desk.

Stewart talked to Green, who agreed this might be just the move for him. Stewart was coming along fine, but no way would he be ready to take over when he, Green, was discharged. He would do what he could for Stewart.

Green talked to Chief Nevil about letting him strike for Radioman instead of ET. Stewart did know international Morse code for each letter and number. He had learned flashing lights, semaphore, flag hoists, and wigwag in the Boy Scouts and Sea Scouts. Chief Nevil agreed to listen to Stewart and give his request some thought.

"So Stewart, you say you know the code and you want to strike for Radioman instead of ET. Is that right?" Stewart noticed the Chief was looking at him with interest, instead of amusement or contempt as he had when Stewart first reported aboard. Stewart was a little bit sweaty as he nodded yes. Right now, he was in a no win situation. They were going to keep him a seaman deuce for six years the way things were shaping up.

The Chief thought for a minute. "Okay Stewart, you said you know international Morse code. I want you to sound out the code for the word—AND. Just use a normal tone but like you hear it come over the speaker."

"Right Chief" and he began in a high falsetto voice—"uh DOT DASH   DASH DOT   DASH DOT DOT." Stewart had spit it out without hesitation. He did know the code.

"Hmmmm. Okay, give me your first name."

"DOT DASH DOT DOT   DOT   DOT." The Chief looked at him with growing interest.   They only had one RMSN, Burns, and that was because he had been busted from RM3.

"First three digits of your serial number." Lee responded with more confidence. "DOT DOT DOT DASH DASH   DASH DASH DASH DASH DOT   DOT DOT DASH DASH DASH."

"So you DO know the code," said the Chief, with surprise. "But you speak it this way, DI-DI-DI-DI-DAH, not DOT DOT DOT DOT DASH. Got that?" Stewart nodded. He self-consciously repeated the code just like the Chief. "Let me tell you something else: we refer to Morse code as CW, for continuous wave. So, remember that."

Across the room, a couple of radiomen had been listening and watching. Suddenly, they broke into code conversation to each other as they pantomimed tuning a receiver. The chief stopped what he was doing and listened for a second, then began to grin.

"Okay, Stewart, better get used to those guys. One's crazy and the other's weird. I'll talk to the Commander about this."

All three laughed. Stewart relaxed a shade.

Maybe, just maybe, things won't be so bad after all.

Chief Nevil knocked on the door and waited.

"Come."

The Chief walked over to Mr. Bowser's desk. "Got a proposition for you, Mr. Bowser."

The Comm Officer raised his eyebrows, stuck his pen in its holder, and leaned back.

"I'd like to let Stewart strike for Radioman instead of Electronics Technician. . ."

"After what he's done to us, you want to give him that?" Mr. Bowser had a look of disbelief in his eyes.

"Sir, he didn't do anything to us. He got screwed by a mistake in the system. He's bright and eager. If we give him a chance, we may get a damn good sailor. Right now, he's pretty sour on the Navy."

The Comm Officer looked at him pensively, chewed on his lip, then stared out the window for a moment.

"Not only that, sir, we can remove him from the ET allowance list. That frees up the ET billet again."

Mr. Bowser reached for his coffee and took a sip. He looked at Chief Nevil, making up his mind.

"All right, make up the paperwork and I'll sign it for Personnel to handle. Then I'll talk to the Exec to see if he can push for a real ET."

The Chief nodded, returned to the Comm Center, and sent for Green and Stewart.

"You wanted to see me, Chief?"

"Green, Mr. Bowser has approved the transfer, effective immediately. Stewart, we're going to try you out as a radioman striker. If you don't work out, you'll be transferred to another department. If you work out, we will get you transferred to Radioman A-school in San Diego. If you work very hard, you can take the test for Seaman in June."

Stewart swallowed and smiled. This was better than he had hoped for. Green smiled and disappeared.

1300, March 14, 1950
Communications Center
Naval Station Tongue Point
Astoria, Oregon

Stewart's training as a Radioman Striker began immediately. The Chief explained, at great length, the importance of maintaining and keeping accurate radio circuit logs. Logs were legal entities, sometimes used in an investigation, maritime hearings, or court-martials. Chief Nevil paused as he thought about Stewart's order of training.

Let's see: will Stewart like voice radio or be scared of it?

He looked around the room and spotted Burns doing absolutely nothing.

"Burns," called the Chief across the Center to the duty radioman, who immediately trotted to the Chief.

"Take Stewart in tow. I want you to go over Voice Procedures in JANP 125, page and paragraph. He won't have CW skills for a long time. So teach him how to be a superior voice operator. Make him watch you for a couple of days, then let me know when you think he is ready to call the net, use the log, send voice messages properly and sign a message cross. Then we'll start him on the weather messages."

"Right, Chief," Burns answered, beckoning to Stewart with his head.

"When you're completely satisfied, test him on the manual, and I want to know the results. 'Cause after he's qualified on voice, we're going to make a teletype and tape machine operator out of him. He has a lot to learn."

"Gotcha' Chief."

In short order, Stewart handled all voice messages during the Day Watch, under close supervision of one of the radiomen. Voice radio circuit procedures seemed easy enough.

"I'm getting good reports on you, Stewart. Keep up the good work. It's time to start on other things, in addition to handling voice traffic."

Stewart nodded his appreciation. "Thanks, Chief."

"Now, listen to Ned while he explains the message board and teaches you a few things about teletype operation and those teletype publications."

Mr. Wetter explained the importance of walking the message board around to specified departments and obtaining the correct signatures for delivery. Mr. Wetter let him watch as he worked on the teletype messages, explaining the different processes. He let Stewart look up and assign teletype routing addresses, while he discussed the spider web of the teletype network. Stewart was getting dizzy from studying all the manuals.

Stewart's mother had insisted he take Typing 1A in his senior year at Bremerton High School. As a result, he could type with a better than average degree of skill. He always typed his letters to family and friends because of his scrawling penmanship.

Stewart thought it should be a snap to learn how to handle the Navy Teletype circuits with its intricate address coding. All this time, the Chief had been watching Stewart and getting good reports from the radiomen and the old Chief.

Life on $62.50 a month cannot go very far in a miserable place where staying aboard the base was better than going three and a half miles to Astoria on liberty. Ten cents for the Base Movie was fairly expensive on his pay. If Stewart were a country boy, he could have gone to the Astoria Train Depot to watch the passengers get on and off the train.

Unfortunately, the Seattle, Portland and Spokane Railway stopped passenger service through Astoria two years before. Freight peddlers still came down the line from Portland, passing right by the closed and padlocked gate of World War Two Tongue Point Naval Station railroad yard. SP&S RR still delivered and picked up goods all the way to Seaside and back.

Lee's love life started gradually in Astoria. He became acquainted with Jeannie, the Western Union operator, first. The Comm Center and the local Western Union Telegraph Company office exchanged messages over a special teletype circuit nicknamed the Pony Line. The Navy sent official messages to Navy personnel at home, or to their families, through Western Union. Lee and Jeannie exchanged one-line jokes and notes on what was nicknamed The Pony Line.

```
JE THIS IS LS XXX YOU ON TONIGHT?
JE  HERE
LS  WHAT COLOR ARE YOUR EYES?
JE  ONE BLUE ONE BROWN  TAKE YOUR PICK
LS  DIDN'T KNOW MOVIE OSS AT THE COLUMBIA
JE  SAW IT AT HOME IN BUTTE XXX BZ NOW BYE
```

Finally, Lee got up enough nerve to visit Jeannie and eventually asked for a date. That didn't go anywhere at all. She told him that before she would go to a movie with him, he had to get some civilian clothes. She would not go out with him while he was in uniform.

Jeannie was in her mid-Twenties.

Really! After all, dating a teenager was desperation, even if he was cute!

Jeannie let him hang around for a while just for something to do. 'Liberty' wasn't much better for her. She knew he could not take her out night clubbing and barely had enough money to take her to the movies once a payday. Mostly, they just sat on a porch swing at Mrs. Bonniford's Ladies' Boarding House and talked.

During the Day Watch, Stewart's duties were similar to those of a Seaman Apprentice striker in any Navy office. He made coffee and polished all brass and copper fittings until they gleamed. His cleaning duties included swabbing, waxing, and buffing the deck, washing woodwork and polishing windows. His Radio duties also involved walking the Message Board around to specified officers and offices. As a young striker, he was available for any other devilment his superiors could think up.

Stewart transmitted the voice weather message every day. The Chief and Mr. Wetter agreed he was ready to begin preparing outgoing teletype messages by looking up address codes in the code manual.

Mr. Wetter taught him to punch the teletype tape properly. Mr. Wetter very carefully checked and pointed out every mistake. He could be cranky when Stewart backspaced and typed LTRS to blot mistakes. He said that was unprofessional and took up valuable transmission time.

"Stewart, why don't you grab some coffee and come into Mr. Bowser's office. We want to ask you a few questions."

"Right, Chief, right away."

Oh shit, what have I done now?

He grabbed his coffee cup and hurried into the office. Helen walked out smiling at him. He felt relieved by that smile as he walked in. Mr. Bowser wasn't there. That relieved him even more. Mr. Wetter dragged a chair in and shut the door. Chief Nevil pointed to a chair and motioned for Stewart to sit.

He had a thick filefolder in his lap and now opened it. "You've made a lot of mistakes these past few weeks, Stewart. One thing that Ned and I have noticed, though, is that you don't make the same mistake again, once it has been brought to your attention. That's very good." Stewart flushed and smiled a little smile.

"Burns tells me he almost never gets you anymore when he questions you on voice procedures. That's impressive because many A-school grads still fumble after they've been in the fleet awhile."

Stewart nodded and relaxed just a little bit.

"Ned also tells me you've got a good handle on teletype routing indicators and can determine incoming message routing, too. You're a fast learner, Stewart." Stewart felt a little embarrassed as Mr. Wetter smiled at him.

"Mr. Bowser is a tough officer to impress. Believe me, Stewart, when I say he has been trying to prove us wrong. We think you'll make a very good radioman. He doesn't. That's what this meeting is all about." The Chief paused and looked at Stewart for a moment.

Stewart swallowed because he felt something was coming.

"I want a straight answer outa you, Stewart. Do you really want to be a Radioman, or are you going to wait a little while and put in for ET school?"

The question caught Stewart off guard. They both were looking at him pretty closely, watching for some reaction. He reached for a cigarette, then paused.

"Answer first, Stewart."

"Chief, I don't know how good an ET I might make. But I do know that working in the Radio Shack where all the traffic moves lets me see what's going on. I like sending and receiving messages. It's kinda like a power or something. I just wish I could copy CW like you, Mr. Wetter." Both smiled, Mr. Wetter nodded. "I'd like to go to A-school where I could learn to copy the fleet broadcasts."

I'm not about to say I know I wouldn't come back here.

Chief Nevil had a big grin on his face and handed him a special request form that had been filled out. He saw that Chief Nevil had requested Stewart's Navy Job Code be changed from SN-0000 (unskilled deck ape) to RM-2354, a designated Radioman Striker who has certain skills but has not attended RM A-school. It was signed by Chief Nevil, initialed by Mr. Wetter, and approved by Mr. Bowser.

Wow! Holy Toledo! It's official.

"Sign it, Stewart," ordered Chief Nevil.

Stewart grabbed a fountain pen and scribbled his signature. He looked up with a big grin on his face and saw Mr. Bowser staring at him from the other doorway. Not quite frowning, but not smiling either.

Stewart gestured with the chit. "Thank you, Mr. Bowser." The Communications Officer inclined his head, turned and went into the Radio Shack.

"That's not all, Stewart. Mr. Bowser doesn't want a Seaman Apprentice hanging around the Communications

Department. You're recommended for Seaman. The Seaman's exam is on June 12.

Yaa hooo!

"You need to brush up for that test. What else? Oh, yes. You are on watch rotation beginning with tomorrow's evening watch. Ned will cut you in with a list of things you need to watch for. Most of them are under his glass top on the desk."

"Anything else?" The Chief glanced at Mr. Wetter who shook his head.

"Well, I guess that's it, Stewart."

"Jeez, Chief, thanks for everything. Errr, can I sew Radioman flashes to show I am a Radioman Striker now?"

"No, not until you make Seaman. Don't thank me yet. We'll have you busting your ass in no time at all. This isn't a give away. You've earned some things and we're giving you additional responsibility."

Stewart felt like walking on water at that moment.

Everything was all right.

Eve Watch was different. In this peace time Navy, the Comm Center closed down at 2400, midnight local time. The Main Comm Center in Seattle had approved this arrangement some time in the past. Besides, the total daily traffic count between Seattle and Tongue Point seldom exceeded ten messages and three of them were weather messages. The duty Radioman always notified Main Comm Center Seattle before securing for the night.

There was very little message traffic received in the evenings. Reading and listening to the radio on the Eve Watch was permitted. Studying on the Eve Watch was encouraged. Sleeping on any watch was verboten!

Chief Nevil arranged the watch rotation so that Stewart usually caught the Thursday Eve Watch, because the man on duty also held Field Day for Friday Morning Material Inspection. Field Day had to be complete before shutting down the Comm Center for the night. He washed most vertical surfaces to remove hand and finger marks and dusted all horizontal surfaces.

Stewart stripped everything from desktops and lifted a seventy-pound buffer up to polish the desk tops until they glistened. He swabbed, waxed, and polished the deck with a big electric floor polisher. Then he restored each desktop to its regular appearance with papers under glass. He also polished the brass ashtrays. This job was perfect duty for a Seaman Apprentice. It had the advantage of keeping him in top physical condition, too.

The Chief stood watches as Station Duty Chief once per month. The only time Stewart ever saw the three senior petty officers was Personnel Inspection, payday, and when he relieved them for the Eve Watch on weekends. It simply wasn't proper for any petty officer to hold Field Day when a seaman apprentice was available.

At Mr. Wetter's pointed suggestion, Stewart practiced typing on the Model 15 and Model 19 teletype machines to improve his teletype skills in procedure, accuracy, and speed. Mr. Wetter did not care what Stewart typed, so long as he typed something. Stewart left his punched tape and paper copy on the desk of the old Chief who would check them carefully for accuracy, and to see how many times he had backspaced the tape to correct mistakes.

One night during typing practice, Stewart typed

WHEN I MAKE SN CMA I AM GOING TO ASK FOR A XFER OUT OF HERE

(When I make Seaman, I am going to ask for a transfer out of here.)

Stewart typed this repeatedly. He forgot a very important lesson Mr. Wetter had pounded into him about security. The old chief always checked the trashcans for classified material.

In the short time Lee Stewart had been stationed at Tongue Point, he discovered there was nothing for a nineteen-year-old sailor to do. He had taken a city bus tour of Astoria. The old passenger train depot had been deserted —with trash and boarded up doors and windows. There were a few salmon canneries operating next to the Columbia River and he had arranged to be on the city bus arriving there at quitting time to look for likely girls: they had all been older women. He would have to wait until later to watch high school baseball or football games.

APRIL

Friday, April 14
The Boardwalk
Seaside, Oregon

Lee had a seventy-two hour liberty and little money. He decided to stay aboard on Friday and spend some time in the Barracks Recreation Room. The Station Recreation Fund had just purchased and installed one of those new 12-inch Crosley television receivers as an experiment for entertainment and Stewart wanted to see what it was like.

The Executive Officer established and promulgated television hours on the barracks Bulletin Boards. Viewing hours were 1800 to 2130 Monday through Thursday, 1700 through 2200 on weekends and holidays. Operation, programming, and hours were enforced by the duty Master-At-Arms. Stewart decided purple and gray figures on that television screen weren't as good as black and white movies at the Base Theater, even if the movie did cost ten cents.

Lee had begun frequenting the Roller Rink in Seaside when he had the money. It didn't cost much: fifty cents entry fee for all evening and twenty-five cents to rent skates. He had progressed to the point where he could skate backwards with some confidence.

Lee watched couples dancing for a while. Didn't matter what record the manager played, they were all organ music. Bravely, he moved out to the center with other beginners, and while watching other skaters dance, tried to imitate the dance steps.

Lee listened to the organ playing another Straus waltz. He concentrated on moving his feet in the simple dance steps he had seen as if he were waltzing with a girl.

Now let's see. Shove off with my left foot going to the left—

okay, now lead back with my right foot and go into a reverse turn.

A girl, also in the center area, was gliding backwards and did not see Lee. They collided back to back hard enough to knock his breath out. Down they went tangled in a heap. Taking deep breaths and trying to help her up, his skates went out from under him and down he went again—with her beside him. Laughing, Lee and the girl both struggled to get to their feet, busily apologizing to each other as they dusted themselves off.

"Gee, I'm sorry. I was thinking about my steps and didn't look where I was going."

Hey, she's not bad at all.

She laughed. "Me too. I was doing the same thing wishing I had someone to dance with."

Gee, he's got nice blue eyes and light brown hair.

"Uh, look, I'm a real beginner at dancing on skates but I'd like to dance with someone, too. Can we team up for a little bit?"

Nice knockers.

"Okay, what's your name? I'm Betty Echols."

He's kinda cute.

"Thanks, Betty, I'm Lee Stewart. Wanna cross hands and see if we can get out in the stream of people without crashing again?"

Cute smile. Warm hands and small waist!

One thing led to another and soon they were skating, albeit awkwardly, as a couple. Both of them really had to concentrate on their moves while dancing. Between waltzes, they talked.

"You live around here, Betty?"

"Not far away. How about you?"

"Oh, I'm a sailor stationed at Astoria."

"Tongue Point?"

"Yeah. Uh, you from Astoria?"

"Um hmmm. I'm a Senior at Astoria High. You know where the Astor Memorial is, up on the hill?"

"Yeah, I hiked up there from the bus stop when I was looking around."

"Well, I live right around the corner by the old Lewis and Clark fort above Astoria. How old are you, Lee?"

"Just turned nineteen. Why?"

"I'm seventeen and not supposed to date older men, that's why."

Ah Ha! She is thinking dates.

Lee laughed at that. "Do you think I'm an older man, Betty?"

"No, but my folks might. I've been on restriction for poor grades."

The music started again. She kept stealing glances up at him as they danced.

"This is the first time I've been out of the house for three weeks, and that's only because they went to an I.O.O.F. dinner dance at Sunrise. If I don't get my grades up in math and physics pretty soon, I won't graduate in June. They'd really be upset then." She looked glum as she talked about that.

I'm pretty good at math and physics, maybe I could tutor her and get to take her out.

"How about us sitting the next dance out and have a Coke?" he asked.

Betty led the way to the fountain and found a table. Lee watched her as he waited his turn at the counter.

He held up two fingers to the boy behind the counter. "Two Cokes, please." Paying twenty cents, Lee balanced the glasses, hoping not to fall as he skate-walked to their table. Rolling up to the table edge, he balanced for a moment and set the glasses down on the table. Sitting down with skates on was a little tricky, but he made it without embarrassing himself.

They sipped their cokes and watched the skaters, studiously avoiding looking directly at each other. Lee dragged out his Camels and offered one to Betty. She shook her head and watched as he lit up.

"Maybe you just need some tutoring in physics and math to get better grades, Betty. Maybe we could meet somewhere after school and I could help with your homework."

Betty looked sideways at Lee and smiled a little bit.

Maybe he has more than just physics and math homework in mind.

"My folks would never go along with that. They might let you come over to the house, though. We could study in the kitchen. If my weekly test grades start coming up, I can have dates again."

"Betty, if I help you get your grades up, do you think we could go to the movies, or something?"

Betty looked at him some more, didn't answer directly and while they were sipping their Cokes, she wrote down her address and phone number so he could call her Monday afternoon to find out what her folks thought of Lee helping her.

They returned to the rink floor, skating together, and dancing for the rest of the evening. Lee's brow wrinkled in concentration as he held her, while making long gliding skate steps. His concentration was deep enough he didn't talk. Betty, a little better skater, had time to glance at Lee from time to time.

The skating rink always played The Tennessee Waltz as the last dance. As the dance ended, she held on, breaking apart gradually and squeezed his hands. He didn't meet her folks, but he saw her walking out with them.

I wonder if they saw me skating or dancing with her?

Monday, Mr. Ned Wetter, a retired Chief Radioman turned Civil Servant, looked around for Stewart and called his name. When Stewart looked around with raised eyebrows, Mr. Wetter smiled and crooked his finger.

"Stewart," he said, "I think you're ready to take on some new stuff, and it is very important.

He proceeded to give instructions on correcting pubs: print neatly with ink, avoid red ink because you can't see red ink in red night lights, and follow directions carefully.

Mr. Wetter said that was a good way to become familiar with all the different communication publications. Stewart spent his day bringing two call sign books and one teletype routing book up to date.

When he could break away to the barracks pay phone, he called Betty.

"Lee, there's a real tough physics test about friction and heat on Wednesday and I don't understand it. Can you help me out?"

"That's easy, Betty, but I have to be there to show you."

"That's okay. Mom said you could come over now as long as she's here, too."

"Okay, I'll be over in a little while—bye," he said with elation.

Stewart cleaned up for liberty and caught the next bus to town. Hiking three blocks almost straight up slowed him down but he managed to get to Betty's house before it was dark.

Lee was huffing and puffing by the time he knocked on the side door and waited. Betty opened the door, smiling.

"Come on it, Lee. Mom and Dad are waiting to meet you. Have you had dinner?"

Lee was sure he could smell one of his favorite dinners —meat loaf, and would have eaten a second dinner just to have something great for a change.

"Nope. Got cleaned up and headed out right away."

A slender woman in a blue wool dress just a little taller than Betty came up behind her and put her hands on Betty's shoulders.

"Mom, this is Lee Stewart. Lee, this is my mother, Jane Echols."

"How do you do, Mrs. Echols?" He asked politely with a shy grin.

Mrs. Echols, nodding and smiling with a wide, warm mouth, looked him over carefully while she wiped her hands on her apron and hung it up behind the kitchen door. She had dark green eyes, almost no eyebrows, and black hair with threads of gray. Her hands were strong and warm as she shook hands with Lee.

"Lee, you hung up the phone before Betty had a chance to invite you for dinner. If you're going to tutor Betty, the least we can do is feed you once in a while." She led him the rest of the way into the house as she talked. A place had already been set for him next to Mr. Echols who was standing in back of his dinner chair.

"Daddy, this is Lee Stewart. Lee, Fred Echols."

"Hello, sir. How are you?" Lee felt a little uncomfortable under the scrutiny of Mr. Echols. It wasn't that he frowned, his gray eyes seemed to pierce his skin, as he looked Lee up and down. Lee and Mr. Echols were of the same height, although Mr. Echols was rather thick around the waist. His round face was smooth and clean-shaven. His head still had fringes of brown hair, but he was mostly bald.

"Just fine, Lee. I understand you're some kind of expert with physics and math. Is that correct?"

"At least as far as high school and beginning college courses are concerned, Mr. Echols."

"I see." It was plain he was somewhat dubious of Lee's scholastic skills.

When the ladies were seated—Mrs. Echols and Betty—Mr. Echols gestured to Lee to sit down. Lee was picking up his napkin when Mr. Echols began praying. Lee bowed his head and listened.

I wonder which church they go to?
I don't remember this prayer.
Long prayer.
Very long prayer!

As he ate, he fielded questions from Mr. Echols, who studied him very carefully.

"Did you attend college, Lee?"

"Yes sir—well, I started but ran out of money and had to enlist."

"I see. What makes you think you can help Betty with physics and math?"

"I got straight A's in physics and A's and B's in math, Mr. Echols. Besides, a little demonstration followed by formula drill ought to put her in shape."

Mr. Echols grunted as he buttered a piece of bread. As dinner progressed, the Echols learned about Lee's family and being a Navy brat, what Lee hoped to do with his life, and what life was like in the Navy.

By the time dinner was over, the Echols family had relaxed, listening with interest as Lee told stories about life at sea on the Chilton, his last duty assignment, and now here at Tongue Point. Obviously, Lee was not going to kidnap Betty and do bad things to her.

After the dinner table had been cleared and dishes washed, Betty and Lee settled down at the kitchen table with her books.

"Now, tell me about this friction and heat you don't understand, Betty."

She told him why she was confused—that pulling different objects up an incline to measure friction didn't register in her mind.

Just as I thought, she didn't feel the heat, so she didn't get the connection.

"Go wash and dry your hands to get all the oils off your palms. I'll do the same." He had her press her hand against his and try to slide it.

"Can you feel how your hand suddenly got warmer?"

"A little bit."

Suddenly from behind them came her father's voice: "A better demonstration is to briskly rub your hands together. That way, you don't have to hold hands."

"Daddy!"

"Fred," came the drawn out warning tone from his wife.

"Be right there, dear."

Lee flushed with embarrassment for getting caught. That was exactly what he was doing. Fred Echols chuckled as he walked back into the living room to his newspaper and his wife. He had accomplished his mission.

"You ought to be ashamed of yourself, Fred."

"Just keeping his fingers out of the cookie jar, honey. Slow them down a little bit, you know."

"Guilty conscience, Fred?"

He rattled his paper in answer and settled back to read.

Betty and Lee concentrated on getting ready for her physics test tomorrow. Finally, Lee rubbed his eyes and stretched.

"Guess I oughta head back to the base, Betty. Don't think your father likes me."

She handed Lee his jacket and walked with him to the kitchen door. Lee turned at the door hoping for a kiss.

Nope, not this time.

She laid her hand on the back of his arm and smiled up at him.

"Thanks for the help, Lee." Betty said, softly. "I know I'll get a good grade on the test this time. Call me Wednesday after school and I'll tell you how it went."

Lee nodded and smiled as he stepped into the light rain.

Think I've got myself a girlfriend.

He hummed "I've got my love to keep me warm," as he turned down hill to the bus stop.

Betty lit into her parents after Lee left.

"Daddy, how could you do that? He's helping me understand the incline a little bit."

"Well, I just don't want an older boy take advantage of you."

Betty tossed her head and glared. "At the kitchen table? Where you can hear us?"

Jane Echols looked between Fred and Betty. "Money doesn't grow on trees, Betty. Try to explain to him that he shouldn't expect dinner here every time he calls on you," Jane said.

"Mother, you were the one that suggested he come for dinner tonight."

"That's true, dear, but I wasn't thinking far enough ahead. I think it would be best if he came after dinner—say 7p.m. He would have time to eat dinner on his station before he came up here."

"Okay, I'll tell him next time he calls."

"No dating yet, young lady. Just tutoring."

"Yes, Daddy."

When she got an 'A' on the physics test, her folks announced Lee could take Betty to the movies to celebrate her grade. They walked hand in hand downtown to a movie at the Columbia Theater. Betty wouldn't sit all the way in the back row but she didn't object when he put his arm around her. "Abbott and Costello Meet Frankenstein" kept her cuddled up to him most of the time.

Lee and Betty held hands on the way home. The hill was steep to climb, and again, Lee began panting with exertion. They walked into shadows under a bushy tree.

"Let's stop here a sec, Betty, and catch our breath."

She stopped with him and shivered a bit. Lee gently pulled on her coat sleeves and she shyly snuggled up next to him, her face close to his neck. Betty put her hands on his hips and looked up into his face.

Oh boy, here we go.

Lee tipped his head forward and brushed his lips slowly across her forehead. She moved her head around to let his lips find more of her face and then her lips—tightly together, but full and firm.

Such a nice warm mouth, Betty.

"That was nice," she whispered and squeezed his hips. He nodded and stood silently and slid his hands down to the very top of her bottom and gently pulled her to him. She hastily pulled away from him and announced: "We better go, Lee. Daddy knows how long it takes to walk home."

"Okay," he said, as he slowly moved his hands over her bottom.

But she didn't tell me to take my hands off her ass.

Lee nodded, and arm-in-arm, they began walking up hill. There was another deep shadowy spot in the next block. This time they both came to a stop and turned for more kisses. Lee's throbbing erection became an object of embarrassment to both of them. Betty, conscious of it, moved back just far enough so she couldn't feel it.

They discovered another dark spot just before her house. Lee backed up against the tree and pulled Betty to him. He could tell everything was in the right places. This time she didn't pull back. Lee took a chance and telegraphed his move. He brought his hand up between them very slowly until her breast was just under his hand. Moving his hand around, he gently squeezed her breast.

Oh, that's wonderful. So soft—even under her sweater.
She's not stopping me yet. I wonder how much she'll let me do?

Betty didn't move; she spoke instead.

"Lee, take your hand away now, please."

A final small squeeze and Lee let his hand slide back down and away.

"You're really nice, Betty," with a strangled whisper.

Even though Betty had noticed his erection before, she appeared to notice his erection for the first time and stepped back suddenly.

"We'd better go."

In a few steps they were around the corner and in view of her house. The front porch light came on and Mr. Echols stepped out, arms folded across his chest.

Oh shit, I'm in trouble now.

He dropped her hand and moved an inch away from her.

It was funny, really. They walked toward the house as Mr. Echols walked toward the sidewalk.

"Good evening, Mr. Echols. Isn't it nice it didn't rain tonight?"

"You're late bringing Betty home, Lee."

"Sir?"

"I know exactly how long it takes to walk from the movie house to our house. You should have arrived about ten minutes ago. Can you explain that?"

Betty's eyes rolled in her head and she turned away from her father in anger.

"Fred, come in the house and leave them alone," called her mother from the front door.

"Mr. Echols, that's a steep hill back there. It's three blocks long and I am not in shape to run up that hill. Sorry it took so long."

"You can run along now, Lee."

"Daddy!" Betty covered her face and ran for the house.

"Fred Echols. You apologize to Lee and get in here this minute."

"In a moment, Jane."

Mr. Echols stuck out his hand. "Perhaps, I have been a little too hasty. Do come back again, Lee." They shook hands formally without much warmth.

Lee nodded stiffly and watched Betty's father rigidly march back in the house. He could hear Betty crying as the front door opened and closed behind Mr. Echols.

Lee and Betty persisted with the tutoring efforts in both subjects. Betty's homework and pop quiz grades began to improve. Mrs. Echols wanted Lee to continue tutoring Betty. He was kind of like the kid next door now.

One Friday evening during dinner, Mr. Echols asked him to come over Sunday afternoon to go to church with them. Lee thought about it briefly and agreed even though his Baptist upbringing was a little different from their sober Mormon services. He had learned that tidbit only last week.

Two Sundays later after dinner, Mr. Echols picked up his napkins, dabbed his lips, and glanced at his wife with arched eyebrows. She nodded and smiled.

"Lee, Jane and I have a surprise for you."

Lee looked up from his plate with a question in his eyes, raised eyebrows, darted a look at Betty, and put his fork down. He picked up his napkin and dabbed his mouth to hide his anxiety.

"Mrs. Echols and I think you are a very nice young man and good company for Betty. You have really helped our daughter improve her grades. There was some question whether she would be able to graduate this June. Now, there is no question that she will wear a cap and gown."

Lee sneaked a look at Betty who was staring in surprise at her father.

She doesn't know what her father is up to, either.

He turned his head the other way as Mrs. Echols spoke.

"Lee, we have this guest room going to waste, and Fred and I want you—well . . .

"What my wife is trying to say, son, is we would be delighted if you thought of this as your second home. You can use the guest room every time you want to get away from the base. Besides, Betty still needs your tutoring."

Lee just did not know what to think. He stole a quick look at Betty. She was crimson with embarrassment.

Wow! This was news to her, also. Never had an offer like this before. Sure more opportunity to get closer to Betty, that's for sure. Somehow, I don't think I want to come over here every liberty.

"Gee, that's swell of you, Mr. Echols. I don't know what to say."

"I'll even let you have the keys to the old Franklin once in a while," Mr. Echols tempted, holding out the keys to him.

Betty was looking at her father in shock.

This is definitely something new.

"Well, thank you both. I'd like that very much. But you know I can't afford to come over every night, but I'll come over as much as I can."

Betty beamed at him and reached across the table for his hand. Lee stammered his thanks and reached for the keys to their 1938 Franklin.

The Franklin scared the hell out of him when it started free wheeling down the steep hill. Everything worked fine after he stopped the car and pushed in the overdrive knob. Betty cuddled up to him in the car and didn't mind if his hands wandered a little bit and played outside her panties and bra, so long as they didn't stay too long in one place.

Betty finally let him get his fingers under her panties. In turn, she began stroking Junior through his pants. Petting was fun but it sure didn't go very far and caused sleepless nights. Now that Lee had a friendly place to go every liberty night, he could relax. Betty's folks were great and rather like family.

MAY

2:30PM, May 14
Astoria, Oregon

Lee had fallen into the pattern of attending church with the Echols when he didn't have the duty. Besides, it was swell sitting with Betty and her folks. Her high school graduation was in two weeks, and Lee was invited to attend the celebration with Mr. and Mrs. Echols.

Mr. Echols, an Elder in their church, stood up and looked around at the congregation.

"You all know that the sailor, Lee Stewart, has been tutoring Betty and stays with us occasionally. Lee and Betty have been dating since March, and now with our blessing, they are keeping company. Jane and I ask you to welcome Lee, as well." Abruptly, Fred Echols sat down while the congregation looked at Betty and Lee, smiling in warmth and recognition.

Betty slid closer to Lee until her hips and shoulders were touching his, and reached for his hand. She beamed at him and looked around the congregation, smiling with pride and possession.

Lee swallowed a couple of times as his heart thudded and tried to maintain a strained friendly face as he looked at the people.

Holy Mackerel! Does that mean what I think it means? Oh shit! How am I going to get out of this?

That night, riding the city bus back to Tongue Point, Lee thought it over and decided to stay aboard the station for a while.

4:25PM, May 15
Barracks
NavSta Tongue Point
Astoria, Oregon

Lee walked up to the pay phone outside the Master-at-Arms shack, hesitated a moment, and stuffed a nickel into the slot and dialed Betty's number.

"Hello?"

"Hi, Mrs. Echols. Is Betty around?"

"Sure, Lee." She muffled the phone and Lee could hear her yelling upstairs to Betty that he was on the telephone.

"Hi Lee. You coming over this evening?" Betty asked, breathlessly.

"Uhh, Betty." He paused for a moment. "I got in trouble this morning. Did something wrong. Now, I have been restricted to be base for a month and more than that, I can't even have visitors here."

I hate to give her up. I know it wouldn't be long before we start making love.

"Oh no, Lee. What did you do?"

"I'm sorry, Betty, I can't talk about it. It's classified."

"When am I going to see you again, Lee? Oh", she gasped, "you're going to miss my graduation and party."

"Yeah, baby. I'm sorry."

"Oh, Lee, me too." Lee heard her voice break as she hung up.

Not only that, I've left a few clothes over there I am not going to pick up.

0915, May 27
Barracks
U.S. Naval Station, Tongue Point
Astoria, Oregon

The narrow sun shaft, intensely white, silently crept across the pillow and burned his eyelids. Lee Stewart grunted and turned away from the white-hot light. The back of his head, not to be outdone, cried out from the heat on his close-cropped head.

Damn it. It's Saturday morning, I've got a 48-hour weekend, and I can sleep in.

Finally opening his eyes, Lee stared at the floor and realized this was his barracks, not the Echols' spare room. The bright sunlight suddenly connected; he looked out the barracks windows into the sky.

Hey! No rain, no clouds.
This might be a good weekend to go find a new girlfriend. School is out and everyone is heading for the beach. Yeah, Seaside's the place to go. I'll have to be careful around the skating rink. Betty might show up. She's got more serious ideas than I can deal with. Too bad, Betty is a neat girl.

Lee sat up in his bunk, then jumped down to the floor.

I wonder if I have enough moolah to go to Seaside today?

Opening his combination lock, he reached in the locker for his billfold and checked the contents.

A lousy six bucks and payday is Monday. Better find someone heading that way to bum a ride or I gotta hitchhike.

He could hear some of the guys kidding around in the shower room. Lee quickly stripped and grabbed his towel and shaving gear. Five guys were in various stages of showering and shaving. He recognized Swensen who had a big Ford sedan.

"Swensen, can I catch a ride with you to Seaside?" Swensen, with his right arm raised to wash under his arm, turned as his name was called and looked Lee up and down. He let his arm drop to his side.

"Well, maybe. Depends on whether I get a full load to Portland. If there's room, I'll let you ride for a buck."

"Jeez guy, I only got six bucks altogether. Maybe I better hitchhike again."

"Do that and that fat old queer will be after your dick. Tell you what, fifty cents is my best offer."

Hmmm, I certainly don't need to waste my juice at the beginning of the weekend.

"You're on, Swensen."

Maybe I'll get lucky and stay with someone instead of having to hitchhike back to Tongue Point.

Lee was in civvies and carrying his gym bag with trunks, towel, toilet articles, and a change of skivvies. Swensen dropped Lee off in Seaside at US-101 and Main Street. He grabbed his bag, stretched, and began the long walk to the beach boardwalk and amusements by the ocean. Strolling along, he that the motel parking lots were mostly full. People were out and about already.

Hey, this just might be a great weekend.

The Greyhound Bus Station manager who had served on the U.S.S. New Orleans—a Light Cruiser—during World War Two, didn't mind if sailors from Astoria changed in the lavatory so long as they did so quickly and left. Lee planned to leave his gym bag in one of those small lockers in the Bus Station. The breeze off the Pacific was still cold. Right now he was thankful he had worn his sweater.

Lee turned into the narrow walkway and hunched his head down against the stiff breeze. He walked toward the

Bus Station entrance and abruptly stopped. Then stepped aside, then back the other way, and back again. Beginning to get annoyed at playing sidestep, he looked up as a nice, laughing voice said, "I guess this means you want to dance with me, huh?"

Oh ho!

That was a girl's voice, but she had covered her face with a woolen cap and muffler. All that showed were her red nose and dancing eyes.

She must be cold because that's a heavy coat she's wearing. Can't see much of her body.

He took a better look at her eyes that were smiling at him.

Holy Cow, they're violet!

Lee had never seen eyes that color before.
"Wow, your eyes."
He continued to stare at them without knowing he was staring. She laughed at him this time and stepping back a bit, removed her cap and muffler. She shook out her jet-black hair and looked at him again.
"There." She said as she plumped her hair with both hands. "Is that better?"
Lee flushed, nodded shyly, and smiled as he tried to check her out without moving his eyes from hers. He was looking down at the top of her head.

She must be about five foot six. The bulky jacket hid her body.

He couldn't tell if she was heavy set or skinny or anything else about her.

"Wonderful. I mean I was just going in the Bus Station to drop off my bag." Following a hunch, he added, "I was going for a walk along the beach."

"That's where I was heading, too. My folks and I are in that hotel for the weekend," she continued, pointing behind her. "They come down to this beautiful place and do nothing but sit around the hotel room the whole time. Drives me crazy."

Lee nodded and decided to try.

"Would you wait a sec 'til I get rid of this bag in there, and I'll walk along with you?"

"So long as you won't be long," she smiled.

Lee excused himself, and dashed into the Bus Station, grabbed a locker, fed it a dime, and tossed his bag in. Shoving the key in his pocket, he was back in less than a minute.

They sized each other up. Lee liked more of what he saw now that she had unbuttoned her jacket. Not a raving beauty, but rather a neat looking girl who seemed to have enough of everything in the right places. She was wearing a blue Pendleton shirt tucked into faded yellow cord pants that hinted at a nice pair of legs.

"My name's Lee—Lee Stewart. What's yours?"

"Ruth Verlock, a working stiff of Seattle. You're either Joe College from Portland or a sailor from Astoria, right?"

He looked at her in amazement. "Sailor. I give up. Is there a sign or something on me?"

"Your crewcut. Only guys in the service or in college get that kind of haircut."

As they walked towards the beach, Lee and Ruth just naturally compared notes. Eventually, Ruth learned of his misgivings with the way things were working out at Tongue Point. In turn, Lee found out she was happy in her job as a buyer for Abercrombie and something-or-other, in Seattle. She preferred to live at home so she could save her money to buy a car. However, she often used her Dad's car at home, but not down here where she could have some fun.

She had gone to Ballard High School while he was going to Bremerton High School, but two years ahead of him. They hit it off, talking about familiar things, as they walked along the edge of the surf.

"Lee, let's just have fun and go dutch treat."

Lee started to interrupt indignantly. That was just not done.

"Forget it, Lee. I know you don't make much, and you know I work. It's not as though you came over and picked me up at home for a date, you know. Let me pay my own way. That way we can have more fun together. It's no skin off my teeth."

He thought about protesting. Then he got it.

If she is willing to pay her own way, she wants me around for a little bit. Besides, fat chance of a piece of ass on the first night.

The sun was getting hot and sand fleas were more active. So, they steered each other back toward the boardwalk and arcades with games, rides, and food. Ruth rode with Lee in one bumper car several times. Naturally, there was a certain amount of jostling and unexpected touching as a way of getting a little better acquainted.

Damn, stay down, Junior!

Both were happy and smiling at each other as they stopped for hotdogs, then roller-skated.

I don't know what I'll do if Betty sees me here.

He didn't know what kind of a graduation party Astoria High School had, but Lee knew it was this weekend. He hadn't called Betty and he didn't think she had called him at the Base.

It was very late in the afternoon when they stepped back on the beach again and headed for the low tide surf's edge.

Ruth moved closer to Lee as the sun dropped over the horizon. Mist rose from the sea and a light breeze chilled the air.

Ruth announced she was cold but didn't want to return to the hotel room where her folks were sitting and rocking. They walked quietly. Lee took a chance and slid his hand around her waist. His belly was thumping as he waited to learn her reaction.

He just about died when she backed off, but that was just to open her jacket. She pulled his hand around closer to her and held it to her waist. Then she slid her arm around his waist, too. Now hip-to-hip, thigh-to-thigh, they slowly headed back across the wide, flat beach in the gathering darkness.

Lee didn't have much experience with girls.

Wonder when I'll make a girl.
Alice and June certainly don't count. Edith? Ha! That ugly Panamanian Indian woman just lying in bed like a dead fish for ten bucks was so bad he didn't even get it up, so that didn't count.
Betty counted for leaners, though. I've gone further with her than any other girl without making out.
Ruth now? I'm pretty sure she will, even if nothing else ever happens.

His hardon was so strong that if it were a light, he could have illuminated the whole damn beach!

Attracted by the sound of singing, they approached a beach fire surrounded by a crowd of young people. They stayed in the shadows behind the circle of people, and watched. She leaned back close to Lee and pulled his arms around her soft, warm belly and held his hands there. Ruth swayed slowly back and forth in time with the cowboy music, rubbing against Lee.

Junior got harder, achingly so, throbbing with engorgement. She stopped moving as Junior continued to pulsate. He was having difficulty breathing. It was so exquisite. Ruth slowly moved until she found the point where they molded together. His hands trembled as they moved lightly back and forth across her belly. She turned her head back and up to his face, kissed him softly on his lips for the longest time, and turned back to watch the fire. The night was pitch black with the orange of the fire flickering on their darkened faces. Lee let his eyes do the moving as he checked to see if anyone was watching them.

Slowly, savoring each moment, he slid his hands, under hers, tingling on the wool material, until they covered her bra.

Oh my God, where can we go?

He gently squeezed and slowly slid his trembling hands all around, feeling the softness, curves, and two very hard nipples that tickled the palms of his hands.

He was in the highest kind of agony.

Oh Lord, I just gotta kiss them.

Her hands squeezed his and gently pulled them back down to her heated lower belly, but Ruth would not let him reach any lower.

She turned around inside his arms and slipped both arms around his neck. His hands eagerly sought her bottom and pulled her gently against his aching throbbing. She wriggled back and forth a moment and then stopped, pressed against him.

Oh, Mother Macree, it's just like a phonograph needle and record groove.

Ruth and Lee were both breathing raggedly as Lee began trying every trick he had ever read or heard about (many), but Ruth wasn't having any of it. She pressed against him.

"Lee, just accept this much or I'll stop right now. Then, you won't see me again!"

Her hand slid up his pants and caressed Junior who was already leaking a little, then gave it a gentle squeeze. Lee backed off, shaken, and struggled for control. Ruth understood and waited. Then, taking his hand in hers, she led him back to the boardwalk.

"We will, Lee, I promise. You need to meet my folks, Lee. That way, when I invite you up to Seattle for a weekend, Daddy will be happy to pick you up at the Greyhound Station downtown. I have a job and can't get home until 8:30 PM on Fridays."

I gotta get early liberty with a 72-hour pass, just to get there by 8:30 PM!

They walked hand-in-hand back to her hotel and up the back stairs to her folks' room on the second floor.

"Mama, Daddy, this is Lee Stewart."

Mr. Verlock, who had been reading a newspaper, got up from the stuffed chair and walked across the room to shake hands with Lee. His green eyes smiled at Lee. Mrs. Verlock smiled and nodded from the rocker where she sat knitting.

"Glad to meet you, sir—ma'am."

"You too, Lee. I hope you two are having fun around here. I'm glad she found someone to play with."

Play with?

"Oh, Daddy, I met him on the boardwalk and we have been having a fine time. He will be back after church tomorrow and we're going swimming in the ocean."
Lee looked at Ruth and smiled with pleasure. He just found out he had a date for tomorrow and what they were going to be doing. Ruth stepped out into the hall to kiss him goodnight and arrange to meet him after church tomorrow. The way her tongue curled against his brought everything to jangling attention again. She giggled, pushed him away, and whispered, "Don't forget your bathing suit and towel,

tomorrow. I'll keep you out in the cold water to calm you down. You can change here afterwards."

Make the water boil, you mean.

"Now, Lee, do you want to plan on coming up to Seattle next weekend? Like I said, Daddy will be glad to pick you up at the Greyhound Station and bring you home. I have a job and can't get home until 8:30 PM on Fridays."

"I sure do, Ruth. I have a 72 next weekend. Gotta check to see if I can get away early on Friday to catch the afternoon bus to Portland and I'm not sure what time it gets into Seattle."

"Well, even if you get in late, Mom and Daddy will put you in the bedroom in the basement. Our two bedrooms are on the second floor and they are both sound sleepers." With that, she quickly whirled back into the hotel room and shut the door.

Stewart walked out to highway 101 and stuck out his thumb.

Let's see, who can I borrow some money from for tomorrow?

JUNE

2030, June 1
Barracks
U.S. Naval Station Tongue Point
Astoria, Oregon

"Deposit ninety cents for three minutes, sir."

DONG DONG DONG DANG DING

"Lee? What's up?"

"Hi, Luscious. I thought I was going to get up to there this weekend, but it will not work out. Just can't do it."

"Oh, that's too bad, Lee." The disappointment was in her voice. "I can't get down there, either. Wait a minute." Lee could hear muffled voices in the background. "Lee, if you can get off next weekend, my folks promise to come back to Seaside for the weekend. What do you think about that?" She paused for a second. Then continued softly. "It's not exactly what we had in mind, is it?"

Lee swallowed, trying to moisten his throat so he could talk. He squirmed, then exploded. "Oh Baby, I want you in my arms so bad."

"I know, Lee. Next weekend, okay?"

"Your three minutes are up, sir."

"Okay. Goodbye, Luscious."

"Bye, Lee."

0730, June 12
Tongue Point Communication Center
U.S. Naval Station Tongue Point
Astoria, Oregon

Stewart was in the Comm Center bright and early having his first cup of coffee. He had already checked the message board for routing. He wanted everything cleared right away.

His Special Request chit for early Friday liberty next week was ready for the Chief to sign. Stewart wanted nothing to interfere with this day. This was the day he would take the Seaman Examination.

His eyes were scratchy because he had been with Ruth and her parents from Friday evening through Sunday afternoon. Surprising Lee, they reserved and paid for a room at the hotel for him—on a different floor, of course. Her father had asked Lee to drive the family around Tongue Point Saturday afternoon. That was interesting because before this, Lee had to walk everywhere on the station. Her parents stuck to Ruth and Lee like flypaper. No chance to hold Ruth or anything else until Sunday.

Sunday, Lee and Ruth frolicked in the cold Pacific surf. Lee didn't mind the cold. They were busy exploring each other's bodies. This time Ruth let his hands go wherever they wanted. She was busy doing the same thing. The weekend had been wonderful. He had gotten back to the base very late.

Stewart came back to the present. He knew he would pass the test. He had been studying hard, wanted to get out of here, and back to the fleet. He was primed and ready for the test. Mr. Bowser walked in. Stewart was very happy and greeted him cheerfully.

"Good Morning, Mr. Bowser."

He glared at Stewart silently, got his cup of coffee, and marched into his office.

Uh oh! Something was definitely not good.

He came back out and announced rather harshly, "Stewart, you know you're not taking the Seaman's Examination this morning, don't you?"

Stunned, Stewart stammered, "No, sir, I didn't know that; what did I do wrong?"

"Do you want to know why?"

Why does this guy have a hard on for me?

"Yes, sir. What's wrong?" Stewart asked. Life just went behind a cloud.

"Because of this, Stewart." He jammed something at him and Stewart reached for it automatically.

"I am not going to let you make Seaman and transfer out to the Reserve Fleet on the Pier. Why in God's name would you want to leave here, anyway?"

The Chief walked in and looked at Stewart with a pained expression on his face. The Comm Officer shoved the crumpled piece of yellow teletype paper in Stewart's face again. Stewart took the paper, smoothed it out, saw his typing practice, and looked over at Mr. Wetter.

WHEN I MAKE SN, I AM GOING TO ASK FOR A XFER OUT OF HERE

Mr. Wetter looked down his pipe at him.

Shit! I forgot. Mr. Wetter always checks the trash cans for classified material.

"We'll transfer you to the Pier all right, but as a Seaman Apprentice, as soon as we can get another Seaman or Seaman Apprentice in here as a striker."

"But sir, I meant to go back to sea duty, not duty on the Pier. I like striking for Radioman."

This did not mollify him at all. If anything, it made him angrier.

"Sea duty? You want to go back to sea duty?" Mr. Bowser asked incredulously, his face turning redder.

"You want to leave the comfort of shore duty for sea duty? Why in God's name would you want to do that?"

He was really pissed off at Stewart. Stewart also was upset.

Careful, Lee, careful what you say to this idiot, or you'll remain a peon for the rest of your days.

"Because I didn't ask for shore duty, Mr. Bowser. I asked for ET school as part of my shipping over choices. Instead, I ended up," hesitating to find the right words as his hands closed in furious anger, "here with you screaming at me for not being the ET I was supposed to be. I'd rather go back at sea. I don't have a wife or kids here. The only time there's someone in the barracks is when they have the duty. There's absolutely nothing here for me, sir."

By this time, Lieutenant Commander Bowser was really red in the face and shouting.

"Well, if you want to go to sea so badly, make out a request chit and get the Chief to sign it. I'll forward it approved and write your letter."

"Yes, sir," Stewart answered angrily, "I'll have it ready for the Chief in just a minute."

The chief quickly looked at him and shook his head slightly. The Comm Officer stopped short and started to say something more. Finally, he turned without another word and went into his office.

Stewart's hands shook as he wrote out a request chit requesting transfer back to sea duty anywhere, as soon as possible. His stated reason was, that he didn't like shore duty, had not asked for it, and was here by someone's error. The Chief shook his head at him, signed his request chit, and whispered, "Stewart, keep quiet. Don't say another word. You're in deep enough shit as it is!"

Stewart grabbed the chit from the chief, still burning over the injustice of it all.

"Thanks, Chief, I've been fucked ever since I got here because someone else screwed up. I just gotta get out of here before I get in real trouble." He paused for a moment and looked down at the message board.

Scratch early liberty.

He pulled the Special Request chit from the board and tossed it in the trash. Chief Nevil looked at Stewart's retreating back, looked in the trashcan and leaned over to pull that sheet out of the trashcan. Reading it over, he looked up at Stewart's back again as he headed toward Mr. Bower's desk. He shook his head, crumpled the request chit and tossed it back in the can.

Stewart marched into the Comm Officer's office without knocking and laid his request for transfer to sea duty on his desk. This led to a final one-sided shouting match with the Comm Officer. Stewart was deserting him. Stewart maintained a stony silence.

"You have one last chance to change your mind."

"No, sir," he replied, coming to attention and staring at the wall behind the Comm Officer, "I want outa here. I want to go back to the fleet, sir."

"Then, by God, I'll make sure you get sea duty in a few weeks."

He grabbed his pen from its brass USN stand, checked APPROVED, and signed the chit. Stabbing the pen back in its holder, he glared at Stewart. "I'll take this to the Executive Officer in a few minutes, Stewart. You are dismissed."

Stewart remained silent, about-faced and marched out of his office, anger etched in his stiff-legged march.

Swensen, the same Yeoman who checked him into the Station, typed up Stewart's letter requesting return to sea duty. The Captain signed the letter and sent it to BuPers that day. Stewart's misery continued.

1845, June 15
Barracks Lounge
U.S. Naval Station Tongue Point
Astoria, Oregon

Stewart had eaten dinner and was in the reading room stretched out in an overstuffed chair with an Earl Stanley Gardner mystery. He had seen the shitkicker movie that was playing tonight and did not want to waste ten cents seeing it again.

"Now Stewart, Lee, Seaman Apprentice, lay to the Master-At-Arms office, you have a long distance phone call."

Who the hell could that be? Mom? Something happened to Dad?

He raced to the office and picked up the phone.

"Seaman Apprentice Stewart speaking, sir."

"Lee, this is Ruth. Do you always answer the phone like that?"

Hoo boy! I was supposed to call her tonight and tell her when I was getting up there. Shit!

"Hi, Ruth. Is something wrong? I've missed you."

"No, Silly. I just wondered why you haven't called me. Is everything all right with you—with us?"

Oh yeahhhh.

"Everything is beautiful, Luscious. I can't get off early tomorrow, so it will be very late when I get up there. Maybe close to midnight."

"That's why I'm calling, silly. I wanted to make sure you were coming up to see me," she interrupted. "Daddy is going to a business meeting in Spokane and is taking Mama. Can you think of anything you might like to do with me?"

Man oh man. Down, Junior!

"Cat got your tongue, Lee?"

"No, I'm thinking."

"Thinking? What about?" The pout came over five by five.

"Listen, Luscious, there's a chance I can get a ride with someone going to Seattle. I'll call you when I hit Seattle tomorrow night."

"Okay, Lee, meanwhile, I'll think of some kind of games we can play to keep busy. Bye for now." She hung up before Lee could respond.

Stewart made a long three-legged walk back to the lounge, oblivious to all in the lounge who reminded him to wear boxing gloves when he went to bed tonight. He coulda' hung his white hat on the front of his pants.

8:30PM, June 16
Ballard Hill
Seattle, Washington

They were in near dark. Ruth sat curled up in his lap on the sofa, their heads close together, listening to 'Your Hit Parade.' The band had gotten up to Number Six: 'My Foolish Heart.' Ruth liked his kisses and Lee liked feeling the soft, warmth of her inner thighs. Lee had never gotten any farther than that with a girl. He wasn't sure how to get from here to there, what to do next. Suddenly, Ruth stopped humming My Foolish Heart, sat up straight and looked closely at Lee.

"Lee, are you a virgin?" she asked. Stunned by her question, he swallowed hard and didn't know what to say.

I don't think this is the time to tell her about that whore in Panama or Alice and June. She's definitely figured out I don't know how to get there from here.

He pulled both hands back to her lap and hung his head in embarrassment. Then he nodded. Ruth looked closely at Lee.

"You mean you never made a girl in the back of a car or at the beach? You were sure trying the last time we were together." He shook his head; glad the lights were low. He knew his face had to be beet red.

"Oh, Lee, are you ever going to have fun this weekend! I'll teach you everything I know, and then we'll learn some more together."

She squirmed around delightfully as she moved more to face him in his lap. Then she took his two trembling hands in her warm hands and brought them to the top of her buttoned blouse.

"Unbutton my blouse, Lee—slowly, and don't tear any buttons off."

The embroidery on the blouse felt like it was an inch thick as his fingers fumbled and unbuttoned each button. He could see her brassiere and the crease between her lovely breasts clearly in the half-light. She leaned toward him and with her hands signaled him to pull her blouse out of her skirt and take it off. His mouth was hot and dry as he stared.

"Don't stop now, Lee. Unfasten my bra hooks in back and pull the straps off my shoulders." She giggled softly. "If you knew what you were doing, you could do it with one hand."

She leaned forward pushing her bra'd breasts gently in his face as his hands fumbled for a second and the hooks fell away. Lee brought his hands slowly up and brushed the straps from her shoulders and lifted the bra away.

Oh God, they're so beautiful.

He reached up with one hand and stroked gently along the side and bottom of one.

Ruth was beginning to breathe a little raggedly herself. Goose bumps sprang up suddenly and her nipples that had looked kinda light in the low lights suddenly darkened and rose. He barely touched one and she gasped and shivered.

Now, here's something I've wanted to do for a very long time.

He cupped her breast, leaned over, and began kissing the nipple with his lips and tongue. The last thing he heard—

or remembered—was her low moan and breathing into his ear as he began to suckle.

Ruth lay on her side, with her head propped up in her hand. Her other hand delicately traced Lee's abdominal muscle patterns with one fingernail. She watched in admiration as Junior rushed to attention.

"Hey, Big Fella," she said, and leaned over to softly kiss it.

Lee stirred sleepily and reached for her. Ruth had really been teaching him some interesting things the last two days. She rolled over on top of him, stopping long enough to get some hairs out of the way and let Junior slide in. She didn't move. She just snuggled up and listened as Lee's heart began to beat faster and his breath got a little ragged.

Oh, Lee, I truly am going to hang on to you for a while. Just don't screw up and say you love me.

"Lee, you have to catch the Greyhound in less than two hours." He nodded agreement.

"Okay, Luscious, one more piece for the road" he murmured as he began kissing her.

"No, no, no," she giggled, "it's time you showered and dressed," she whispered through his kisses.

"Wanna wash my face again?" he grinned, knowing how that drove her crazy.

She showed off by squeezing and squeezing, as Lee shuddered with pleasure. Then she moved backwards off him and out of bed.

He looked at her in disbelief and gasped in shock. "That's not fair, leaving me hung like that." She laughed at him, staying out of reach and ran for the bathroom. Lee waited until he heard the shower running and ran to join her.

Maybe in the shower . . .

June 19
Communication Center
U.S. Naval Station Tongue Point
Astoria, Oregon

Stewart managed to work through the day without falling asleep. His thoughts were with Ruth and the fantastic weekend. He was wide awake enough to have noticed a memo posted on the barracks bulletin board this morning, looking for a Seaman or Seaman Apprentice who was interested in striking for Radioman to call Chief Nevil. He knew his days were numbered.

I wonder if they will change my Navy Job Code number back to SN-0000?

1800, June 24, 1950
Communications Center
NavSta Tongue Point
Astoria, Oregon

Lee was listening to KAST radio music while he held Field Day on the communication offices. He had already swept and swabbed the deck. It was time for a coffee break.

Lighting up a Camel and filling his cup, Lee settled down in Mister Wetter's chair. The music came to an end followed by a commerical and KAST's ID music. The announcer began speaking breathlessly.

> **THIS IS K A S T, ASTORIA, OREGON, 1160 KILOCYCLES ON YOUR RADIO DIAL. (pause)   THIS IS JIM PERSONS, YOUR ANNOUNCER.**
>
> **JUNE 24TH, TUESDAY, WITH YOUR SIX O'CLOCK EVENING NEWS FROM THE**

WIRES OF UNITED PRESS AND INTERNATIONAL NEWS SERVICE.

IN THE HEADLINES—REPEATING EARLIER BULLETINS, THE NORTH KOREAN ARMY CROSSED THE THIRTY-EIGHTH PARALLEL INTO SOUTH KOREA ABOUT NOON TODAY OUR TIME, OR 4 AM JUNE TWENTY-FIFTH KOREAN TIME.

ACCORDING TO REPORTS COMPILED FROM THE NEWS SERVICES, THE NORTH KOREANS HAVE ATTACKED SOUTHWARD ON FIVE ROADS CROSSING THE THIRTY-EIGHTH PARALLEL. ON SCENE REPORTERS STRESS THIS IS NOT THE USUAL BORDER CLASHES BETWEEN NORTH AND SOUTH KOREAN TROOPS.

IN WASHINGTON DC, OUR GOVERNMENT HAS NOT MADE ANY ANNOUNCEMENTS ABOUT THIS DEVELOPMENT.

LOCALLY, SUNRISE GRANGE WANTS ME TO REMIND YOU OF THE SQUARE DANCE FRIDAY JUNE THIRTIETH JUST OFF HIGHWAY TWENTY-FOUR . .

June 28
U.S. Naval Station Tongue Point
Astoria, Oregon

War came quickly to Tongue Point. A heightened sense of security was evident. Armed sentries manned the Main Gate. A roving armed patrol in a WW2 Jeep drove along the perimeter fence, lighted for the first time since October 1945. Broken light fixtures and burned out lights along the perimeter road were being replaced. Potholes were being filled in and other crews were cutting back four-year-old green growth.

Significant amounts of war material would be shipped by rail from several Naval Supply Depots, Naval Supply Centers, and Naval Ammunition Depots. The railroad gate had new padlocks issued by the Seattle, Portland, and Spokane Railroad, installed because the gate had not been used since 1947. Its hinges were freshly greased. Public Works personnel were checking and cleaning the railroad spur from the gate through every switch to all sidings to prevent derailings. SP&S RR inspectors passed judgement on their work.

The U.S. Navy Pacific Reserve Fleet at U.S. Naval Station Tongue Point began receiving urgent secret messages through the Communications Center. Their collective meaning was to prepare specific ships for recommissioning.

To his surprise, Stewart had not been replaced. His clipboard began carrying more messages to the regular offices around the base, plus a few reactivated offices closed since 1947. When Stewart and the other Radiomen pointed out delays in delivery of important messages because they had to walk the entire messenger route, Mr. Bowser arranged to have a jeep assigned to the department. Stewart was able to maintain rapid delivery now.

To everyone's annoyance, The Captain decided to reinstitute Friday morning Materiel Inspection over the entire base. Not only that, Personnel Inspection would be conducted every Saturday morning.

Adding insult to injury, the Captain decided that division officers would conduct a bag inspection on all their personnel. There were cries of anguish in the Communications offices. SA Stewart snickered because *his* bag was full!

The two Naval Station Yard Tug Boats (YTB) began earning their keep. They were busy slipping designated mothballed ships from their mooring in Oyster Bay. Pairs of tugs pushed and pulled the dead ships, mostly LST's, into the Reserve Pier.

Crews of men attached to the Reserve Fleet at the Naval Station began removing the silver mothball covers and restoring each designated ship to its operational readiness condition, ready to go to war.

The full mothballing procedure was to seal a ship against rust, humidity, and infestation from insects, birds, and other pests. On de-mothballing, the mothball designers stated that full readiness, including crew and all stores, would take no more than thirty days from the order to proceed.

Ship crews hadn't started arriving yet.

JULY

July 2, 1950
Communications Center
U.S. Naval Station Tongue Point
Astoria, Oregon

Teletype message traffic leaped to forty or fifty messages per day. Ships' supplies and new equipment began to arrive by rail and truck. Regular Navy personnel, transferred from other ships and stations, started to dribble in by Greyhound bus to man and help prepare these World War Two ships for war. Public Works opened closed barracks and prepared them for use by several hundred enlisted men of the re-commissioning crews. The B.O.Q. (Bachelor Officers' Quarters) and Chief's Quarters were expanded to original sizes. The enlisted men's Club and Officers Club underwent a hurried renovation. The Chiefs Club, which had been closed since 1947—not enough chiefs attached to the base—really required a hurried rebuilding. A gray Navy bus met each Greyhound bus at the Greyhound station in downtown Astoria.

Sullen, Inactive Duty Naval Reservists (USNR-R) began to arrive, recalled to active duty. Truman had decided it was more important to recall old warriors who had fought in battle during World War Two than to activate trained Reserve units whose personnel had never seen combat.

Lieutenant Commander Bowser discussed the traffic load with Chief Nevil and Mr. Wetters. The Navy Communications Facility in Seattle had been complaining that important message traffic was piling up during the early hours, waiting for Tongue Point to open at 0800. Following the meeting, the Communication Center converted from the more casual peacetime atmosphere to a much tighter War footing.

New security provisions closed the previously open door into the Comm Center to all but Communications personnel and senior officers. The increased message load required round the clock service, which meant starting the Mid Watch. Stewart would now stand Day, Eve, and Mid watches in rotation with other Radiomen. Tongue Point advised the Main Comm Center in Seattle to send traffic around the clock.

July 6
U.S. Naval Station Tongue Point
Astoria, Oregon

Message traffic really began to increase. There was so much traffic about reactivating these ships that one man could not prepare all of it for distribution before 0800 the next morning.

The entire command, economizing and enhancing efficiency due to expected personnel shortages, had canceled all 72-hour liberties until further notice. Additionally, early liberty on Friday and Rope Yarn Sunday—always Wednesday afternoon—were canceled until further notice. Liberty on Saturday would not commence until 1200, even for personnel who should have qualified for a 72-hour liberty.

Without a 72-hour liberty, Lee could not visit Ruth in Seattle. Ruth and Lee schemed and hit upon a plan. He could easily get to Portland and rent a hotel room or she and her parents could come down to Seaside or Astoria so Ruth and Lee could play around. They had time for one of each.

THIS IS K A S T, ASTORIA, OREGON, 1160 KILOCYCLES ON YOUR DIAL. (pause) WE HAVE JUST RECEIVED A UNITED PRESS BULLETIN DATELINED UNITED NATIONS PLAZA, SATURDAY JULY EIGHTH.

THE SECURITY COUNCIL HAS ASKED THE UNITED STATES GOVERNMENT TO

APPOINT GENERAL OF THE ARMY DOUGLAS A. MACARTHUR AS SUPREME COMMANDER OF ALL UNITED NATIONS FORCES IN KOREA.

SO FAR NINETEEN NATIONS HAVE PLEDGED ACTIVE PARTICIPATION. THERE HAS BEEN NO COMMENT FROM MACARTHUR'S FAR EAST COMMAND HEADQUARTERS IN TOKYO, JAPAN. REPEATING, WE HAVE JUST RECEIVED . . .

Ships' recommissioning detail radiomen were coming by for their message traffic on a regular basis. The ships' radiomen started complaining to Stewart and the other Radiomen handling the 'door' traffic, about the single-ply yellow teletype paper for their traffic. The station supply officer okayed three-ply paper for the ships' message traffic.

To handle those messages inexpensively, Mr. Wetter would wait until there were several messages for all the ships. Then take the ditto paper out of the runoff teletype machine and insert the three-ply for these ships. Stewart was going quietly crazy trying to keep up with the different procedures.

July 15
Communication Center
U.S. Naval Station Tongue Point
Astoria, Oregon

Today, the first two glistening LST's with all four LCVP's in their nests, were recommissioned, well ahead of schedule. Until they departed following shakedown, NavSta Tongue Point had their inport communication guard. The two LST's began receiving coded messages. That was a whole new ball game. Ned Wetter threw his hands up in despair. The Comm Officer and Supply Officer had a heated discussion about the Communications Department's over-budget expenditures.

July 20
Communication Center
U.S. Naval Station Tongue Point
Astoria, Oregon

Recall notices for retired and reserve military service personnel who lived in Northwestern Oregon and Southwestern Washington were coming in at the rate of five a day average to Naval Station Tongue Point Comm Center for onward delivery by Western Union. Mr. Wetter personally handled all commercial traffic when he arrived each morning; those arriving on Saturday or Sunday were held for him until Monday. The first KIA message came in for Western Union less than a week after the Korean War began.

AUGUST

1600, August 29
Communication Center
U.S. Naval Station Tongue Point
Astoria, Oregon

Stewart had just relieved the Day watch—the fat, old Radioman First Class Martin—and was leaning out the window watching him get into his car and leave.

It's time I called Ruth to let her know I'm not sure when I can get up there again. Of course, she did say she only dated one guy at a time usually until he declared his undying love. Then Ruth would be off and running looking for a new boyfriend.

Stewart understood that as long as he could maintain the difference between the emotion of love and the passion of lovemaking, Ruth and Lee would be a scene until one or the other got bored.

Bored? Of making love with Ruth? Never!

Stewart heard the teletype motor energize and the Model 14 printing tape machine clutch release as a message started printing on the teletype.

Boy. the messages are really coming in these days. Already the first two LST's are gone, and two more will be recommissioned in a couple of days.

He listened to the teletype and tape machines rattle on at 60wpm long enough for some of the address to arrive. Stewart turned to look at the message, and stared in surprise.

```
DEFERRED
28 AUGUST 1950
FM BUPERS
TO NAVSTA TONGUE POINT
INFO USS LST 1071
COMWESTSEAFRON
NAVRECSTA TI
COMFLTACTS YOKOSUKA
GR47
BT
REF YOUR LTR 12 JUN CMA 037/12 X
UNODIR XFER ON OR BEFORE 31 AUG
STEWART CMA LEE H SA 3925144 USN
RM2354 CMA TO NAVRECSTA TI FFT
NAVRECSTA YOKOSUKA JAPAN FFT USS
LST 1071 FORDU X AIRPRI 3 X NO DELREP X
100 POUNDS AUTH BAG
BT
```

(Unless otherwise directed, Tongue Point will transfer Stewart, a Radioman Striker, on or before August 31 via Treasure Island, California and Yokosuka, Japan, for duty in the USS Landing Ship Tank, hull number 1071, carrying his seabag and a small bag weighing no more than 100 pounds total.)

[Note: LSTs were assigned county names several years later.]

Holy shit! Back to the fleet in the Far East.

Uh oh. This is going to mess up my love life with Ruth something fierce. Gotta call her before I leave. They must need me right away because sailors on overseas assignments usually got up to thirty days delay in reporting, taken as leave he had on the books. Not only that, Naval

Receiving Station Treasure Island was going to send me over by air, instead of going out on some ship.

Holy Toledo. Tomorrow is going to be a busy day. I have to check out and get any shots from the Corpsman. I damn well better make sure my yellow International Inoculation card is up to date. Then, get paid and pack my seabag for departure the next morning.

Stewart already knew the daily Astoria to Portland local bus left promptly at 9:15 AM, down town and he wanted to connect with the 1:30 PM, Portland to San Francisco Greyhound Express.

It's going to be tight. I don't want to catch that damn local Greyhound that makes every stop all the way to San Francisco.

On a hunch, he called the Astoria Greyhound office and made reservations for the Portland Express to San Francisco. Good thing he did. Almost all the seats were taken.

0830, August 31
U.S. Naval Station Tongue Point
Astoria, Oregon

Stewart was ready to leave. The Naval Station Personnel office arranged to have Public Works drive Stewart to the Astoria Bus Station in the Dodge van. Stewart stopped in the Comm Center long enough to say good-bye to a couple of the radiomen, Chief Nevil and old Ned Wetter, as a courtesy more than anything else.

"Stewart, now aren't you sorry you asked for sea duty?" asked Chief Nevil with a smile.

Stewart hesitated and mentally shrugged. "Chief, that Large, Slow Target I'm going to is a hell of a lot better than this rust bucket. I'd rather have a destroyer but anything is better than this place."

The Chief and Mr. Wetter stood and shook his hand. Stewart pointedly ignored Mr. Bowser who was watching from his office.

Someone called out, "Smooth sailing, Stewart."
He looked around and couldn't tell who it was, so he waved at the other sailors and left. Stewart had worked for and with these people for a few months. It still stuck in his craw.

This had been a complete zero as a command, even worse.

He heard Helen's comment to Mr. Bowser as he left. "I don't think he likes you." Bowser turned back to her and glared.

Stewart stopped at the pay phone booth near the back entrance.

"Deposit ninety cents for the first three minutes, please."

Lee picked up his change and pushed the coins into the slots.

DONG DONG DONG   DANG DINGDING.

"Go ahead with your call, sir."

"Abernathy and Holcomb Certification Service, may I help you?"

"Yes, please. This is Lee Stewart in Astoria. . ."

"Lee—Ruth's boyfriend?"

"Uh, yes. Can I speak to her, please? I don't have much time."

"Oh just a moment, Lee. We know ALL about you."

All? Jeez, I thought only guys talked!

"Lee? What's up? Got another liberty?"

"Ruth, I got bad news, Luscious. I got my orders yesterday. . .

"Oh no!"

`"And right now, the driver is waving at me to hurry. I'm on my way to Japan and Korea for the war."

"I thought that was a little police action, Lee. Nothing to get excited about."

Good Lord, Lady, read the fuckin' paper!

"Since the North Koreans are about to beat South Korea to a pulp, the United States Navy is in action out there to help the rest of our own forces and South Korea."

"Oh, Lee, baby. When will you get back?"

Down, Junior!

"Just as soon as I can, but I have no idea when. Will you write to me?"

"Oh, baby, you know I will."

"Okay, when I get settled, I'll write. Send some me some new pictures. The one I have in my wallet doesn't do you justice."

"Lee, I don't know anyone who would take the kind of pictures you'd like, but I will get some nice ones out to you. Be good and come back safe."

Ruth put her phone down and leaned back, staring at the wall.

Damn, damn, damn! Now I have to find another sweet guy.

Then she shrugged and picked up the paper she had been studying when Lee called.

Stewart picked up his seabag and ran for the van. He threw the seabag in the back of the van and held onto his records and orders. Those he kept in hand. You can replace a lost seabag. Jumping in the front seat, he shut the door and gave a fast look around.

"All set, Stewart?" asked the driver.

Stewart nodded to the driver, "Yeah, let's go!" They drove around the building and up the hill. He knew one other thing for sure: the last weekend in Seaside was probably the last time Ruth would be in his arms.

Ah, well!

> **. . . AND NOW, GABRIEL HEATTER WITH THE WORLD NEWS TONIGHT.**
> **AHHHH, THERE IS TRAGIC NEWS TONIGHT.**
> **THE UNITED STATES ARMY HAS RELEASED INFORMATION THAT TWENTY SIX MEN OF THE FIFTH CAVALRY REGIMENT WERE FOUND BOUND AND EXECUTED BY NORTH KOREAN FORCES NEAR WAEGWON.**
> **WE OFFER OUR SYMPATHIES TO THE FAMILIES OF THESE VALIANT SOLDIERS.**

- - - The End of the Beginning - - -

Lee's adventures continue in the U.S.S. HOQUIAM PF-5 series named

> RESURRECTED,
> ROAD TO HUNGNAM,
> HOCKY MARU, and
> KNOCK OFF SHIP'S WORK.

These novels can be ordered directly from the author or from major booksellers. You may email the author at "markdgls@me.com" with questions or comments.